T0003323

Look for:

Daddy's #1 Girl
by Earl Sewell
ISBN-13: 978-0-373-83079-4
ISBN-10: 0-373-83079-3

Spin It Like That
by Chandra Sparks Taylor
ISBN-13: 978-0-373-83080-0
ISBN-10: 0-373-83080-7

Fast Life
by Cassandra Carter
ISBN-13: 978-0-373-83076-3
ISBN-10: 0-373-83076-9

www.KimaniTRU.com

Joyce E. Davis

can't stop the shine

KIMANI
TRU
™

CAN'T STOP THE SHINE

ISBN-13: 978-0-373-83078-7
ISBN-10:   0-373-83078-5

www.kimaniTRU.com

Printed in U.S.A.

KIMANI TRu™

FRESH. CURRENT. AND TRUE TO YOU.

Dear Reader,

What you're holding is very special. Something fresh, new and true to your unique experience as a young African-American! We are proud to introduce a new fiction imprint—Kimani TRU. You'll find Kimani TRU speaks to the triumphs, problems and concerns of today's black teens with candor, wit and realism. The stories are told from your perspective and in your own voice, and will spotlight young, emerging literary talent.

Kimani TRU will feature stories that are down-to-earth, yet empowering. Feel like an outsider? Afraid you'll never fit in, find your true love or have a boyfriend who accepts you for who you really are? Maybe you feel that your life is a disaster and your future is going nowhere? In Kimani TRU novels, discover the emotional issues that young blacks face every day. In one story, a young man struggles to get out of a neighborhood that holds little promise by attending a historically black college. In another, a young woman's life drastically changes when she goes to live with the father she has never known and his middle-class family in the suburbs.

With Kimani TRU, we are committed to providing a strong and unique voice that will appeal to *all* young readers! Our goal is to touch your heart, mind and soul, and give you a literary voice that reflects your creativity and your world.

Spread the word…Kimani TRU. True to you!

Linda Gill
General Manager
Kimani Press

 KIMANI PRESS™

To Yanick Rice Lamb
Thank you for the continuous encouragement. Your example,
guidance and unwavering belief in me have been instrumental in
both my professional and personal development. I'm so blessed
that God put you in my life. Love you always, jd

Acknowledgments

There are many people in my life who have helped me along the way to this first novel, and it would be impossible to acknowledge them all. First, I must give thanks to my parents, James and Mary Lee Davis, for literally sacrificing twenty years of their life (and still some) to put me on the right path to independence, self-worth, righteousness and a lifetime appreciation for learning.

Being a Kimani TRU author was a perfect fit for me because it has always been important for me to communicate, relate and be a mentor to young people without them feeling like I was preaching to them. My mother, who kept a book in my hand, nearly from birth, first taught me this. So a heartfelt thank-you to Ma for making brother Rayford and me participate in library summer reading programs, limiting our television time and not ordering me to sleep when I wanted to stay up late and finish a book. Because of you, I fell in love with reading—the greatest gift you could have ever given me.

Thank you, Gerry, for your patience, understanding and love, when I was in the throes of getting those final chapters completed and not quite the most pleasant person to be around. Thank you, Kenyatta, for being the special young man that you are. I hope that you enjoy this book when you get to high school a few years from now.

I give special appreciation to the friends and family who read chapters of *Can't Stop the Shine*. Rayford, Asata Reid and my PowerFlow Media partner, Vanessa Lipske (God is sure blessing us!!), your critical feedback was invaluable. Cousin Toni Lee and friend Amani Wimberly, you guys were my barometers of young people's pop culture. I still consider myself a youngster, but it was the two of you that let me know what was really happening and "fresh," as an eighties high school graduate would say, with high schoolers in the millennium.

Thank you to my agent, Sha-Shana Crichton, for helping me through my first publishing deal. Thank you, Linda Gill, for giving me yet another chance to flex myself in the literary world. I'm grateful that you continue to keep me in mind for such wonderful opportunities.

And to the many other family, friends, and friends of friends— Danielle Withers, Karen Good, Sylvette Jackson, Grandma Hattie Lee, Ingrid Sturgis, Kimberly Seals Allers, Nigel Killikelly, Denene Millner, Mitzi Miller, Tara Roberts, Jessica Care Moore-Poole, Dana Wimberly, Danyel Smith, Mikel Husband, Gina Toole, E. Monique Johnson, Angela Burt-Murray, Lorraine Robertson and others— thank you for your regular prayers (you are my spiritual warrior, Vanessa), conversations and tons of e-mails, filled with encouragement, understanding and love. I needed all of you to get through this project.

Not only do I need to thank God for the gift of creating me as a woman who appreciates creativity, but thank you, Lord, for my newest blessing, Miss Amber Mariama Loyd. When I was writing this book, I had no idea that you would come into my life. But I do know that when you're a teenager, you'll meet plenty of the girls I created in *Can't Stop the Shine* from my own experiences. I hope that you'll get as much enjoyment and empowerment from the lessons they learn as I got out of writing their story.

chapter 1

Kalia looked around the room slowly, realizing the significance of the moment. Everybody she knew and loved was there. Her mother, Elaine; her father, Ronald; her crazy sister, Mariama; and her best friend, Dewayne. In fact all of her friends were there and so were all of the other folks who made up her world. For a hot second she let this special moment eclipse her anger. She knew she would go off if she didn't get away for a minute.

The object of her venom came up behind her as she walked into the kitchen.

"What's up, sis?" said Mari. "Happy birthday!"

"I wish it was," said Kalia, whipping around, "but it's not because you messed it up!"

"What are you talking about? Everybody is kickin' it."

"Yeah, they sure are, but that's not what we agreed on. It wasn't just supposed to be a kick-it party. It was supposed to be special, but as usual you went ahead and did what you wanted to do. Why do you have to be so selfish?"

"K, it's hot outside. I'm burning up. Don't get on my nerves today, okay? It's my birthday," said Mari, getting a bottle of water out of the refrigerator.

"It's my birthday, too, Mari, and you're turning it into a straight hip-hop party. We said we'd compromise."

"I can't help what the deejay is playing," Mari said, smirking.

"If you'd hired DJ Spin Nice like we talked about you wouldn't have to help what he was playing. It'd be a mix, just like we said. You make me sick, Mari. You always have to have your way," said Kalia, pointing her finger at her smug sister.

Mari moved closer to Kalia.

"I know you're not talking about somebody having to have their way, Miss Priss. You're the queen of selfishness. I told you earlier, DJ Spin Nice costs too much. We didn't have enough money for him. So that's right, I got my way this time, and there's nothing you can do about it."

"You think so? You think there's nothing I can do? *Phhh,*" said Kalia, folding her arms across her chest.

"Look, I'm sixteen. I'm getting my license next week. You're eighteen. You can…uh…vote. Anyway, what I'm trying to say is that the food is great, we look good, it's our birthday party. Let's just have fun," reasoned Mari.

"I'm not hanging out there with you and your little ghetto friends."

"Fine. Stay in here and be a crab at your own birthday party," said Mari, turning on her heels. "God. You must be on your period or something," she mumbled, walking out of the kitchen.

Enraged, Kalia stamped up the back stairs and into her room to look at the party through her huge open windows. *Who the hell does she thinks she is?* Kalia thought. *This is probably my last birthday at home, and it looks like a hip-hop video.* She surveyed the teenage crowd in her backyard, spotting Mari and her crew of girls up front near the deejay table. They were with some thug-looking guys, bouncing around in their baby T's, low-riding jeans and sneakers, and were shaking their behinds to the empty boasts of some rapper claiming he had a girl in every city in the world.

The beat is hot, Kalia thought, tapping her fingers in time with the baseline against the ledge. She spotted her friend Dewayne staring at her and motioned for him to come up to her room. Sitting at her desk, Kalia logged on the Internet to find her horoscope, wondering every year like always if her parents had planned to have her and her sister in the same month so they could always knock out both birthdays in one party. At least they came correct, ending the summer with blowouts every year.

Their birthday parties were the best. Anything could happen and anybody could show up. They had in-home puppet shows and cartoon-themed parties when they were little. When Kalia and Mari were ten and twelve, Elaine, a yoga instructor, used her connections at the National Black Arts Festival to arrange for an African dance performance with live drummers. A few years later, for their fourteenth and sixteenth birthdays, Elaine and Ronald blew their kids' minds when they threw them a Caribbean-themed party with a steel pan band, Carnival decorations and Caribbean-prepared food.

And this one would have been the best ever, thought Kalia. This party was the only one that their parents had let the Jefferson sisters plan by themselves. Kalia wanted something a little more sophisticated and formal, while Mari just wanted a good hip-hop deejay, so she and her crew and all their friends could sweat it out on the dance floor. Kalia had envisioned high heels, dresses and finger food in the living room around their piano, not hot wings and crunk.

"Everybody looks like they're having a great time," said Dewayne, entering Kalia's spotless room. "What are you doing hiding out in here?"

"I cannot believe that Mari got DJ Love. He's played the same five songs all night," said Kalia, getting up from her desk and looking back out the window.

"Aw, girl, ain't nuthin' wrong with a little hip-hop—a little Jay-Z, a little Ludacris, some OutKast," said Dewayne, bouncing his shoulders a bit.

"You know I like hip-hop, but just not 24-7."

"Stop pouting," Dewayne ordered, sliding his lean body halfway out of the massive window next to hers. "The only reason you listen to other stuff besides hip-hop is that you sing and play the piano. That's your gift. She's just listening to everything everybody else is listening to."

"What are you doing? Defending her now?" snapped Kalia, yanking herself out of the window and sitting down on her well-made bed.

"What you need to do is go out there and show them young girls how it's done," said Dewayne, looking down at Mari and her girls dancing, and ignoring Kalia's question.

"I'm not putting one foot in that yard," said Kalia, stopping her head from nodding to DJ Love's hip-hop beats.

"Come on. You know you want to walk it out. I've seen you shake it like a saltshaker before," teased Dewayne. "You'd probably cause an earthquake if you got to trippin' on the dance floor."

"I told you, Dewayne Craig, I am not dancing to that deejay. I wanted some variety in the music. Mari just had to have her way. She is so selfish."

"Well she may be selfish, but she's the one having a blast at y'all's birthday party. There's nothing you can do now," Dewayne reasoned, "so you might as well go on downstairs and get your dance on."

Kalia looked hard at her best friend. He always knew how to reason with her and make her see the logical and practical sides of situations. He was the calm yin to her high-strung yang, and so their friendship was a natural fit.

"All right, well I guess you're right," acquiesced Kalia, combing through the stylishly funky flip in her hair, which she'd been wearing ever since her mother let her get a perm at age twelve. "We can go downstairs, but I'ma get Miss Mari. Believe that."

"Cool, but let me check my e-mail first since we're up here," said Dewayne, scrunching his long legs underneath her computer desk.

"Okay, Dewayne, but as soon as you sign in, I'm turning the timer on," warned Kalia. "Ten minutes and that's it. I think I'll change clothes while you do that."

Standing in front of her closet, Kalia knew she needed to cheer up if she was going to get the happy back in her birthday. Surveying her conservative but cute wardrobe, she glanced back at Dewayne, who'd already gotten sucked into the Internet. Ever since a drunk driver had killed his older brother, Spencer, five years before, Dewayne had been obsessed with anything animated and technology oriented. He'd even started referring to himself as the Chosen One, a character he'd created.

"I'll be right back," she said to Dewayne, grabbing a change of clothes, kicking off her high heels and flouncing out the door in her lace dress. Minutes later when she reappeared in a pale yellow sleeveless blouse, lime green Capris and matching lime flip-flops with yellow rhinestones, Dewayne had that same engrossed expression on his face.

"I'm back," she announced.

"Kalia, come over here and check out this site," he beckoned. "I've been looking for something like this for a—"

"Time's up," interrupted Kalia, speeding the timer up until its bell rang.

"For real? Okay, just let me—"

"I'll see you outside."

"I'm coming right now," he said without budging from the computer.

Dewayne could hear Kalia's "umm, hmm" moving down the hall. "The Chosen One is left alone again to save the world," he said to no one in particular.

The next voice he heard a few minutes later was Mari's. "Boy, you need to come downstairs and dance with one of these ladies," Mari said, thumping him on the head.

Grabbing her wrist without turning around, Dewayne said, "You're right, 'cause there sure aren't any ladies in this room."

"Whatever, man," said Mari, rolling her eyes and thumping him again with her other hand. "I'm a grown-ass sixteen-year-old woman. Did you hear me? Woman!"

"Real women don't hit men on the head, and they definitely don't get themselves in situations they can't get out of," said Dewayne, standing up from the desk and tightening his grip on Mari's wrist.

"Stop playing, boy! You're gonna make me hurt you," Mari said unconvincingly, even to herself. She caught a glimpse of her five-foot, petite frame next to his lengthy six foot two and felt the ridiculousness of her empty threat. Squirming to break Dewayne's hold, she knocked over one of Kalia's glass-blown picture frames, breaking it.

"Ooh. You're in trouble now." Dewayne laughed, letting her go and backing toward the door. "You know how Miss Perfection is about her room. You're not even supposed to be in here, right?" With a "See ya, wouldn't want to be ya," Dewayne left the room.

Mari picked up the now unframed photo and glared at a Kalia who was a few years younger in the picture, but still had that same flip in her hair and self-satisfied look on her face, like she knew exactly what her life was going to be like. She kicked the broken glass under Kalia's bed, making a mental note to clean up the mess later and to try and replace the frame before Kalia knew it was missing. But that was going to be hard, she thought, looking around her sister's room, which was more a work of art. Kalia had her music keyboards in the corner, schoolbooks stacked neatly on her desk, an unwrinkled spread on her bed and a ridiculously color-coordinated closet with all of the clothes hung on hangers facing the same direction.

Envy washed over Mari as she left Kalia's neat-freak room and shoved open the door of her own, which looked like it was arranged by a hurricane. Stepping over almost every item of clothing she owned, Mari threw Kalia's picture on her dresser. Sometimes she wished she had some of the same characteristics as her big sister. It would be nice to be organized and talented, but that just wasn't her.

Mari smoothed the building oil off of her cocoa-colored skin, pulled her ponytail tight and slid some gloss across her thick lips. She admired her well-toned athletic build in her full-length mirror. She worked hard, running year-round, to perform well during track season. She winced at the thought of running cross-country in the fall, as all track athletes were required to do at East Moreland, the private, mostly white high school she attended. She loved running, but anything over two miles was just a waste of time to her. "It is time for him to notice me," she said aloud, spraying a little Tommy Girl behind each ear and bounding down the back stairs to find one of her girls, Colby, in the kitchen.

"You know Qwon's here, don't you?" asked Colby, reading her mind.

"Yep. Shauntae told me he was on his way with one of her boys. Have you seen him?"

"Umm, hmm. He just got here with like a gang of fine guys."

"Girl, you might catch a holla tonight, but stay away from Qwon. He's mine," Mari half joked.

"You don't have to worry," said Colby. "Those type of guys never even look my way."

"What are you talking about, Colby?"

"I'm too skinny. Those guys either go with the dance team girls, ones with curves like Shauntae or the kind who wear that expensive designer stuff—Baby Phat, Coach—and get their hair and nails done like every other day. You know, the popular kind."

"That's not always true. And it sure ain't true tonight 'cause

I'm none of that, but Qwon is going to kick it to me—tonight," said Mari.

"I hear ya. He does look good, and Shauntae did say he asked about you when he came in."

"For real? Where is he? Wait, what did he say? What's he got on?" demanded Mari, taking Colby by the shoulders and shaking her.

"Girl, you're so crazy. Let me go," said Colby, backing away from her excited friend.

"Well?" said Mari, putting her hands on her hips expectantly.

"He's all geared up. Got on a light blue hoodie and some Girbauds. He's rocking some of those new Carmelo Anthony Jordans, too."

Mari let out dreamy "oohs" all through Colby's description. "What's going on with his hair? It's always so tight," said Mari.

"He's got one of those old crazy braided styles that you dig, going every which way, all symmetrical and stuff," said Colby, squinching up her face. "And he's got his full shine on. His neck, his wrists and his ears are all iced out. I don't know if it's real or not, but he's probably out there blinding everybody at your party."

Mari clapped her hands in glee.

"I gotta go find him," she said, heading out of the kitchen. "Oh wait." She stopped. "What did he say?"

"I don't know, Mari," said Colby. "Shauntae just told me he was here. You better go find him, too, 'cause she was getting that look on her face. You know how she gets when she sees a dude she wants to get with."

"Please," dismissed Mari, "Shauntae knows better. She can get with, and probably has got with, every dude at Crunk High, but she betta keep her hands off Qwon. She ain't no fool."

"Whatever you say. Anyway, he's probably out back. Come on. I'll go with you," said Colby.

Outside, the party was jumping. DJ Love was putting it down, and about a hundred teenagers were working it out on the grass dance floor. Mari and Colby stood against the back of the house, craning their necks, looking for Qwon. Spotting him, Colby pulled Mari toward the side of the house. "There he is. Over there by the cooler," she said.

As they walked up behind Qwon, he and his boys were crowded in a circle around something.

"Haaay, Qwon," said Mari, tapping him on the shoulder.

Qwon turned around and grinned a crooked smile. "What's up, birthday girl? Happy birthday," he said, bending down and giving her a peck on the cheek.

"Thank you," said Mari, wrapping her arms around his neck so he couldn't get away.

"Dog, girl." Qwon laughed and disengaged himself from her. "Don't choke a brother."

"Oh," said Mari, slightly embarrassed.

Spying Colby, Qwon said, "What's up, slim?"

"Hey, Qwon."

"Girl, when are you gonna gain some weight? Mari, you need to take your girl to IHOP and get her two big stacks of pancakes."

"Shut up, Qwon," said Colby.

He laughed, rubbed one hand over his intricately woven braids and started to turn back toward his boys. It was then that Mari saw Kalia in the middle of the group, looking slightly guilty. When she spotted Mari, she looked at Qwon and started smirking.

"Your sister is looking kind of tight tonight," Qwon whispered in Mari's ear.

"You think so, huh?" she said, seething.

"I'm thirsty. I think I'm going to get something to drink," she heard Kalia say.

"Aw, baby, I'll get it for you," said one tall, gangly guy.

"Hold up, man. I got it," said another, dipping his hand in the cooler for a soda.

"Oh, I think I want some water. I'ma go inside," said Kalia, satisfied with the heated look on Mari's face.

"Can I come with you?" asked Qwon as she sauntered away.

"Have a few more birthdays and maybe," she threw over her shoulder.

Mari balled up her fist and Kalia stuck out her tongue at her sister.

"She gets on my nerves," said Mari to Colby.

"Your sister can't help that Qwon 'n 'em like her," said Colby.

"You gettin' on my nerves, too," said Mari, stepping away from Qwon and his boys. "Where's Shauntae? I wanna know what Qwon said about me."

"I saw her trying to push up on Dewayne earlier."

"For real? That's like a waste of time 'cause Dewayne is so gone over Kalia that it ain't even funny. Plus, he's like the biggest nerd *evah*."

"He is kinda cute though," said Colby.

"Who? Dewayne? You must be joking. There that fool is now. Him and Shauntae," said Mari, waving her over.

"I gotta give it up to you, Mari. Your party is *the party* of the summer," said Shauntae, walking up.

"Thank ya very much." Mari grinned. "So what's up with you and Dewayne?"

"Ain't nuthin', girl," said Shauntae, wiggling her hips and throwing her arms in the air as DJ Love cranked up T.I.'s latest hit. "This is my song."

"It's mine, too," said Qwon, turning around. "Come on. Let's make it happen."

Before Shauntae could even answer, Qwon pulled her into the dancing crowd. Mari stood by, stunned.

"What the hell just happened here?" she said. "How is she gonna…" Mari couldn't even finish her sentence and Colby didn't know what to say. Helpless, they watched Shauntae get into a groove with Qwon. They hadn't been on the dance floor two minutes before they were bouncing up against each other, Shauntae's arms around Qwon's neck and her massive breasts bumping against his chest. Mari thought she was going to throw up at the totally enthralled look on Qwon's face as his hands slid up and down Shauntae's back.

"I know he is not rubbin' on her butt at *my* party," said Mari.

"I don't think so. That's kinda like her lower back," said Colby.

Mari swung around and glowered at Colby, opened her mouth to say something smart, but then realized it wasn't Colby who had her angry.

"I'm going inside," she said and walked off. Colby followed. Passing through the dining room, they stopped to look at the humongous triple-layered red velvet cake, inscribed in red frosting with Happy Birthday, Kalia and Mariama.

"At least the cake will be good," said Mari.

"Umm, hmm," seconded Colby.

Just then they heard a familiar tune coming from the piano in the living room. Someone was playing some Stevie Wonder. She couldn't tell until she got around the corner what song it was, or that, to her surprise, it was her mother playing. Colby was still following, and behind her, streaming in from outside, was more than half of the party, drawn in by Elaine's singing. After he was told, DJ Love took a break.

It had been years since Mari'd seen her mother sit down at a piano, and she was playing her favorite Stevie song, "As." Also standing in awe around the piano were Dewayne, her father, Kalia and lots of other family and friends of their parents. As soon as Elaine got to the chorus, everybody who knew the words started singing. Old and young alike were rocking back and forth and dancing.

There was a thunderous applause when Elaine finished, and Mari went up to her mother and hugged her. Kalia just stared at Elaine, dumbfounded. Mari dragged her mom over to Kalia, screaming, "I told you Mom could get down! I told you! I bet you can't get down like that.

"All you play is that classical stuff," she added. "I wanna see you rip it."

People were still hugging Elaine and clapping.

"Is that a challenge, Mari?" demanded Kalia.

Kalia marched over to the piano, sat down and started one of the longest, most elaborate runs of the keys that she'd ever attempted. Whatever song she was playing was ominous in its introduction. She slowed her pace, segueing into a slower R & B flow, and by the time she started singing, she knew where she was going.

Kalia sang the words from Alicia Keys's "If I Ain't Got You," dripping with emotion. As she progressed, she threw her everything into it. Her fingers were flying over the keys, and she was belting out the chorus. No one was talking. The whole party had moved indoors and was wrapped up in her performance.

Mari loved to hear her sister sing and play, but she was really surprised to see Kalia performing for a crowd. Besides competitive or official school concerts, Kalia did not sit down and play for anybody, and she certainly never sang for just anyone. It took them years to convince her to join her junior high school chorale. Though she always seemed nervous before her group had to sing in front of the entire school, that night she was totally confident.

Mari looked across the way at her dad, who surprisingly had

his arm around her mom's shoulders. Ronald was grinning at his elder daughter and proudly nudging folks around him. Pangs of jealousy set into Mari's heart. He rarely looked at her like that, she thought.

Ronald Jefferson was hardly ever at home. The owner of three fast food restaurants, The Fish Frys, he was always working. Between worrying about the competition from the more established Captain D's and Long John Silver's to being a micromanager of his own locations, the forty-four-year-old was barely able to support any of his daughters' extracurricular activities, and he certainly hadn't attended any of the yoga classes his wife taught or the events she helped organize as a part of the committee for the National Black Arts Festival.

Turning her attention back to Kalia, who was jazzing up the bridge of Alicia Keys's hit, Mari couldn't even remember the last time she saw her parents get dressed up and go out anywhere together. She recalled when she and Kalia were children how her parents used to leave them with family or babysitters at least once a month and get fly and go out to plays or dances or even just dinner with friends. Their house was always filled with people for card parties and get-togethers, and there were family vacations to Disney World, Busch Gardens and Savannah.

Mari missed those happier, carefree times. And she knew her mom did, too, even though she couldn't tell it that night. As Kalia crescendoed toward an impressive ending, a petite Elaine hugged her husband's waist. Mari pictured her parents back when she was in elementary school. A former dancer, Elaine, now forty, was a beautiful young mother and a fabulous host. Every once in a while, Elaine would perform with a dance troupe. A slight woman, extremely graceful, always with her head held high, she could do it all—ballet, modern, jazz and African dance.

Her parents were acting like they did when she was young. Ronald and Elaine were being loving and supportive parents. The only problem for Mari was at the moment all of the love and support was focused on Kalia, who was receiving a standing ovation, applause and cheers for her performance. Half-heartedly clapping, Mari walked over toward where Shauntae and Colby were standing.

"I guess y'all are all caught up in my Alicia Keys wannabe sister, too?"

"Don't hate on your sister, girl," said Colby. "She sure can blow—and play, too."

"But she need to let them lime-green pedal pushers go. She looks like she's been fishing in those high-water pants," Shauntae snickered.

"I know you are not talking about my sister," warned Mari.

"You were," said Shauntae, the penciled-in eyebrows on her smooth fair skin arching in attitude.

"She's my sister, so I can."

"Stop being so protective about your prissy-ass sister," said Shauntae. "She ain't all that now. So what, she can sing and play the piano? A lot of people can do that."

"Well, I think she's tight," said Colby. "She's got skills."

"Who asked you for your opinion? You always got something to say," said Shauntae to Colby, who looked away to hide her hurt feelings.

"Why don't you leave her alone?" Mari said to Shauntae.

"For what? I can say what I want," said Shauntae, adjusting her ample chest in the too-tight blue halter she was stuffed into. She smiled at a couple of guys who were staring at her thick hour-glass frame and shoulder-length sandy-brown naturally curly hair that kept her the center of male attention wherever she went.

"Not at my party you can't," said Mari, moving closer to Shauntae.

"You just think you all that because your sister can sing. *She* can sing. You can't."

Mari heard a bunch of "oohs" from around the room and realized that all eyes were on her and Shauntae.

"What is your problem? Why are you always roastin' on people? That is so childish," said Mari.

"No, what's childish is you trying to front on me because Qwon is all up on me and not paying you any attention—at all."

More "oohs." Louder this time.

"Now what are you gonna say?" challenged Shauntae.

Mari was on fire. She could feel the heat rising up the back of her neck. She wanted to knock Shauntae down, but she settled for something just as satisfying.

"The only reason Qwon is on you is because he knows you're the biggest freak at Crunk High."

Hoops, hollers and laughter erupted. People slapped palms and gave one another dap. Embarrassed, Shauntae tried to play it off with a "Whatever," and a flip of her hand. She ended up rolling her eyes and walking out of the room.

Mari was satisfied. She hated the way that Shauntae treated Colby, but she also felt that Colby needed to stand up for herself. She'd been letting Shauntae run all over her since Mari met them both five years ago at a YWCA sleepaway camp. When they got back from their two-week stay, they found that they lived right across town from one another. Shauntae lived in a mixed-income apartment complex, Colby stayed with her grandparents in a shabby house not too far from Shauntae, and they both were juniors at Samuel Odette Williams "Crunk" High, where Kalia was a part of the magnet performing arts program.

"Let's take a group picture," said Kalia, walking up. "This may be the last time we have a joint birthday blowout 'cause who knows where I'm going to be next year."

"Mom and Daddy are outside," said Mari, reflecting on Kalia's words. Kalia was right. This was probably their last birthday party together. Mari hadn't even started her sophomore year yet, and she was already wondering what her junior and senior years were going to be like without Kalia around. True, her sister annoyed her, but it was an annoyance that she'd gotten used to having around.

The four of them—Mari, Kalia, Elaine and Ronald—hugged up together under a big Happy Birthday banner. Flashes were popping and the summer was ending. There was a good vibe in the air, and everyone was having fun. It would be a long time before all of the Jeffersons were this happy again.

chapter 2

Mari walked into Greenbriar Mall in her normal gear—a denim miniskirt, white sneakers and a too-tight white baby T that screamed It's All About Me! in red across the front. Bopping down the mall, she slathered on lip gloss and pulled her ponytail tight. She was supposed to be meeting Colby for some back-to-school shopping, but her heart wasn't really in it. Peering at the latest styles in the store windows while navigating the massive number of black teenagers kicking it at the mall, Mari realized she wasn't ready to go back to school, especially since she'd just passed her driver's test. She wanted a little more time to get her skills up before she had to get back in the grind. Even though Shauntae had acted a fool at her birthday party, she'd really enjoyed her summer, hanging out with her girls.

In the beginning of the summer her mom had her in a local leadership development program for a few weeks with a bunch of nerds, and she also went to a cool summer camp for track-and-field athletes for about ten days. She'd been to like five or six hot parties with kids from public school in the past two and a half months.

Mari wished she went to Williams High with her friends. She'd hung out with the Crunk High crowd all summer, and now she was going to have to go back to boring, stuffy, mostly white East Moreland. Even Kalia got to go to the livest high school in the city, Mari thought as she spotted Colby standing in front of their favorite shoe store.

"What's with the grumpy face?" said Colby as Mari walked up.

"Hey," said Mari. "I am so not ready to roll back to the most uppity school in the city."

"Well, at least you get to do cool stuff at your school," said Colby. "I wish we got to go to plays and the symphony and go out of town like y'all do."

"Well, that's what rich people do," said Mari, walking into the shoe store. "But y'all ain't just sitting around over there at Williams. You've got best football and basketball teams. Our games are so boring, and we lose every time. Your parties and talent shows are tight, and everybody says your proms are off the chain. I don't know why Kalia didn't go to her junior prom, but you'll get to go this year."

"Yeah, if somebody asks me," said Colby, twisting her long braid extensions into a messy bun.

"Somebody will and you'll get to go. You'll probably end up being the queen of the hypest prom in the city. I don't know why my parents put me at East Boredom anyway."

"Uh…'cause you're smart. Smart enough to get that full scholarship to go to that private school," said Colby.

"Everybody knows that Mari's got some big brains," said Shauntae, walking up behind Colby. "You don't need to remind us."

Mari opened her mouth to say something, but was stunned into silence when she saw who was with Shauntae.

"Hey, look who I found," said Shauntae, grabbing Qwon's hand.

"What's happening, ladies? What are y'all doing up in here?" said Qwon, slipping his hand from Shauntae's grasp.

Seeing that Mari still wasn't able to find her voice, Colby stepped in. "You know, trying to get some new gear for school. Catch some of these sales."

"Me, too. Check out my new kicks," said Qwon, stepping one foot forward.

"Those are hot, baby," cooed Shauntae, tightening the belt on her hot pink Apple Bottoms jeans, which accentuated her Coca-Cola bottle shape. "You should get me the ladies' version and then we'll be matching. That would be *so* cute."

"What's up with your money, chicken?" asked Qwon, eyeing her.

"You weren't calling me that a few minutes ago when you were all up on me in the movies," spit Shauntae.

"That was different," said Qwon, glancing around the shoe store. "Look, I'm about to be out. I just came over here to check out what they had in here."

"Ain't nuthin' in here for you." Shauntae smirked with her hands on her hips.

"Cool, 'cause I know everyone else been up in it anyway," Qwon threw over his shoulder as he left the store.

"Whatever," said Shauntae, eyeing some hot-pink stilettos.

Mari hadn't said a word through their whole exchange. She didn't know if she was more disgusted with her choice of men or how Shauntae could let herself be so insulted by a guy.

"What's wrong with you, girl?" said Shauntae, snapping her lime-green freshly painted inch-long acrylic nails in Mari's face. "I know you ain't trippin' over Qwon. He ain't even got nuthin' goin' on."

Mari regained her voice. "How do you know?"

"Didn't you just hear me say we were in the movies? He can't kiss or nuthin'. He don't even know what to do with his hands."

"Just shut up, Shauntae," said Mari, raising her voice and her hand. She was more disgusted at Shauntae's behavior.

"Who are you getting loud with?" Shauntae demanded, rolling her neck. "I can't help if Qwon knows what he likes, but like I said, he ain't about nuthin' no way."

Well, they did agree about that, thought Mari, watching Shauntae pick up the stilettos.

"Colby. Girl, I bet you couldn't even walk in these." Shauntae laughed, holding up one shoe by the heel. "Your skinny foot would probably slip out of the front and you'd bust your butt."

Mari had totally forgotten that Colby was even with them. She walked over to where she was sitting and plopped down beside her.

"I thought y'all were gonna throw some blows for a minute there," said Colby.

can't stop the shine

"I ain't trippin' over that girl."

"But you were trippin' over Qwon."

"*So*," Mari said a little too harshly.

"I'm just saying, you should be happy that Qwon got with Shauntae. At least you know what kind of girl he likes," said Colby.

She didn't see Shauntae behind her.

"If you've got something to say to me, Colby, you need to go on and say it," said Shauntae. "Personally I think you're just hatin' 'cause you couldn't catch a holla if you walked through this mall butt-ass naked.

"Well, at least half the dudes in this mall haven't seen me butt-ass naked," said Colby, shocking both Mari and Shauntae. Colby rarely stood up for herself.

"Whatevah, trick," said Shauntae, with a wave of her hand.

"This is ridiculous. I'm tired of arguing, and I need to get some new clothes," said Mari. "I'm going to Rainbow."

They all had attitudes with one another as they walked out of the shoe store. Mari was thoroughly annoyed and considered ditching her friends to finish her back-to-school shopping alone. As they walked through the mall, Shauntae did get the most attention, but Mari and Colby were used to it. Shauntae had had a grown woman's body since she was thirteen and she knew how to handle it. Mari did wish she would slow up on the number of guys that she got with, but Shauntae was headstrong, and it was hard to tell her anything.

"I'ma dip into Rich's," said Shauntae, finger-combing her curly hair and slinging her empty backpack over her shoulder. "I'll catch up with y'all."

"Get something for me," said Colby as Shauntae walked off. They knew the next time they saw Shauntae that her backpack would be full, but she wouldn't have spent a dime.

"Does that girl ever pay for anything?" asked Mari, already knowing the answer to her question.

"Nope," said Colby. "She's got that thing down to a science. She racked up at the jewelry spot last week. Check out these silver hoops she got me. I hope she doesn't get caught again."

"Don't be putting that bad energy out there, girl," said Mari.

"Well, we won't be minors anymore in a couple of months when we turn seventeen," said Colby, "and if she gets caught stealing as an adult, she'll probably get in some real trouble, not juvenile stuff anymore."

"Aw, you just said Shauntae had skills," said Mari as they walked into Rainbow. "The only reason y'all got caught before is because she forgot about the cameras in the dressing room, right?"

"Yeah. Anyway, I've boosted for the last time. I'd just rather pay for my stuff and not risk it again," said Colby.

"That'll probably keep you out of jail, which is good," said Mari, "but I won't front. I loved that CD player y'all got for me that one time. I still use it."

Colby stopped at the tennis dresses, picked one up and placed it in front of her thin frame in the full-length mirror. At nearly seventeen, she still had the underdeveloped body of a twelve-year-old, and her glasses sometimes made her look just that age.

"This would be cute if I had something to fill it out with," she said. "Shauntae would look like a Barbie doll in this."

"Nothing's going on in here," said Mari, ignoring Colby's comments. "Let's hit the food court. Shauntae knows we always end up over there anyway."

A half an hour later, Shauntae flopped down at a table with Mari and Colby and dropped her bursting knapsack on the floor.

"I guess you racked up," said Colby. "What did you get me?"

"Now you know I don't discuss the goods before I go home and check them out," said Shauntae, grabbing one of Colby's French fries.

"You could have asked," said Colby.

"What are you going to say? No?" dared Shauntae, taking another fry.

"Maybe," said Colby, scooting her plate over. "Get your own food, greedy."

"With your string bean of a body I guess I should leave your food alone. That's why I didn't get your stingy butt anything," said Shauntae. "I had a close call up in there, but I worked it out. I think this'll be my last time for the summer. I basically got all the gear I need anyway. I'ma sell some of this stuff and get me a little dough to get some smoke, too."

Colby looked around quickly to see if anyone was listening to their conversation. "I wish you wouldn't be so loud about what you do," she whispered to Shauntae. "Everybody doesn't have to know that you smoke."

"Fool, everybody in this mall is probably high right now," said Shauntae with a sweeping gesture.

"Well, I'm glad you didn't get caught. My grandma was pissed when she had to come and get us from the police station last time," reminded Colby.

"We probably would have gotten away if you knew how to handle the security guard, but your skinny butt doesn't give a man much to look at," said Shauntae.

"You've got one more time to say something about me, Shauntae," threatened Colby.

"Or what, punk? What are you gonna do?"

Colby just kept eating her fries.

"At least your grandmama came and got you," said Shauntae. "When I got home, my mama just told me I was too stupid to even know how to shoplift without getting caught."

"Your mama ain't the brightest color in the box, you know?" Mari snickered. "Only Mrs. Washington would name her child after some old eighties rapper, Roxanne Shauntae. Your mama really wanted to be a rapper, huh? That is *so* funny."

"Shut up, Mari, before I have to come across this table," said Shauntae, standing up. "Your mama ain't all that, either. She looks like a played-out old hippie with that wild hair."

"Keep talking, Shauntae, and I'll knock you so silly that you'll feel as drunk as your mama always is," said Mari, rising from her seat as well.

"Y'all are just ridiculous," said Colby. "Ain't nobody's mama perfect, so cool it now."

"What are you? The long lost member of New Edition?" teased Shauntae. She started singing the group's old school hit "Cool It Now," and when Mari joined in the singing, they drew some applause from tables nearby.

Colby laughed at her friends, slightly embarrassed at the attention they were getting in the food court. "Y'all are so crazy, but I love ya," she said. The mood was lifted, attitudes were gone, and all three girls laughed and joked the rest of the time they spent in the mall, shopping until they were nearly broke.

All the talk about mothers made Mari think about hers as she was standing outside the mall later, waiting for Kalia to come and pick her up. She really wondered what other people thought about her mother.

"Do you think Mama's happy?" she asked Kalia, getting into the champagne-colored 2001 Camry she hoped her sister would be willing to share with her since she was a newly licensed driver.

"I guess so. What do you mean?" Kalia questioned.

"You know how she's always acting so free-spirited and stuff, but lately she's just been kinda down."

"Well, she and Daddy haven't been really talking. Something's going on."

"Something is always going on between them, but this something is a little different."

"Yeah, you're right," Kalia admitted, "but at least they put up a good front at the party."

"As usual. You don't think they would ever get a divorce, do you?" Mari almost whispered.

"*No*, of course not," Kalia lied, knowing she'd been thinking the same thing for months. "They're just going through it like they always do. There's nothing really wrong. They'll snap out of it soon enough, and things will be back to normal."

"Okay. If you say so," said Mari, not really as comforted by Kalia's reassuring as she wanted to be. "I just really worry about them sometimes. They're never together really and when they are, they're either ignoring each other or screaming and yelling."

"I told you they'll be fine," said Kalia. "They've just got a lot going on. Ma just finished with the Black Arts Festival and she's nervous about that application for the loan to get her yoga studio. Daddy's opening a new restaurant, and you know how he gets all crazy when he's doing that. Plus, they were helping us plan our last party, and school is starting and all…you know, they're just stressed."

"Umm, hmm, but I thought that married people were supposed to be happy. They always look happy on TV, even when they're fighting. They always end up working it out, you know, and laughing about it," said Mari as they pulled up to the house. "Our parents haven't seemed happy to me in at least the last year."

"That shows how much you know about marriage, silly. TV

is fake, okay? Married people are happy sometimes, and they argue a lot of the time. That's just how it is," said Kalia authoritatively.

"Umm, hmm. Whatever you say. I hope I don't have a marriage like that."

"Don't worry. Nobody's gonna marry you because you're too messy."

"Shut up, neat freak."

A few weeks later Kalia saw just how serious things were getting between their parents when the night before school started, she got up to go to the bathroom in the middle of the night and caught her father sleeping in the guest bedroom. On the ride to school that morning, while Mari chattered away about her first day of tenth grade, Kalia debated about whether to tell her sister about her parents' new sleeping arrangements.

"Tenth grade better be fun. I mean, aren't your high school days supposed to be the best days of your life?" asked Mari. "Well, if ninth grade was any indication of what the rest of high school is going to be like for me, I might as well quit now and work at the post office."

"I think you have to finish high school to carry mail," said Kalia. "You've just gotta find something that you'd like to get involved in at East Moreland—some kind of activity or club or something."

"I don't want to be in their boring old clubs. I wanna kick it."

"Too bad for you 'cause you sure don't go to a kick-it school."

"Shut up. I know that." Mari pouted. She hated going to private school—or at least the lack of people who looked like her at East Moreland.

"You shouldn't be so smart," teased Kalia.

"Well, smart and boring is the last thing I wanna be. What good is all this brainpower if I'm bored to death? You're lucky. All kinds of stuff is going on at your school."

"I can't help that I get to go to Williams. Like I said, you shouldn't be so intelligent."

"I'll trade you my brain for your talent," offered Mari, getting out of the car.

"Never."

"Why not?"

"Because creativity will take you farther than intelligence any day," said Kalia, putting the car in Drive to pull out of the parking lot.

"Thanks for the ride, chauffer."

"Later."

As Kalia drove toward Williams, she realized she had not told Mari about seeing their father sleeping in the guest room. "I guess I'm not supposed to tell her," she said out loud. She watched the landscape of the city changing as she navigated her way downtown. Mari's school was near the governor's mansion, where there were gated estates and several country clubs with meticulously mani-cured grounds. She bypassed the upscale shops and boutiques that she'd only been in a few times with her mother, when Elaine was splurging on an outfit. The closer she got to Williams, the more skyscrapers and concrete she encountered. Sure, there were land-scaped city parks carved out here and there, but the lush greenery of the East Moreland area was not duplicated downtown, and being that it was the last week in August in HotLanta, the heat was so stifling that steam was rising off the street at seven-thirty in the morning.

Only in Atlanta could it be nearly eighty degrees first thing in the morning, Kalia thought, looking at many of her schoolmates mixed in with the throng of mostly businesspeople pouring out of the Five Points MARTA train station. As a senior, Kalia was finally going to get a space in the school's parking deck, and she couldn't be happier. She hadn't ridden the train in from their Southwest Atlanta neighborhood since tenth grade, but now she would no longer have to hunt around for parking on the street.

"Good morning," said Dewayne, nearly scaring the life out of Kalia, opening the passenger door of her car and sliding in as she was stopped at a streetlight. "What did I tell you about locking your doors, girl?"

"I know…I know," said Kalia. "Somebody's gonna jack me one of these days."

"And then whose house am I going to hang out at?"

"'Cause it's all about you, right? Who cares that somebody's just grabbed your girl and probably hauled me off somewhere?"

"They'll bring you right back as soon as you open your mouth. Nobody but me can take all of that bossing around."

"Get out of my car, right now," ordered Kalia.

"See. You just couldn't wait to tell me what to do."

"Shut up."

"And you can't stop. It's a good thing it's all love between us," said Dewayne. "So how do you feel being a senior and all? This is it. We've got one more year of frivolousness, then we'll be thrust into the world as starving artists."

"I don't know about you," said Kalia, "but I'm not trying to miss any meals. I've got a plan."

"Oh, do you really? Tell me about this grand scheme, and of course don't forget to include where I fit in. You know it's all about *moi!*"

"Look, *moi,* my plans are just that right now—my plans. I ain't ready to share yet. I'll let you know when I am."

"All right, OO7. Keep your little secrets to yourself. I've got some secrets of my own. Maybe one day we can rendezvous for a clandestine meeting and exchange classified information. You know the Chosen One is always down for adventure."

"Okay, you're trippin'. Get out," Kalia said, pulling into a parking space. "You need to disengage yourself from that creepy comic strip world and concentrate on some real art."

"How many times to do I have to tell you that the universe of the Chosen One is real art? People get major recognition for these types of illustrations. Plus, there are new ways that I'm finding to combine some Web stuff with animation and..." said Dewayne.

Hustling down the steps of the parking deck, Kalia shook her head at her friend. "Boy, I just don't want to see you end up at one of those comic book fairs with all the overtattooed, over-pierced grimy guys who only leave their mother's basements to go to those weirdo conventions."

"You just don't understand what I'm trying to do."

"Yes, I do. You're trying to create some X-Men–Spider Man thingy, and I still say that's not real art. What's up with the styles of Romare Bearden and Jacob Lawrence? I'm sure if you worked at it, you could create art like theirs."

"But that's not me, K. I don't want some sterile, museum exhibit-type art style," Dewayne insisted.

"Well, you're never gonna get recognition from the important people in the art community," said Kalia as they entered the halls of Williams, which was teeming with a mix of urban hip-hop kids and alternative artistic teens.

"Who says I want their recognition? Who cares what they say? I'm doing my thing, just like you," said Dewayne, swooping around a dancer stretching against the wall and swerving to nearly miss getting clipped by a guitar case slung over the shoulder of another student.

"What do you mean, like me?"

"I know how well you can sing classical like Denyce Graves and jazz and stuff, but to me you're more like an Alicia Keys. You're always trying to appeal to the highbrow crowd, singing traditional stuff, but you've got some Jill Scott funk in you or something. You can create your own style with your talent. I know you wanna do it anyway. You blew everybody away at your birthday party."

"What the hell are you talking about, D? The only reason I sang that song is because Mari didn't think I could," said Kalia, quickening her step. "I'm a serious singer—a trained musician. I work hard on my voice and my playing. I do not…hold up…will not be pimped out in some skimpy outfit grinding on some man talking about how I can do it to him better than the next chick can!"

"Slow down, mama. You're missing the point. What I'm trying to—"

"I know what you mean, and I'm not trying to hear it. I gotta find my first class, so I'm out," said Kalia, turning on her heels and marching off down the hall, leaving Dewayne to make his point to himself. She hated that he knew how to break her down so well. How did the conversation get turned around to be about her anyway? she wondered. Weren't they talking about him and his comic book obsession? She didn't want to admit it to herself, but she did enjoy singing that song by Alicia Keys, who *was* a classically trained vocalist and pianist. So if she performed more Alicia Keys-style music, would she really be turning her back on years of serious training?

chapter 3

Two weeks later, Kalia, Mariama and Dewayne were on the way home after Mari's cross-country practice.

"We need another car in this family," said Kalia, "'cause I'm sick of hauling your stinky butt around."

"You were the one who was rushing me after practice. If you'd given me ten minutes, I could have taken a shower," said Mari, stretching out across the backseat.

"I think you're gonna have to fumigate this car," said Dewayne to Kalia.

"Whatever, man," said Mari. "You know you love my natural fragrance."

"If that's natural, then you need to visit a doctor because that's the worst body odor I've ever smelled," said Dewayne.

"Cut it out, you two," said Kalia. "I'm serious. I think we should ask Elaine and Ronald for another vehicle."

"Now you know Mr. and Mrs. Jefferson are not going to get me a car," said Mari. "They hardly let me drive with them. It *so* sucks that I've got to have like a kazillion hours of driving with them before I can drive by myself."

"I had to do it, and you certainly need the practice," said Kalia. "I've seen your skills. Daddy is still trying to get the grass to grow back from where you ripped it up. Remember when you almost backed into the bushes? Ooh, he was hot!"

Dewayne and Kalia burst out laughing.

"Shut up," Mari said.

"If you get better, they might get you a car." Kalia chuckled.

"You ask Daddy and see what he says," Mari said, twisting up her face. "That old cheapskate is going to launch into that story about how he didn't have a car at this age and how he was able to do everything he had to do on public transportation," said Mari.

"And how we should be grateful that we have one car to share…yeah, yeah, yeah… I know the speech…but we might as well ask," said Kalia. "Nothing beats a failure but a try."

"You are so corny," said Dewayne to Kalia.

"You can walk, ya know?" said Kalia.

"Yeah, put his skinny butt out," encouraged Mari.

"I'll put both of you out of this car, then you'll both be walking," said Dewayne.

"I'd like to see that," said Mari, thumping him in the back of the head.

"Stop playing, girl," said Dewayne, catching Mari's arm. "See, you just can't leave well enough alone."

"You better quit before I put my stank on you," Mari said, threatening him with an armpit.

"You win," said Dewayne, letting go. "That skunk funk has the power to kill, but the Chosen One knows how to avoid smelly evil."

"Ahh, shad up. Hey, did y'all hear about that talent contest?" asked Mari.

"Yeah, I heard something about Fire Records doing some type of show," said Dewayne.

"It's supposed to be open to anybody in high school in the metro area. They're going to have the preliminary contest in October when they'll pick twenty people to compete again in December, where they'll narrow it down to eight. Then the last eight will be in one more contest in March and that's who they'll pick the winner from," said Mari.

"You sound like you work at Fire Records," said Dewayne.

"I don't, but that would be cool," said Mari. "Hey, Kalia, you should enter."

"Umm, yeah. I'll enter, right," said Kalia.

"That would be tight," said Dewayne. "I could be your manager. That would be a perfect alter ego for the Chosen One."

"Shut up, Dewayne," said Kalia. "I'm not entering any singing contest. They probably don't even have a good prize."

"How did you know it was singing?" asked Mari. "I said it was a talent contest."

"So you heard about it, too, huh?" said Dewayne to Kalia.

"I didn't hear what you get for winning," said Kalia.

"Well, I think I heard something about a record contract," said Mari.

"That settles it. We're entering," declared Dewayne.

"What do you mean 'we'?" asked Kalia.

"So you do want to enter," said Mari.

"I didn't say that," said Kalia. "Contests are stupid anyway. I've got more important things to do with my time. I've got to write a song for my music theory class and the chorale is doing Handel's *Messiah* again this year. We're going to be practicing like crazy. Plus, I just found out that a large part of my grade in my piano class this year will be based on me being able to play some really complicated pieces. I'm not entering a dumb singing competition, just to get all stressed out about it. Nope. Not me."

"Umm, hmm," said Dewayne and Mari, both eyeing Kalia.

"For real. I'm not doing it," Kalia insisted.

"Well, you'll be the dumb one if you don't," said Mari. "A record contract? Do you know how great that would be? I'd be the sister of the new Beyoncé. Just call me Solange."

"Now see, that's why I'm not going to enter right there. You won't catch me shaking my behind like that," said Kalia.

"Shake, bake, whatever. Every time I see her she's strutting like she's on a catwalk or something, in Dolce & Gabbana, Armani or Gucci. And look who she's with. Jigga is the ultimate baller."

"I thought you were a Lil Jon-T.I.-Ying Yang Twins girl," said Dewayne.

"I am, but ain't none of them rollin' like Jay-Z, *okay?*"

"Right, right," agreed Dewayne.

"I can't wait for you to win," said Mari, returning her attention to her sister.

"I can't believe we agree on something, Mari," said Dewayne, "but I think you're right. I think Kalia could win."

"Thanks for the vote of confidence," said Kalia, "but you're wasting your breath."

"That is shocking that we agree on something, but we do," said Mari. "Kalia, if you don't enter this contest, you'll be making a mistake."

"Good thing I'm old enough to make my own decisions, ain't it?" Kalia said, huffing.

"You don't have to get all snotty about it," said Mari.

"Well, I told y'all I wasn't doing it, and you're still talking about it. Give it a rest, okay?" snapped Kalia.

Mari and Dewayne got the picture. Dewayne turned up the radio, and the rest of the ride home was spent in silence, each one thinking of how they'd be affected if Kalia entered the contest.

The next day at cross-country practice, Mari ended up being the pacesetter for the team. As she was leading them through a winding path in the lush green forests around the campus of East Moreland, she noticed someone gaining on her. Looking sideways, she realized it was, of all people, Asha Wright, the only other black sophomore at her school. When she reached Mari, Asha began keeping Mari's exact pace and breathing. This had never happened to Mari before. It was kinda weird, and she tried to speed up and change her breathing a few times, but that was weird, too, because it wasn't natural.

"So what? You're running cross-country now?" Mari breathed heavily to Asha.

"I just thought I'd give you a little competition," said Asha, quickening her pace. Mari noticed that Asha was not nearly as winded as she.

"Whatever," said Mari, speeding up as well.

They almost killed themselves running the final half mile, trying to outdo each other. Both came flying down the last hill, arms flapping and legs looking like spinning spokes on a ten-speed. Instead of tapering off into a warm-down, each flopped out on the front of the gym steps, spent. Mari hoped it would go unmentioned that, if they were racing, she didn't come in first place.

"That's quite a stride you've got there, Miss Thing," said Mari, resting on her hands.

"I've been running all summer," said Asha, flipping her nearly waist-length braid back over her shoulder as she bent over stretching.

"So you like these long distances? It's just not my thing."

"They're not too bad if you know how to run them."

"What do you mean?"

"You know, get your breathing right, your stride right. My trainer, Pierce, used to work with Jackie Joyner Kersee, and he said the three most important things in track are being strategic, becoming one with your body and you've gotta have a lot of heart."

"Oh yeah. I've heard that before," lied Mari.

"Really?" Asha smirked. "He told me he got that from Jackie's personal coach, so I don't know how you would have heard it."

"Well, you know I watch a lot of ESPN," said Mari, lengthening the lie. She wasn't going to let Asha think she didn't understand what she was talking about. She'd already beat her at her thing. Knowing more about it would be unbearable.

"Umm, hmm," said Asha, rising to her full five foot ten. "I hear we're running the horse trails tomorrow. I hate them. You never know what kind of smelly, unpleasant surprises those beasts will leave behind."

"That's why you can have this cross-country mess," said Mari, getting up, too.

"Oh, I'm just doing this so I can run track in the spring," said Asha, walking into the gym.

Mari didn't know what to say. Track was her thing. Only one person in the whole school—a senior—could run as fast as her. Why was Asha running track? she wondered.

Following Asha into the locker room, Mari felt her anger rising.

"So I thought you did plays and stuff in the fall," she said. "Aren't you going to join that theater group this year?"

"Well, yes, I am. They have auditions this week," said Asha, grabbing her shower caddy. "I know I'm going to make it, too. Professor Ritchie said he wanted to cast me as Eponine in *Les Misérables,* which is great because you know I speak French, and I went to a theater camp this summer where I boned up on my projection in *A Raisin in the Sun* playing Beneatha. I was great—got a standing ovation."

"That's lovely and everything, but how are you gonna do cross-country and theater?"

"Coach Little said he'd work it out with Professor Ritchie. When he called me this summer, he told me he really needed some more speed on his team."

But I'm the speed, Mari thought. *Coach called her this summer? He's never called me at home.*

"Oh well, I guess I'll have to show you the ropes," Mari tried to say nonchalantly, realizing that Asha was recruited for the track team while she'd had to try out last year.

"I think Pierce knows what he's doing. He's had me doing aerobics and weight training to prepare, and Coach told me that I needed to run cross-country as well," said Asha. "Thanks anyway. I'll let you know if I need some of your help. If I keep beating you like I did today, you might need my help. I'm hitting the showers."

"Be careful," Mari yelled after her. "Wouldn't want you to fall in there and break a leg or anything."

Her spoken wishes didn't make her feel any better, especially since Asha didn't respond. She didn't even know if Asha heard her. Sitting on the bench in front of her locker, Mari daydreamed about an ambulance pulling up to the gym and hauling off an injured Asha, who'd slipped in the shower and fractured her leg. A grin spread across her face.

Walking outside to wait for her father to pick her up, Mari spotted Randall Davidson, a guy from her Early World Literature class. She wasn't normally the intimidated type, but Randy was different. He and his family were entrenched in East Moreland. His parents and grandparents had attended the school, at least one relative sat on the board, and the fine arts building was named after his great-uncle, who'd been a huge benefactor forever. But that wasn't what really got Mari about Randy.

What bothered her was that Randy had been getting the best of her in class lately. He had a good answer to every question their teacher, Mr. Wills, asked and all of his comments were insightful. Mari had liked the class immediately. It had most of the elements to engage her competitive nature. The subject matter they were going to cover was interesting. She'd always liked Greek mythology and stories set in faraway places, and she was ecstatic when she found out the grade for the class would be heavily based on papers and participation in class discussions as opposed to pop quizzes and tests. This was just the type of class she not only enjoyed, but in which she knew she could perform well.

Looking around the classroom one day as class was nearly over, she wondered if any of the other students felt the same way—that Randy was just taking over the class. But unlike Mari, no one else looked or acted like they felt overly competitive with him. The class was having a deep discussion about the myth of Hades and Persephone. Randy was intensely defending his interpretation of the myth. Mari told Mr. Wills that she had a different understanding.

After being corrected by her teacher, who sided with Randy, Mari sulked through the rest of the class. She didn't even speak up to answer questions to which she knew the answers. Randy ran away with the discussion.

Walking out of Early World Literature and toward her locker, she was so wrapped up in how to dispose of Randy that she almost knocked Asha over in the hallway.

"You need to watch where you're going," said Asha, avoiding their collision.

"Oh yeah. Sorry," said Mari.

"Hey, I think you've got some visitors here."

"What?"

"There were these two black girls up here asking for you."

"Who were they?"

"I don't know," said Asha. "I do know that one of them was really loud and her clothes were a lot on the eyes."

"What are you talking about?" asked Mari, scanning her brain for who could be at East Moreland looking for her.

"They were down by the boys' school. The one with the plastic pink stilettos and the pink Tar-zhay jeans was talking to Derrick. He's such a nerd. I don't even think he noticed how skanky she looked."

Mari realized that Asha was most likely talking about Shauntae and Colby. She knew she had to find them before Shauntae caused a problem.

"Where did you say you saw them?" asked Mari.

"On the steps in front of Royal Hall. You better get down there if you know those girls. They were driving some kind of hooptie-looking thing and blasting some hip-hop. They won't last long around here with security."

Mari ran down the covered steps from the girls' school through the administration building and out the side door. She was right. There was Shauntae leaning against a beat-up white Caprice Classic, which Mari thought would be perfect for MTV's *Pimp My Ride.* Derrick Travis, a black junior at East Moreland, was standing right up against her. Mari knew that half the campus could hear Lil Jon and the East Side Boys. At least thirty students, mostly white, were milling around in the courtyard and outside the sliding glass doors of the lunchroom. Everybody's attention was directed at Shauntae's display. Glenn and Ed, two other black male juniors, were making their way to the car where Colby was sitting in the driver's seat.

She was just about to head toward Shauntae when she saw Mrs. Reeves, the black senior adviser, step out of the lunchroom. *Oh Lord,* Mari thought, jogging down the hill.

"Girl, what are you doing up here?" she yelled, running up on Shauntae.

"I tried to call you on your cell, but you weren't answering, then Derrick here rolled by and, well, you know," said Shauntae, touching Derrick's face.

"You know I keep my phone off when I'm at school."

"That's your problem right there—ever heard of vibrate? And what? I can't come up here?" she asked as Mari shoved Derrick out of the way. "Hey, don't push him. He's a cutie."

"Yeah, don't push me," said Derrick, moving back toward Shauntae.

"Colby! Turn that down," shouted Mari, turning toward the car. "Y'all can't play music like that up here."

"What do you mean 'music like that'?" asked Shauntae, raising her right penciled eyebrow. She had grabbed Derrick back by his belt loops. "Black music? Hip-hop? You know all these white kids listen to is Eminem. They need to hear some of this crunk."

"That's n-not what I meant, Shauntae," stuttered Mari, wondering what she really did mean. "I meant that you can't play music loud like that on this campus."

"Umm, hmm, whatever," said Shauntae, reaching in through the passenger-side window and bumping down the volume. Derrick's eyes widened as her pink thong peeked out at all of East Moreland. "Why didn't you ever tell me y'all had such fine men up in here?"

"I don't know," said Mari, annoyed, watching Glenn and Ed on the other side of the car talking to Colby.

"So can I get your number?" asked Derrick, touching Shauntae's waist.

"I was looking for a pen, baby," purred Shauntae.

"Look, what's up? Y'all got a holiday or something? Why aren't you at school?" asked Mari.

"I didn't feel like going," said Shauntae, not taking her eyes off Derrick.

"Yo, G," Derrick called to Glenn, "you got a pen, man? I need to get this girl's number."

"Hold up, man," said Glenn. "I'm trying to talk to this honey right here. What's your name again, slim?" To Mari's dismay, Colby smiled as Glenn took her hand.

"Ooh. That's my part," said Shauntae, all of the sudden shaking her hips. "Crank that up, Colby."

"No, Colby, don't crank that up," Mari ordered.

"Girl, you know how we do. When Lil Jon says 'Ohhh-kaaaaay,' you know we gotta let the masses know," said Shauntae, grinding against Derrick. "I said crank it up, Colby."

Colby obeyed, and no one but Mari paid any attention to the growing crowd of white kids watching them and the two Mercedes and one Jaguar that were stopped behind them.

"Hey, you gotta move. There's people behind you," Mari screamed. She thought she would die of embarrassment.

"Shiiii…they can go around," said Shauntae, dancing around Derrick.

Fed up, Mari pushed Shauntae and Derrick aside, reached in the car and turned the radio off, ripping her new Baby Phat blouse on a jagged lock that was not pushed down.

"Hey! Why you trippin'?" said Shauntae.

"Yeah, Mari," said Derrick. "What's wrong with you?"

"I told you you need to move. People are trying to get around you," said Mari.

"Damn, girl," said Shauntae. "Colby, pull over."

"You're not about to leave, are you?" asked Derrick, following Shauntae over to the steps.

"Yes they are," said Mari. "'Cause I have to go to class."

"I've got a free period next," said Derrick. "Shauntae, I can give you a tour of the campus."

"They came up here to see me, and I have to go to class, so they're leaving," said Mari.

"Ladies, can I be of some assistance?" asked Mrs. Reeves, walking up behind them. "Mari, if you have guests on campus, they need to sign in in the administrative office."

"No, Mrs. Reeves, they were just leaving," said Mari, glaring at Shauntae.

"Help me up, baby," said Shauntae, reaching to Derrick. "We do have other places ta be. Other peoples ta see."

With a cutesy "whoops" and a devilish smile, Shauntae fell against Derrick as she popped up. Mari grimaced and avoided looking at Mrs. Reeves.

"We were just coming up here to check you out. You never invite us up here. Like this school is so damned special or secret or something," said Shauntae, writing her number in pen on Derrick's hand.

"I'll take you on a tour myself sometime really soon," said Mari, hoping to pacify Shauntae. "Hey, Glenn, don't you have physics next? Professor Tungsteen locks the door."

Continuing to talk to Colby, Glenn ignored Mari.

"Stop being such a hater," said Shauntae. "You know Colby don't get no play. Let her talk to that little nerd if she wants to."

"Y'all gotta go," Mari pleaded. "For real."

"We're going, dawg," said Shauntae, getting into the car.

"Ladies, if you would like to visit Mari again at East Moreland, you should let her know that you're coming, so she can be prepared," said Mrs. Reeves. "Guys, let these ladies leave. Don't be late for class."

At Mrs. Reeves's direction, Derrick, Ed and Glenn immediately said their goodbyes and headed back up the steps. Shauntae was outdone.

"Who asked you?" she questioned Mrs. Reeves, rolling her eyes. "You need to mind your own business."

"This is my business, young lady. I suggest you develop some respect for your elders," said Mrs. Reeves.

Shauntae pursed her lips, looking Mrs. Reeves from head to toe and back again. "You right about one thing. You sure are an elder," said Shauntae, turning to Mari. "We're leaving your stuck-up-ass school. Happy now?"

Intense embarrassment and helplessness to improve the situation left Mari speechless. Bending over, the best she could do was throw up the peace sign to Colby, who waved back sheepishly. Mari knew coming up to the school was Shauntae's idea.

Shauntae flicked a bird to East Moreland as the car sped off, smoke and loud backfire adding to Lil Jon's lyrics. Mari hung her head, wishing the ground would swallow her up. She felt a hand on her shoulder and looked up to find a warm smile accompanying Mrs. Reeves' touch. "Come on, Mari. I'll walk you to your next class," she said.

As they made their way up the steps under the burning gaze of at least fifty students, Mari thought about how she'd met Mrs. Reeves. The stately, well-coiffed, suited-down black counselor was the very first person Mari met who was associated with East Moreland. Mrs. Reeves attended the same church as Mari's great-aunt. She came over to the Jefferson house a few days after Christmas when Mari was in seventh grade and somehow, Mari remembered, she'd ended up in the living room with Mrs. Reeves, just the two of them together. Mrs. Reeves asked her about everything that day—sports, school, even boys. But she liked Mrs. Reeves's vibe so she didn't mind the questions. Mrs. Reeves treated her like an adult.

But she was afraid of what Mrs. Reeves would say about Shauntae showing up at East Moreland, and she sure didn't expect her first question.

"So why haven't you invited those young ladies to East Moreland before?" asked Mrs. Reeves, ushering Mari toward a gold-rimmed plush red sofa and seating herself upright in the matching chair.

"I don't know," said Mari, wondering how they got to her office. She didn't even remember the walk.

"They are your friends, aren't they?"

"Uhh…yes."

"So…"

"I don't know," Mari said, picking some imaginary lint off the sofa. "I guess I didn't think they'd like it or something."

"Why not?"

"I don't know. They wouldn't understand it up here. It's just easier for me to go to school here and not have to explain a lot of stuff to them about what it's like here."

"Well, what is it 'like' here?" asked Mrs. Reeves, making the quotation marks sign with her fingers.

"You know, there are a lot of rich people who go to school here—rich white people."

"You don't think your friends would understand rich white people?"

"Not really. They're just different."

"Different how?"

"They don't really get to see a lot of the stuff I see up here," said Mari, "like going on out-of-state trips and to plays and museums and stuff."

"Would you go and do those things if you didn't go to school here, Mari?"

"Probably, because my mother is a dancer, you know, and she used to take me and my sister to all of this creative stuff when we were younger."

"Sweetie, you're blessed to be exposed to lots of different types of experiences," said Mrs. Reeves, taking off her glasses and resting them on the table in front of her. "Everybody doesn't have those opportunities."

"I know. I know, but they just don't know how to act in different places. You can't act the same everywhere you go," said Mari, pulling at the fresh hole in her blouse to distract herself from tearing up. "I'm so embarrassed."

"It's natural to be embarrassed when you're trying to make the best of a situation that's out of your control. I'm sure your friends didn't really mean to embarrass you," said Mrs. Reeves, trying to be hopeful. "They were probably just curious about where you went to school."

"They never asked me, and I just didn't think about it. I didn't even realize I'd never asked them up here until Shauntae said it."

"Well, don't worry about it. I will say one thing, though. Be patient with those who don't have the same advantages or opportunities as you. Sometimes lack of knowledge and understanding manifests itself as petty jealousy."

Sniffling, Mari just nodded and accepted the tissue Mrs. Reeves handed her.

"Sounds to me like you're the lucky one in your group of friends. You're a very smart young lady, Miss Mari. I've seen your test scores. Lead by example. Those who want better for themselves will recognize that trait in you and follow and make their own paths."

"Okay," said Mari, looking at the clock on the wall. "Oh my God, I am sooo late for class. I've gotta go."

"Don't worry. I'll give you a note," said Mrs. Reeves, writing one out. "Whenever you want to talk, I'm around, okay?"

"Okay. Thanks," said Mari, taking the note and hurrying out the door. She'd begun feeling better in the confines of Mrs. Reeves's office, but as soon as she was outside, the rush of embarrassment was so strong she felt naked in the hallway. She nearly sprinted to her next class, hoping no one who'd seen Shauntae and Colby would approach her on the way.

Kalia got out of her last class early and figured she'd go home to practice instead of waiting for an available piano at school. All the way home she couldn't get the idea of her father sleeping in the guest bedroom out of her mind. As she approached the kitchen door, she heard her parents loud and clear. They were yelling. She thought about going around the front, but she knew they'd see her, so she just stayed in the kitchen, listening.

"Elaine, I'm not spending any more money on a car," said Ronald.

"Look, Ron, Mari is going to need her own transportation sooner than later."

"Well, those girls need to get jobs, then, like I had to when I was their age."

"But their lives are different than ours, and we can afford it," said Elaine.

"I can afford it, is what you mean."

"No, us, okay? Everything I do with these girls is a j-o-b, too— a labor of love, true, but it's hard work. You think I want to be hauling them around for the rest of my life? I need a break."

"You're not even driving them really anymore. Kalia's getting her and Mari everywhere they have to go. And what? My money is supposed to finance your break?" asked Ronald.

"That's right, or you can switch places with me. I can be the breadwinner and you can be the caretaker."

"You don't know the first thing about running a seafood restaurant," said Ronald, walking out of the kitchen and through the living room toward the front door. Elaine was in hot pursuit.

"Oh, I'd sell those joints," she declared, slamming her fist down on top of the piano, "then I'd open my own yoga studio. We'd live well off that. Plus, we'd eat better because I'd be a lot more knowledgeable about nutrition, and I'd probably be able to get you to come in and take a few classes to work on that pouch. Maybe you'd even learn to meditate."

In her going on and on about her quest to change her husband, Elaine hadn't noticed that Ronald was frozen. He hadn't moved an inch since she said that she would sell the Fish Frys. He was just staring at his wife of nearly twenty years like she was someone he didn't know.

"You…you…you would sell the Frys," he stammered. "After all of the work that you know that I've put into growing this business? I've worked harder on the Frys than I've worked on anything in my entire life."

"Including this marriage? Or your daughters?"

"I did this for you and the girls. That's why I'm out there nearly killing myself, so you and Mari and Kalia can have everything you need. I don't know why you want to do that yoga thing anyway. I got this. I'm the provider, and I'm providing."

"Well, how come Mari can't have a car then, Mr. Provider?" Elaine reasoned.

"Don't try to twist things around. I said everything they need, not want," said Ronald. "Both Mari and Kalia don't need a car. They might want one, but they sure don't need one."

"Ron, sometimes it's just nice to spoil your children from time to time."

Kalia couldn't believe that her mother was saying that she and her sister should be given anything. She always thought that it was her father who was the giving one. She wondered at that moment how her parents paid for the piano and whose idea it was to get it in the first place. Probably her mother's, she thought.

"I'm not buying Mari a car 'cause she's got one—the one Kalia has. They can share," said Ron.

"And that's just it, huh? You're the man, so you're gonna put your foot down and I'm supposed to obey?"

"That's about the size of it."

"All right then, I'll buy her a car. I ain't getting any younger, and you're probably going to work yourself to death and not even get a chance to enjoy any of what you've been working so hard for, anyway," Kalia heard Elaine say, and she knew the conversation was over. She didn't hear any more voices after that, just her mother walking up the front steps and her daddy starting his car.

"They are so predictable," Kalia said out loud as she went up the back steps to her room. Sitting on her bed, Kalia realized she was initially relieved that this argument between her parents was a short one, but she was also concerned about the frequency of the disagreements and how they never seemed to stay on the subject of that particular argument. Every time Ronald and Elaine got into it, the same two problems came up. Ronald wanted to continue to expand his seafood restaurants, which took most of his time and most of the money that he was making off the three restaurants he already had open, so he wasn't home much, and he appeared overly thrifty to his family.

Ronald was also dead set against Elaine opening a yoga studio at all, and he expressed this to her as often as he could. Kalia had been hearing them arguing frequently in the past six months about the Fish Frys, the yoga studio, money and spending time at home and with her and her sister, and now her sister was noticing, too.

Lying down on the bed, she tried to shake the thought of her parents separating and breaking up their family. Kalia ended up falling into a fitful afternoon nap. Her dreams were filled with terrifying images of her mother and father as old people, living separate lives, lonely, wishing they'd stayed together. When she woke, there were tears on her pillow.

chapter 4

Mari was fuming. She'd had another run-in with Randy. He was just on point, and she must have had on her invisible costume, because as much as she raised her hand, Mr. Wills only seemed to see Randy's. It was more than she could take, so she began blurting out her answers without waiting to be called on. That behavior only got her a short speech on rudeness from Mr. Wills in front of the class. Smarting from a public lecture, Mari sunk into her seat and didn't even attempt to participate for the rest of the class.

Spotting Asha on the way to her locker, she was trying to decide if she was in the mood to be bothered.

"What's happening, Mari?" said Asha.

"There's this guy in my Early World Lit class, and he's a real know-it-all," said Mari, opening her locker. "Do you have any of those types in any of your classes?"

"Uh, yeah…this is private school, silly. Everybody is a know-it-all. You should know that. You've been here just as long as me," said Asha.

"Well, I don't care about everybody else. This dude is really getting on my last nerve. I mean, he's answering like every question better than me."

"Well, maybe that means you need to study harder."

"Okay, so you're not hearing me. He's outshining me, all right? I'm sick of them having everything and knowing everything. Can a black person have something? Damn."

"What do you mean?"

"These people have money," said Mari.

"I know. My family has money, too," said Asha.

"Yeah, but not like they have money. Their great-great-great-grandparents were rolling in it. Can you say the same?"

"Well, no, but why does it matter?"

"The things that we're concerned about, they never even think about," said Mari. "Like, I'm afraid to ask my parents for a new car, but more than one of these lucky rich kids will come out of class on their sixteenth birthday to a brand-new BMW or Mercedes sitting in front of the school with a big red bow on top.

"And they have no idea what chores are because they never have to do any," continued Mari. "Their maids, which look like my grandmama, do everything for them. Some of the kids running around here, like Randy, have buildings on this campus named after their relatives. Their parents are like important government officials and CEOs of big companies. They just get all of these privileges like going to Italy and skiing in Switzerland during the holidays. Shoot, we just go to Louisiana where my mother's people are from."

"Okay, so what does all of this have to do with Randy? It sounds like your problem isn't really with him, but with wealthy people," said Asha.

"Whatever," said Mari, slamming her locker door. "He just thinks he can come in and run the class, and I'm not having it. These rich white people get to have everything and do everything. It's just not fair."

"You've just got to learn how to beat them at their own game."

"Maybe."

"Like the way I'm going to run circles around you at the track," said Asha, and crossed her eyes.

Mari was in a much better mood by the end of track practice. She didn't even let the fact that Asha beat her in the 200 dampen her spirits. But she did get annoyed after waiting outside the gym for thirty minutes for her father to pick her up.

"Your dad's not here, again, huh?" asked Asha, sitting beside Mari on the front steps of the gym.

"Yeah, and I can't find my mother or my girls, either. I've called them all," said Mari. "I don't know how he keeps forgetting to pick me up. This is the third time in like two weeks."

"Your girls? You mean those characters who were up here a couple of weeks ago?" asked Asha, lacing up her sneakers.

"Don't go there, Asha," Mari warned. No one had really brought up Shauntae and Colby's visit since it occurred, and she really didn't want to hear anything about it.

"Look, you want my mother to take you home?" asked Asha, trying to make peace. "There she is. I'll ask her."

Asha jogged to her mother's Lincoln Navigator. After a few nods, she turned around and motioned Mari to the car.

"Mama, this is Mari," said Asha, fastening her seat belt.

"Hello, Mrs. Wright," said Mari.

"It's nice to finally meet you, Mari. And listen, sweetie, Mrs. Wright was my mother. Just call me Roxie, baby. Everybody does," she said.

"Yes, ma'am," said Mari.

"No ma'ams, either. I know this is the Deep South and all, but we're New Yorkers, and I just don't need to get down like that, so it's just Roxie," said Roxie.

"*Okay*...Roxie," said Mari. "Thanks for taking me home. I kinda don't know where my family is. I guess I'm like an abandoned child."

"They want you. They just want a short break," joked Asha.

"Ha-ha. Very funny," said Mari.

"Mari, Asha tells me that you're giving her quite a challenge on the track," said Roxanne.

"Umm...yes," said Mari, reaching around the headrest in front of her and nudging Asha in the back of the head.

"*What?* I did beat you today. Twice," said Asha, pulling down the visor and sneering at Mari in the mirror. Mari stuck out her tongue at Asha.

"It's not nice to brag," said Roxie, nonetheless smiling proudly at her daughter. After a day of wrestling with Randy and her father forgetting to pick her up, the last thing Mari wanted to deal with was Asha's teasing. She began to rethink her decision to let Roxie take her home.

"Mari, I've got to stop by home for a minute, then I'll take you home. You wanna call your parents? You can use my cell," said Roxie. "As a matter of fact, why don't you tell your folks that you're going to have dinner with us tonight? I'm making my famous turkey burgers."

Hmm, a night with the Wrights, thought Mari. "Well…I don't know, Mrs. Wri—I mean, Roxie. I have homework and—"

"Yeah, Mama, you know midterms are coming up, and she's probably got a lot of studying to do," Asha broke in, narrowing her eyes at Mari in the visor mirror.

"Well, she's gotta eat, doesn't she? She might as well do it at our house," said Roxie. "Plus, you never bring anybody home. I don't even know who your friends are. Do you even have any?"

Asha glared at Roxie. "Yes, I have friends. Fine. Mari, do you want to come over for dinner?"

"Uh, well," stammered Mari, feeling caught in the middle of a mother-daughter battle, the kind she knew all too well.

"Great, it's settled," piped Roxie. "We're gonna have beauty night at the Wrights—I love it when I rhyme—and you are going to love my turkey burgers, Mari. They are off the chain."

After Mari left a message for her father on his cell phone that she'd been invited to have dinner at Asha's house, she began to pay attention to the neighborhood through which they were driving to get to Asha's house. She realized they were in the Cascades area of Southwest Atlanta where prominent black families had lived for decades. The houses were humongous, Mari thought. Her place could be the guesthouse behind the two- and three-story all-brick homes she was seeing with their balconies, bay windows, wraparound decks, manicured grounds, over-sized pools and winding driveways.

The ride to the Wrights was filled with get-to-know-you conversation, spearheaded by Roxie, which Mari thoroughly enjoyed. She liked Roxanne Wright and her Farrah Fawcett hair. The cut was so precise that when she bent her head, the wings stayed in place. Roxie wore her feathered do like she'd invented it. Her makeup was flawless, almost like she'd had her face done by a professional makeup artist. Mari wondered how many shades of eye shadow it took to blend that smoky sunset look Roxie had going on on her lids, and the lipstick was a perfectly matching high-gloss color. She wore a cream designer suit—the kind that didn't come from a department store. Her meringue bag and shoes matched, and her three main pieces of jewelry consisted of a pair of dainty but substantial diamond studs, a thin platinum necklace with a heart-shaped diamond pendant and a diamond ring on her right ring finger that had more baguettes than Paris.

She was crisp in style, but her personality was entertaining. Somehow, she knew all about the hottest singers, and Mari was really impressed when she recognized the voice of rapper JD who was being interviewed on the radio about his recent signing to Fire Records.

"You sure know a lot about hip-hop, Mrs. Wri—Roxie," said Mari, shaking her head, correcting herself.

"Well, you know, I gotta keep up with you young bucks," said Roxie. "It's part of my business, staying up on the trends. I'm trying to get with Alicia Keys and Fantasia. I'm looking into getting them to promote my products."

"Oh, what type of product do you…" Mari tried to ask.

"You've got the Wright Touch, baby," Asha sang, and very well, Mari thought.

"The Wright Touch?" Mari exclaimed. "You're like Roxanne Wright of the Wright Touch? My girls wear your makeup, but it sure doesn't look like that on them. Your makeup is great. Asha, why didn't you ever tell me?"

"Baby, you never told your friend about the Wright Touch?" said Roxie, furrowing her brows. "I thought I asked you to tell all your friends."

"My mama owns the Wright Touch line, Mari," said Asha. "You know, the kind all the celebrities wear."

"That is really cool, Roxie," said Mari.

"Thank you, Mari. Now what do you think about my idea to approach Alicia Keys and Fantasia? I like to get the opinions of my target market."

"I think it's a great idea. I really like Alicia Keys. She has really cool style. My girls like Fantasia. They're both really pretty and talented," offered Mari.

"Geez…Ma, this is why I don't like to tell a whole lot of people what you do," said Asha.

"Why? Why not?" asked Roxie.

"Because everybody gets all crazy about it, excited and asking me for products and stuff. You know how it is when I tell somebody."

"And you know I don't mind giving your friends product either. I wanna know what they think. Stop being so silly," said Roxie. "Mari, I'm going to hook you and your friends up when we get home. So what are you, a lip gloss girl?"

"Oh my gosh. How did you know?" asked Mari.

"That's my business, baby—Roxie is always Wright, right?" Roxie smiled, looking at Asha.

"Right," replied Asha.

Asha groaned as they turned onto the long winding driveway to the Wrights' house.

"Wow, you've got a really nice crib. It is so big. You must have twenty-five rooms," said Mari to Asha.

"About that," answered Asha nonchalantly. As Roxie parked, she sang the lyrics to one of the most played songs on the radio, "Game Boy" by Ace, a rapper from Decatur, an Atlanta suburb.

Getting out of the car, Mari and Roxanne joined in for the chorus.

As they were all dancing up the walkway, Mari nearly tripped looking at her surroundings.

"Your lawn is really nice, too," she said. "Is that what you call a yard this big? A lawn?"

"Thank you, Mari," said Roxie. "We have a gardener who comes in once a week to maintain it. Can you imagine Asha out here pulling weeds?"

"Very funny, Mama. C'mon, Mari. I'll show you around," said Asha, sauntering past dozens of sculpted bushes and shrubberies on the massive landscaped and manicured front lawn.

As soon as she entered the front entryway, Mari knew she was in a home that was different from hers. Everything seemed like it was in its right place. African art and artistic photos graced the walls and bookshelves, the rooms were spacious, and there were hardly any doors downstairs—Mari just turned a corner and she was in a different room. There were rounded adobe-styled entryways, and she could tell that Roxie or a wacky interior decorator had gone a little hog wild in the Southwestern motif.

The colors were coral and teal, and there were occasional reds, greens and yellows. Everything complemented everything else—

the intricately handwoven rugs, the hardwood floors and the seat cushions in the wood lounger, the maple dining room set complete with an ornate set of china in a regal marble cabinet and the kitchen bar that was complemented with comfy colorful bar chairs.

"I'll be down in a few minutes, ladies. Asha, fix Mari something to drink and show her where we kick it," Roxie shouted from the top of a wide spiral wooden staircase in the back of the kitchen.

"Your house is great," Mari said to Asha.

"Okay, you've said that," Asha reminded her. Mari immediately missed Roxie's presence.

"Well, it is," she said, wondering why she was there in the first place. If her daddy had shown up on time, she wouldn't be stuck with Asha, whom she was beginning to wonder whether she could ever really like.

"It is nice, ain't it?" Asha admitted. "I do wish it was bigger. I wish we could have a real gym. That would be fabulous, then I'd have somewhere for Pierce to hook me up in the mornings. You know I gotta keep my edge over you," she added, opening the door to the largest stainless steel refrigerator Mari had ever seen.

"Thanks. What kind is this?" Mari asked, taking a bottled water from Asha.

"That water is enhanced with minerals. It's the only kind I drink. You never know what's in tap water, girl. Let's go upstairs."

"Cool. And hey, you've got one more time to bring up track, and it's gonna be you and me. I'm in a slump, but that's how I set up my prey."

"Umm, hmm…*okay*. This is my room," said Asha, flinging open the door with a grand sweeping gesture.

Mari felt like she was in a fairy tale. Asha's room had everything any teenager could ever want. First of all there was so much space in it, Mari knew she could do three back flips and not hit a wall or a piece of furniture. Asha's huge cherrywood four-poster bed, draped with a butter-yellow spread and yellow curtainlike material over the posts, sat in the center of the room on an expansive plush yellow rug into which her feet were disappearing. There were butter-yellow window treatments that matched the cushions in the rocking chair and ottoman set in the corner and the window seats in the side window that nearly rose to the ceiling.

Every piece of furniture was a rich cherrywood, including several overflowing bookcases against the walls, an old-fashioned stand-alone rounded full-length mirror, an entertainment center that held a flat-screen television, a DVD player, a stereo and tons of CDs and DVDs, and the intricately designed desk and chair where Asha did her homework. The multicolored throws and blankets draped across the bottom of the bed and on the window seats matched the green, orange and red throw pillows on the bed, the rocking chair and the cushions of another couple of comfortable oversized chairs placed on either side of a huge walk-in closet that was filled with designer clothes, shoes and bags.

"I can't believe this," said Mari, walking around the room. "Asha, you've got everything in here, plus, enough space to host a track meet. I bet I could run the 100 in here. At least I could long jump."

"I thought we weren't talking about track." Asha laughed.

"Shut up."

Asha kicked off her shoes into the closet and fell backward onto the bed, observing Mari looking at the different paintings on the wall of young black women and then walking over to a wall-mounted photograph of a field with wild yellow flowers growing for miles and miles. The flowers seemed to meet the horizon. Something about the photo gave Mari the feeling it was taken in another country.

"Where was this taken?" she asked, then noticed the outside through what she'd thought were floor-to-ceiling wood-trimmed windows. "You have a balcony, too?" asked Mari, switching gears and swinging open the floor-to-ceiling glass-and-wood doors to step on a balcony that overlooked the side of the house where the gardener maintained a beautiful spread of flowers. Asha joined her on the balcony, and they both sat in a swing that was suspended from the ceiling of the overhang.

"The photo was taken in a little town not too far from Paris," said Asha.

"You've been to Paris? Like overseas?"

"Yep." They were swinging back and forth now.

"So what was it like?"

"The shopping was crazy. I mean, everything in Europe is like three years ahead in terms of fashion. We racked up on all kinds

of gear, and of course everybody smoked a lot and spoke French.
Thank God I speak French, too."

"Paris! That's what's up. When did you go? Was it cold? Were
there any black people? How was the food?" Mari was excited.

"We went last spring. Yes, it was kinda cold, but not too bad
because my mama got us these beautiful Burberry wool coats, and
we were chauffeured around, so we hardly felt the cold at all. The
food *was* different—really rich with lots of creamy sauces. Paris
has way more white people than black people, but we saw a lot
of blacks, especially Africans. Probably because my mama was
there to scout out models for Wright Touch."

"Did she find one?"

"She found a ton. I think they are going to choose one soon
to do some kind of European marketing campaign. We've been
to Jamaica tons of times and London, too. I think she's trying to
go to Brazil later on this year. I'll probably get to go."

"That's really cool that you get to travel like that."

"Well, you know that's how it is when you're a baller," said
Asha. "One day we'll probably have a private jet and everything."

"A lot of people wish they could have a life like yours. I mean
I've never been out of the country," said Mari, closing her eyes
to think. "Well, I take that back. When we went to a wedding
in Detroit when I was young, we drove across the border to
Canada, but we were only there for a few hours. We used to go
on a family vacation every summer to places like Disney World
and Washington, D.C. We did go to L.A. and New York City,
but I don't think I really know any black people who live like
you."

"There are a bunch of us, just not all in one place. Maybe you
can come back sometime when my mama is throwing one of her
fabulous affairs. You'll really see how the grown and sexy get
down then. It's catered, and there's a live band and champagne
flowing everywhere."

"That sounds like a video."

"Well, there are usually celebrities everywhere," said Asha,
hopping off the swing to lean against the wood railing of the
balcony.

"Ooh, like who?"

"Just some singers, rappers and a few actors and models—the

regulars. I'm going to take a shower," said Asha, changing the subject. "I'll use the one down the hall and you can use mine. Towels are in the closet, and just get a T-shirt and shorts out of the top drawer." Asha grabbed a towel and some clothes and disappeared from the room.

After dinner, Asha took Mari on a tour of the Wrights' home. Every room, all sixteen, not including the full basement and the four bathrooms, were just as impressive as Asha's room. There was all kinds of art—from sculptures to paintings and state-of-the-art technology all over the house. When they entered the foyer, Mari noticed the grand piano between two sets of spiral staircases and asked Asha who played.

"Not me," she said.

"I play," said Roxie, coming around the corner, "and Asha sings."

"You sing, Asha?" said Mari, a bit surprised.

"Well, I can do a little something," said Asha.

"Sing a little something for Mari, baby. I'll play," said Roxie, sitting down at the piano.

"Mama, I'm kinda tired from practice, plus, I don't know what to sing," said Asha, moving closer to the piano.

"Girl, please. You know you wanna sing. Stop all that fake modesty," said Roxie.

"Okay, I'll do a short something," said Asha, grinning.

"What do you want me to play?" asked Roxie.

"No, Mama, I don't need accompaniment. I'll just do something a cappella," said Asha.

"All right, Mari. Get ready," said Roxie. "You're gonna get the real deal now."

Asha opened her mouth and a whole 'nother person came out— one who clearly was blessed with such natural vocal abilities that it seemed eerie. She sang Mariah Carey's "Vision of Love." When Asha sang, she seemed to reach deep down in herself, and her emotion drove the song. Her voice was rich, like that of a seasoned singer's, and her range was wide. There were no falsettos in her high notes, and her low ones scraped the bottom of the barrel. Nearing the end of her short performance, Asha was leaning so far back to get those last notes that she was holding her stomach and the banister behind her simultaneously, seemingly needing to steady herself.

"Damn my baby is good," said Roxie, standing up and clapping furiously before Asha finished singing the last word.

Mari was shocked. She didn't expect that much soul to come from Asha. "You can really blow," she said. "How long have you been singing?"

"Oh, I had Miss Asha in vocal classes when she was four years old. She can sing anything, anytime, anywhere," bragged Roxie. "I don't know why she wants to sing that old stuff though. She needs to be singing something more contemporary, like Mary J. She can do it, too."

"Mama, you know I don't like to sing that stuff. That old-school Mariah is a great ballad," said Asha.

"Fine, sing some Jill Scott. I know you like her," said Roxie.

"Okaaaay," Asha gave in—again.

Sitting down again at the piano, Roxie started playing "He Loves Me," and Asha sang effortlessly. As she got into the song, Mari couldn't tell that there was ever any reluctance in Asha. She was ripping it, not as well as Jill, but close.

"I didn't even know you could sing. You should enter the talent show," said Mari.

"She is," said Roxie, "and she's gonna win."

"No I'm not," said Asha. "I am not singing in a talent show."

"Why not? You've definitely got the talent," asked Mari. "You know my sister sings. I've been trying to convince her to get in the show, too. What is it with you singers? Y'all can sing and you don't want to. That is so weird."

"I'm sorry for your sister 'cause my baby's gonna run away with that contest," said Roxie. "Anyway, Asha, you're entering that contest, and that's final."

"I don't want to, Mama," Asha whined. Mari couldn't really tell if she was serious.

"You'll have some great competition if I can get my sister to enter," said Mari. "You should go ahead and do it."

"So your sister sings what? Jazz? R & B?" asked Roxie. Happy for the opportunity to brag about her sister, Mari wasn't going to miss this chance to let Asha know she wasn't going to be able to win easily.

"Kalia's incredible. She can sing anything—classical, jazz, R&B—anything you throw at her. She goes to Williams High, downtown."

"Crunk High? That's where your sister goes to school?" Asha huffed. "I hope she's in the performing arts program because that's the only reason to go to Crunk High."

"Of course she's in the PA program, and I don't know what you have against Williams. It's the livest school in the city. It's sure got way more going on than East Boredom," countered Mari.

"Anyway." Asha waved off Mari and turned to her mother, suddenly changing her mind. "I'm picking out what I wear and definitely what I'm gonna sing."

"Sure, baby," said Roxie, winking at Mari. "Whatever you want, we'll talk about it."

"Umm, hmm," said Asha. "Don't think I didn't see that. Mari, don't let her suck you in. She's convincing. She's a marketer. That's what they do."

"Uh, they also make money, Miss Thing, which is why you get to eat so well and live so well and get such an expensive private school education," said Roxie, ascending the spiral staircase on the right. "I just want you to see what a great position you're in, Asha. All you have to do is study and sing and have some fun. I wish I had it that easy when I was a kid."

"All right, Mama, you don't have to guilt me to death," shouted Asha up the staircase after her mother. "I'm grateful."

She turned to Mari. "And I'm gonna whip your sister's butt, just as bad as I've been whipping yours."

"Whatever," said Mari, sending up a silent prayer to God to start working on convincing Kalia to enter the contest. There was no way Asha was going to beat her *and* Kalia. She'd do anything to see Asha lose, even if she had to get dirty making it happen.

"So how was dinner?" Elaine asked Mari, handing Kalia the glass part of the blender to fill with ice.

"It was cool. They have a big ol' house," said Mari, "and everything is spacious and wood and looks expensive, but is still kinda chill. I liked it… And hey…they have a piano, too—a white grand piano—in their entryway, uh, foyer, between two spiral staircases."

"Two spiral staircases, huh?" mumbled Elaine. She was cutting up fruit to make one of her famous smoothies.

Mari tried to keep talking about the Wrights' house, but

every time she opened her mouth, her mother turned on the blender. Finally she was done, and Kalia asked who played the piano in the house.

"Roxie can play," said Mari, "but get this, Asha sings…I mean really sings."

"Who is Roxie? Asha's sister?" Elaine asked.

"No, Ma. Roxie is her mother. She won't let me call her Mrs. Wright. I tried a couple times, but she said Mrs. Wright was her mother and everybody she knows calls her Roxie. I felt kinda funny, but…"

"Hmm," said Elaine, frowning.

"Asha can sing?" mused Kalia.

"And she's entering the talent contest, too, Kalia. I told her you'd give her some stiff competition," said Mari.

"You said what? Why did you tell her I was going to enter the contest? I told you I wasn't going to do it," said Kalia and stomped out of the kitchen.

Elaine poured a coral-colored smoothie to share with her younger daughter and sat at the kitchen table across from her.

"I don't understand why she acts like that, Ma. She has so much talent," Mari said. "If I was her I would enter that contest in a second."

"Everybody isn't you, sweetie. One of your gifts is that you have a competitive, adventurous spirit, and I love that in you, but Kalia isn't you. She's more cautious, especially with her gift," said Elaine.

"But it's not like she's not good at it. She's a great singer. There's nothing for her to be afraid of."

"What if Kalia isn't afraid, Mari? What if she's just checking out the lay of the scene?"

"Do you think she's going to enter the talent show?" asked Mari.

"Honestly, I don't know. I think she's interested, but this might not be her thing, and you need to be okay with that, baby. It's her talent. You have to let her accept and do with her gifts what she chooses. You have those same choices. Choices is what it's all about," said Elaine, getting up from the table.

Just then Ronald walked in the kitchen door. "Hey," he said, looking around kind of sheepishly.

"Hey, Daddy," Mari said, nearly jumping from her chair to give him a hug.

"So I guess your mother was able to pick you up," he said, patting her on her back and looking at his wife. "Sorry. I just couldn't get away tonight," he said to Elaine, who just nodded at him.

"That's okay," Mari eagerly forgave. "How was your day?"

"Long," Ronald said, slinging his bag on the table and reaching into the refrigerator for a cold beer. He had three long gulps before he even loosened his tie.

"Well, maybe you just need to sit down for a minute, Daddy," Mari said, ushering her father to the kitchen table.

"There's some smoothie left if you want some, or I can throw something on the George Foreman, if you want. You know how quick that grill is," said Elaine.

"Why are you being so nice to me?" Ronald asked sharply.

"What do you mean?" asked Elaine.

"I mean, you haven't been nice to me in months. What's up with the all-star treatment tonight?" said Ronald, kicking his shoes off into the middle of the kitchen floor, wiping one hand down the entire front of his face and letting it rest on his chin.

"Do we have to talk about this now?" asked Elaine, moving closer to Ronald.

"Are you okay, Daddy?" said Mari.

"Yes, I'm just fine," he said, suddenly remembering Mari was in the kitchen, too. "Just fine and tired. Tired of working so damn hard, and for what?"

"What are you talking about, Ron?" said Elaine.

"Nothin'. I'm just exhausted. I'm going to bed," he said and left the kitchen with all his stuff everywhere.

"Ma, you think Daddy's all right?" asked Mari.

"Girl, who knows?" Elaine said, clearly annoyed. "I'm tired of thinking about him and his Fish Frys."

"What do you mean? You think something is wrong with the Fish Frys?"

Elaine erupted. "Can somebody around here worry about something else besides the damn Fish Frys? There *must* be something wrong with the restaurants because that's the only thing he shows any emotion about or really pays any attention to. Your father is about to get on my last nerve with that," she said. Mari was watching her mother, and Elaine seemed to be straightening and restraightening the same thing in the kitchen. She'd wiped off the same counter at least three times.

"Are you okay, Ma?" Mari said.

"Yes, girl, I'm fine," Elaine said, stopping suddenly and staring at Mari. "I'm just fine. Why are you asking me all these questions? Go upstairs and do your homework or something."

"Okay. G'night," Mari said and headed out of the kitchen. Looking back over her shoulder, she saw her mother standing in front of the refrigerator with the door open, peering inside like she was looking for something she knew wasn't there. Mari knew that the next time she opened that refrigerator, it would be rearranged and clean as a whistle. Her mother always found things to do in the kitchen when something was on her mind, particularly if she was stressed or upset.

Mari wondered why her mother and father were acting so weird to her and to each other. Maybe Kalia would have a clue. Figuring Kalia was probably still mad, Mari decided not to knock on her door. She went to bed with her parents' strange behavior on her mind.

Kalia wasn't in her room. She'd needed someone to talk to, and had sneaked out of the house over to Dewayne's. She threw a rock at his window in the back of the house, and he came outside a few minutes later. They sat in the gazebo in Dewayne's backyard, which was extremely overgrown with grass, vines and weeds.

Kalia told Dewayne that on the way out of the house, she'd seen her daddy sleeping in the guest room again.

"You know, I don't know if they're getting separated or divorced or what," she said. "I just want them to stop fighting. The other day Daddy and I were talking about college, and he just went off on me, but it seemed to me who he really wanted to yell at was Ma, and since she wasn't there, he was taking all of his frustrations out about her on me.

"I told him I wanted to go to a college that has a good fine arts program. He said he wanted me to major in business and minor in fine arts. He doesn't understand how serious I am about music and how since I'm trying to double major in voice and piano, I really need an excellent fine arts program. He just doesn't get it.

"And God forbid I decide to enter this Fire contest that Mari is so hyped about. Daddy would probably really go bananas. I have been thinking about auditioning, though—I just don't want to get off track. I mean, what if I qualified? What if I won? That would be kinda crazy, huh?" Kalia half questioned. "Do you think I could win?"

Dewayne didn't answer—partly because he could tell she was warming up to the contest and partly because he knew her question was rhetorical. She was in full monologue mode, the star of her own show. He hadn't said anything since Kalia started talking. He just leaned as he always did.

"I…I…I…just can't think about the contest now… Hmm, I wonder what I'd sing, though… I really like Alicia Keys… I mean, you know, I've been thinking to myself, she is a classically trained vocalist and pianist. And she has great style. She incorporates all kinds of styles into her music and her performance. I mean, she can do it all. If she can do it, I can do it. Don't you think?"

Dewayne didn't even nod.

"Anyway, anyway, anyway—back to what's important… When I tried to explain to Daddy how much I'd thought about getting into a good fine arts program, he launched into this whole speech about Ma and how he didn't want what happened to her to happen to me. He was just talking about her so bad, saying she didn't have any business sense and because of that her yoga studio was going to fail. He was just going on and on about how if she'd had a business degree and wasn't so 'artsy fartsy' she might have been farther along in life."

Dewayne put his arm around her and pulled her head down to his shoulder. He still said nothing because he knew she wasn't finished.

Kalia put her hand on his chest and continued, "He called Ma flighty and clueless. I just couldn't believe it. He said if I knew what was good for me, I'd get a business degree and concentrate less on my singing and my playing. I've been practicing for years. I thought that he loved to hear me sing and play. He was clapping the loudest at the party, but somehow all of the sudden he's changed his mind.

"I think it really has something to do with what's going on

between him and Ma. They've been snapping at each other for months, and now they're sleeping in separate rooms and talking about each other behind each other's backs. It's just terrible. I wish they'd get their shit together.

"I mean could they really break up? Really?" asked Kalia, searching her friend's lean face for answers. He wiped the tears from her cheeks and smoothed her hair down.

"Dewayne, what would I do without you?" she asked him, wrapping her arms around his waist from the side. "Thank you so much for being there for me."

Dewayne's only response was a kiss on the top of Kalia's head. They sat in the gazebo for a long while that night, just holding each other.

"Girl, please keep your mind on the road and not your sister right now," said Elaine, putting down her paper. "You're gonna send that dog to meet his maker."

"Okay, okay," Mari said, swerving to avoid the lost-looking golden retriever. "But really, how did you?"

"Because Kalia is a creative young woman and she's ambitious and competitive, but mostly with herself. She likes to challenge herself, but stepping out of her comfort zone isn't really one of her strong points. So this is a brave move for her."

"When she told me last night that she was going to audition, I almost fainted. I was sure she'd wimp out. And then we, like, planned out her outfits and stuff. I mean, we haven't hung out like that in a while."

"I'm glad you guys are sharing this experience," said Elaine. "Did she tell you why she decided to enter?"

"Well, something about Alicia Keys and being able to sing and play all kinds of music. What if she wins, Ma? Ooooh, she'll be famous. And I'll be her sister, and I'll get to kick it with all the stars on Fire Records. I'ma have to get me some new gear, too. I can't be the sister of a star lookin' busted."

"You're gonna bust us up if you don't watch it. You're following that car too closely. Slow down or we're going to end up in his trunk," Elaine ordered.

Mari slowed too quickly and both she and her mother lurched into the dashboard. Her heart pounding and her life flashing before her eyes, she decided her mother was right. She needed to pay attention. What she really needed to do was go back home. Besides helping Kalia with her style for the Fire contest, midterms were upon her. She needed to be hitting the books and not wasting time fooling with her girls. Nevertheless, she'd agreed to meet Colby at the IHOP at noon to talk with her about whatever the pressing thing was that she swore she could only talk about in person.

As she pulled into the parking lot, Mari's suspicions proved to be true. Colby and Shauntae were visible through the glass window. She parked in a handicap space right in front and hopped out of the car, avoiding her mother's look of disapproval.

"Ahh, parking here is not going to win you any points with me," her mother called to her as she walked around the front of the car, checking out her outfit in IHOP's glass windows. She

chapter 5

Mari adjusted her seat for the third time. For some reason, she just couldn't seem to get comfortable behind the steering wheel. Maybe it was because she was distracted. Her mother looked at her and shook her head.

"If you don't want to drive today, we can do this another time," she said, flipping open the newspaper. "Pay attention. The light is changing."

Mari took her foot off the gas and tried to focus on the task at hand: getting to IHOP, which was right around the corner. As she drove, her thoughts wandered again.

She was still in shock that Kalia had decided to enter the Fire contest. When her sister had sauntered into her room the night before, acting like she wasn't looking at her wardrobe, Mari knew something was up. Kalia did not share her sense of style. After answering one too many questions about hip urban fashion, Mari started to get suspicious and Kalia finally gave it up. She was going to audition and she wanted Mari to be her stylist. They'd spend the rest of the night flipping through magazines and talking about clothes, shoes, hair and makeup. Kalia had really surprised her.

"Ma, how did you know that Kalia was interested in the Fire contest?"

liked her orange nylon track pants and her Nikes, she thought, pulling her orange trucker hat farther over her right eye.

"Oh, it was only for a second," she called to her mother.

"And that's all the time it takes to get a ticket," her mother said as she walked toward Colby, waving goodbye. Although she and Colby had gone to the movies in the last week, it had been nearly two weeks since Mari had seen or spoken to Shauntae. And she wasn't sure if she wanted to see her. Shauntae's performance at East Moreland was still fresh in her mind. She hesitated for only a second before joining them in line.

"What's up, C?" she said to Colby.

"Hey, Mari. We just got here," said Colby, nervously glancing at Shauntae, who was boring a hole into Colby.

"How long is the wait?" asked Mari, ignoring Shauntae.

"Umm...let me go see," said Colby, escaping the tension to look for the hostess.

Uncomfortable dead silence hung heavy between Shauntae and Mari, until Shauntae broke it.

"That dude Derrick called me," she said.

"I'm sure he did," said Mari.

Silence again. Mari spoke up this time.

"Well, did y'all go out?"

"Not yet. He's talking about midterms or something."

"Yeah. They're next week."

"He sure does talk a lot about school. As a matter of fact, that's mostly what he talks about, and he asks me about my classes, too. Talking about how he wants to be some kind of engineer and how he's going to work with NASA and stuff."

"Yep. He's ambitious," said Mari.

"So what? You're gonna do something like that, too? Be a big shot somewhere making a lot of dough?"

"I don't know, I guess," said Mari, surprised at Shauntae's question. In all of the years she'd known Shauntae, they'd never had a discussion about their future professions. "What do you wanna do?"

"I don't know," Shauntae said, looking at the ceiling. "I haven't really thought about it that much, but Derrick thinks about it all the time. He's got like this ten-year plan. Shoot, I don't know what I am going to do the rest of this weekend."

"Well, I'll be studying. I know that."

"Figures."

"What does that mean?" asked Mari, a little annoyed.

"So it'll be about ten minutes," said Colby, walking up. She was grinning, looking back and forth between Shauntae and Mari. "What are y'all talking about?"

"Nuthin'," said Mari and Shauntae at the same time.

"Oh," said Colby, disappointed.

Mari and Shauntae did start talking to each other again, but the conversation between the three of them remained a little strained all through breakfast. As they walked out, Colby tried to convince them to walk down to the drugstore with her to pick up some acne medication. Shauntae wanted to take the train to Lenox Square Mall, and Mari wanted to go home and study. The three were about to part company when they heard a loud screech. Turning, they saw a young man holding several rolled-up signs, dodging cars, across the busy four-way intersection in front of IHOP.

"He must be crazy," said Colby.

"Or have a death wish," agreed Mari.

"I'm glad he made it 'cause he's kinda fine," said Shauntae, finger-combing her hair and adjusting her pink micro-miniskirt.

He stopped just short of them at a light post, pulled some thick tape out of his back pocket and hung one of the posters before jogging over to them.

"Ladies, ladies, ladies," he started.

"Yes, yes, yes," said Shauntae, putting a hand on her hip.

"Do any of you sing?" he asked.

"Why?" asked Mari, eyeing him. He was handsome, she thought, checking out his wavy afro, freckled nose and dimples deep enough to swim in.

"What about you, Miss Lady?" he said, taking Colby's hand.

"Oh no," she said, jerking her hand back in surprise.

"I don't sing," said Shauntae, "but I have other talents."

"I'll bet you do," said the young man, looking Shauntae up and down. "Look, I'm putting up these posters for Fire Records. They're having this singing contest, Who's Got That Fire?, where you can win a record contract."

"Yeah, I heard about it. I know two people who are going to

enter," said Mari. "So what's the deal? Is there a fee or something?"

"Nope," said the guy. "You just have to show up at the label on the day before Halloween for prequalification."

"Do you work for Fire?" asked Shauntae, moving closer to him. "I see you've got all of their gear on. Do they make those shirts in baby Ts?"

"Oh, y'all like my shirt?" He grinned, spinning around to give them a better look. When he stopped, he was facing Colby. "I can get you one, cutie."

"Umm," said Colby, lowering her head.

"Well, I want one. It'll look better on me, don't you think?" said Shauntae, touching the back of his shoulder. When he turned around, she sucked in her breath to call attention to her shape.

He took the bait.

"No need to fight, ladies," he said, speaking directly to Shauntae's breasts. "I can get all of you shirts."

Mari rolled her eyes. "Ain't nobody fighting over a T-shirt. What's your name, anyway?"

"Sorry, ladies. I should have introduced myself. I'm Sean, and I work on Fire's street promotions team."

"What's street promotions? What do y'all do?" asked Mari.

"Right now we're getting the word out about this contest, talking to people, putting up signs and stuff. That's kinda what I do—you know, let people know when artists are coming out with a new album or when there's some kind of special promotion going on like this."

"So do you get to meet any of the artists? Do you know Ace or T-Lo or LaToya?" asked Shauntae.

"Well, I don't really know them, but I've met them a few times at meet and greets and sometimes at store openings and stuff," said Sean.

"So when are we gonna get a tour of Fire?" she purred.

"Umm, I don't know if I can hook that up, but I'll see what I can do," said Sean.

"I just wanna know how I can make sure my sister wins this contest, 'cause she's got that fire," said Mari.

Both Colby's and Shauntae's heads snapped around toward Mari.

"Kalia is entering this contest?" asked Colby.

"So you do talk, li'l mama," said Sean, taking Colby's hand again, "and you've got soft hands."

This time Colby didn't take her hand away, and Shauntae sucked her teeth.

"Well, I'm going to Lenox. Who's coming with me?" she asked.

"So that's where you ladies are heading off to?" asked Sean, staring down at Colby, who was now looking up into his eyes.

"Naw. Colby is going to get some pimple-popping stuff for her face." Shauntae smirked.

"That's your name, sweetie? Colby?" asked Sean.

"Uh, yes," said Colby, looking down again.

"You've got the prettiest face I've ever seen," said Sean, lifting her head with one finger under her chin.

"I'm jettin'," said Shauntae.

"Actually I'm headed that way, too. We've got another promotion going on up there," said Sean.

"Ooh, can I catch a ride?"

"That's cool, baby," said Sean, letting go of Colby's hand and looking at Shauntae's thick legs. "We can kick it."

"Ooh, and you can tell me all about how you got your gig at Fire. I am *so* interested," said Shauntae, looping her arm through Sean's. "What are you driving?"

"It was nice meeting you, ladies. I'm sure I'll see you around," Sean threw over his shoulder as Shauntae dragged him toward the intersection.

Mari shook her head at their departure.

"Girl, you're gonna have to get some game," she said to Colby. "He was feelin' you, but you let Shauntae get him."

"Oh, he was just being nice," said Colby, adjusting her glasses.

"Naw, I think he wanted to kick it to you."

"Well, I'll never win against Shauntae and her body."

"And that's about all she's got. I don't know why we keep hanging with her anyway. She ain't about much."

"She's our friend," said Colby.

"She wasn't acting like a friend to you just then," said Mari, spying Kalia driving up. "Any fool could see that Sean liked you. She saw it, and she didn't even care. She threw herself at him anyway."

"I guess," said Colby, looking lost.

"Come on," said Mari. "I'll ask Kalia to drop you off at the store."

Kalia was nervous. It had taken her and Mari all week just to pick out what she was going to wear—a cream scoop-neck blouse, some hand-painted jeans she'd scored at an overpriced consignment shop and her brown Steve Madden boots. If she sang Alicia Keys's "A Woman's Worth" one more time, she knew that the other students in the practice rooms at Williams were going to ban her from the building, but she had to get it just right. *I'm only getting one chance,* she thought, standing in the lobby of Fire Records. There were at least two hundred other potential contestants there for Who's Got That Fire? Some looked so professional with their throats wrapped in scarves, drinking hot lemon water and doing vocal exercises. Kalia remembered that she knew those exercises, too. She challenged herself not to be nervous. At the moment, she wished she hadn't exerted her independence. She wished that someone was there in her corner. Dewayne would be great. Even Mari would do.

The Lord must have been listening, because she got what she asked for. In walked her sister with Colby and Shauntae. Kalia tried to hide behind a column, but Shauntae spotted her immediately and ran over.

"Girl, I'm so excited for you!" she screamed. "If you win you're going to blow up!"

"What do you mean 'if'?" asked Mari. "She *is* going to win. Okay?"

"Yeah. Good luck, Kalia. I hope you win," said Colby.

"She doesn't need luck," insisted Mari. "She's got talent, and that's all she needs."

"What are y'all nuts doing here?" asked Kalia.

"We came to, uh, give you some support," said Shauntae, looking at a well-built young man standing nearby.

"I see," said Kalia, eyeing Shauntae.

"No, for real," said Colby. "We came to be in your corner. We can be your cheering section."

Kalia's cell phone beeped, and after she spent way too long trying to check her messages, Mari snatched it from her.

"You've got a text message, silly," she told her sister, punching buttons on the phone. "It's from Dewayne. Wanna see?"

Kalia peered at the phone. "Aw, he's wishing me good luck. That's great."

"See, Kalia. Just relax. We all know you got this," said Mari.

"Well, thanks for coming, but I really gotta get my head together. Look at all these people here," Kalia said, looking around.

"Don't think about them," said Mari. "It looks like it's going to be a long wait, so we're going to keep you company."

"Ooh, girl, do you think we're gonna see that fine Sean? I haven't talked to him since we hung out at Lenox. We had a good-ass time, too, and he bought me something to eat."

"What? A slice of pizza?" asked Mari, joining many of the other contestants sitting on the floor.

"No. Well yes. California Pizza Kitchen. It was pizza, but it was more than a slice," protested Shauntae.

"Umm, hmm," said Mari, watching Kalia, who was off in a corner humming to herself.

They sat on the floor for at least half an hour before the first singer was called. A tall, shapely young woman, wearing the short and tight outfit of a video girl, stepped from behind a red suede door and called one name after another. In the next hour they saw all ranges of emotions. Singers tripped in nervous and came out with big smiles on their faces. Others strutted in with the confidence of experienced performers, only to be wiping tears away when they came out twenty minutes later. Some just sauntered away like auditioning was something they did every day. When Kalia's name was called, she just froze—like a deer caught in headlights. Mari, Shauntae and Colby had to walk her to the door, all the while whispering to her that she was the best singer in the place.

It was going to take more than her sister to convince her of that, Kalia thought as she followed the video girl down a long hall lined with encased silver plaques touting the gold and multi-platinum successes of Fire Records. When they arrived at their destination, the video girl opened an oversized blue suede door and motioned for her to go through.

As Kalia entered the massive room, the spotlights directed at her gave her pause. It took her a minute to get adjusted, then she saw a microphone in front of her and instinctively stepped forward.

"Hello, Kaaah-liii-aaaah," a voice boomed from some direction she couldn't quite ascertain.

"Hi," she squeaked out.

"Are you ready? Are you warmed up?"

Kalia was now able to make out three shapes of who she figured were a panel of judges in a glass-enclosed booth about a hundred feet away. When she saw the edge of the stage she was on, her hands started sweating. It would be just her luck to fall off.

"Miss Jefferson? Are you ready?" the voice asked again.

"Oh yes," said Kalia, snapping back to reality. *Pay attention,* she said to herself. *This is it. Don't blow it.* "Yes," she said again in a much stronger voice. "I'm definitely ready."

"Okay, great," said a woman's voice this time. "So, Kalia, have you got that fire?"

"Absolutely," she said, grabbing the base of the mic to steel her nervousness. Her sweaty hands slipped up and down the stand.

"Tell us why you think you've got that fire," said yet a third voice.

Unprepared for an interview, Kalia was happy she was quick on her feet and that one of the few TV shows she'd allowed herself to get addicted to in the past year was *American Idol.*

"I know that I've got a gift that should be shared with the world," she started, letting go of the mic. "I've been singing and playing the piano since I was five years old, and I've known since then that being a creator—a performer—is all that I've ever wanted to do. I'm a talented person, and I want to use my gifts to make people feel something—happiness, sadness, some kind of emotion. I know I can do it, and when I finish you'll know it, too."

"Well, all righty then, Kalia," said the woman. "What are you going to sing for us today?"

"I'm going to do 'A Woman's Worth' by Alicia Keys."

She jumped when all of the sudden she heard the first few chords of the song coming from a piano not thirty feet from her. She hadn't even noticed the person sitting at the piano.

"Start when you're ready, Kalia," said the third person's voice. "Dennis will come right in."

Kalia closed her eyes, flexed her hands and thought three words—*Help me, Lord*. She then gave it up. Zoned out. Became one with her talent. When she opened her mouth, it was like she was singing in one of the practice studios at Williams. She didn't open her eyes until she got to the chorus, but by that time she was into it. She was handling every note like she'd been born to sing that song and that song only. Rocking and rolling with it, she had to place her hands on her hips then stretch them toward the sky to get all of the notes. She enjoyed this performance, and she nailed it. Instead of bellowing out an *American Idol* ending, she tapered off to a delicate, beautiful finish. She stepped back from the mic, spent.

"Thank you, Kalia," boomed the first voice. "Good luck."

Meanwhile, back in the lobby, just as Kalia had disappeared behind the red suede door with the video girl, Asha walked into Fire Records' lobby. She was stunning in a nearly sheer multi-layered fire-engine red top and hip-huggers. The cropped jeans showed off some bloodred eel-skinned stiletto boots. Asha's hair was purposely tousled, and a huge red flower was affixed to the right side. Red lips, red dangly earrings, a million silver bracelets and black face-masking sunshades all gave Asha a star appearance. As she made her entrance, people moved aside like she was Moses parting the Red Sea.

"Look at her," Mari said, huffing.

"Who's that? I dig those boots," said Shauntae.

"This girl from my school."

"She's in high school?" asked Colby.

"Umm, hmm, and she can sing, too," said Mari.

"Well, she certainly looks like she can do something," said Shauntae.

"She ain't no competition for my sister," said Mari.

"Says who?" interrupted a male voice.

Mari, Colby and Shauntae looked up to see Sean standing above them. Shauntae jumped up.

"Heeeey, Sean. I was hoping I'd see you," she said.

"Well, here I be. What's up, ladies?" said Sean, then turned to Mari. "I guess you're here to support your sister?"

"Yep. She's in there right now, probably blowing the house down," said Mari.

"Well, I hope so 'cause there sure is some competition up in here," he said.

"So I guess it's too busy to get that tour today, huh, Sean?" said Shauntae.

"Well, yeah, it is kinda tight today, and I already promised someone a private tour today," he said, turning to Colby, holding out his hand to her. "We can go right now, if you want to."

"When did y'all talk?" demanded Shauntae.

"When we went to the movies last weekend," he said, pulling a smiling Colby up by both hands. "How are you, Miss Gresham?"

"Lovely, Mr. Turner," said Colby, holding Sean's hand.

"She can't even date yet," said Shauntae. "Her grandparents won't let her go anywhere."

"Why do you care?" said Colby. "We went out, and that's that."

"Humph. Whatever," said Shauntae, sitting back down.

"Did you know about them, Mari?" asked Shauntae.

"Uh...well, yes."

"Why didn't you tell me?"

"'Cause Colby asked me not to. Besides, I wasn't paying either of you too much attention last week. I was studying ridiculously hard for my midterms—which I did fabulous on, might I add."

"You are such a nerd. And Colby, that backstabbing trick...I can't believe she stole my man," said Shauntae, getting loud.

"You're trippin', Shauntae. Stop hatin'. Sean wasn't your man, and anyway, if I'm a nerd and Colby's a trick, why do you hang out with us?"

"Just shut up, Mari," said Shauntae, rising to her feet. "Shut your ass up," she screamed and raced to the exit door.

It was 11:45 a.m., and all of Williams High was scheming about how to be near a radio in fifteen minutes. Today Hot 103.5 was set to announce the top twenty contestants who made the cut. Kalia was sitting in her Spanish 3 class hoping she could get out early. She had a plan. She was going to her car and get the news by herself, that way if she wasn't chosen, she could just drive off into oblivion. The 11:50 bell rang, and she flew down the hall and up the stairs to her car. She'd just punched Hot 103.5 when Dewayne popped into the passenger side.

"Damn! If I'd just locked my door," she said.

"See what happens when you don't listen to me?" he said.

"How did you know I was going to be here?"

"Uh…how long have I known you?"

Kalia rolled her eyes and turned up the radio.

"Are you nervous?"

"What do you think, fool?" she asked, punching Dewayne in the arm.

"Don't abuse the Chosen One," he said. "I may have to throw some of my superpowers on you."

"Like what? You're going to…shh shh shh, it's coming on," she said, gripping the sides of her seat.

They heard the familiar Who's Got That Fire? song that had been playing for weeks every time Hot 103.5 was going to make an announcement about the contest. Usually Kalia would sing along, but today she had cotton mouth.

"All right, y'all…hundreds of people showed up to audition for Fire Records' Who's Got That Fire? contest, and now it's time to tell y'all who made it to the top 20, who's going to be in the first competition in December. So we've got JD, a hot new artist signed by Fire to give us the low on who made the cut. What's up, man?"

Kalia threw her head back and hands up. She could care less about this JD, but she didn't speak a word in case he said her name. When Dewayne opened his mouth to speak, she pinched his arm so hard that his lips snapped shut.

As JD shouted out everyone from his barber to his grandmama, Kalia rocked her head back and forth against her seat in agony. Dewayne chuckled at his impatient friend.

Kalia thought she would die. Why didn't they just read the names and stop torturing her? If she ever met JD or that silly Cool Mike, she was going to clock them both. Dewayne looked at the frustration on Kalia's face and held her hand tight.

"So you've got the list, man? The list of the top 20?"

"I got it right here, dog."

"Okay…drum roll please…"

chapter 6

In her haze, Kalia thought she heard a phone ringing. After a few jingles, she realized it was her cell phone. *I really need to use my phone more,* she thought, fumbling around in her bag for it.

"Hello," she said, still dazed.

"CONGRATULATIONS," screamed Mari from the other end. "We're gonna be rich."

"Thanks, Mari." Kalia couldn't help but grin.

"So how do you feel? What was it like to hear your name on the radio? Aren't you excited?"

"It was just unbelievable," said Kalia, leaning back in her car seat. "I just don't know how to feel. I'm really happy."

"Me, too. Where were you when you heard? Let me tell you where I was," bubbled Mari. "No, this is your moment. You tell me. Where were you? Where are you now?"

"I'm still in the car. That's where I heard it. Me and Dewayne," said Kalia, looking at Dewayne, who was doing a celebratory dance next to her.

"Dewayne is there? Hit that fool in the head for me. Anyway, I'm so excited for you. This is so tight. So, what's next? What do we do now?"

"Well, right now I've got to go to class."

"What? You're going to class? You need to be celebrating."

"One of the requirements for participating in the contest is to maintain a B average, so that's why I'm going to class."

"Don't worry, Mari," yelled Dewayne. "I'll make sure she does some kind of celebrating."

Kalia looked at Dewayne quizzically.

"Look, Kalia, I gotta jet," said Mari. "I really do have to go to class. I took a bathroom break from chemistry class and ran to the computer room to hear it on the Internet, so I really gotta get back. I'll catch up with you at home. Lata."

Mari walked into the house one evening after a late cross-country practice and found Kalia slumped over on the piano. She just stared at her sister for a while in total admiration. For the last few weeks, Kalia had been in near hibernation, practicing so diligently for the upcoming Fire competition in December that she disappeared off the scene. Mari could hardly catch her between school and vocal practice—she was hemmed up in both. She walked over and looked a little closer at Kalia. She saw that her sister was tired. She looked exhausted. There were bags under her eyes and her trademark flip had flopped.

Mari couldn't believe it. Had she not witnessed Kalia furiously burning the candle at both ends, she would have taken the opportunity to wake her sister and clown her mercilessly about her appearance. Instead she gently woke Kalia who seemed too drugged with sleepiness to even care who Mari was. After helping her up to bed, Mari sat in a chair in Kalia's room and watched her sleep for a bit, then all of the sudden, she got it. Kalia needed a break. Yeah, she needed sleep first, but after that, she needed to kick it.

The timing was perfect, too, Mari thought as she hopped in the shower. It was homecoming. Kalia had never really been into sports, so all of the hoopla surrounding the event usually didn't affect her, but this year, Mari knew she could get her sister hype about the festivities because Fire Records was producing a big halftime show during Clark Atlanta University's game. Plus, the fact that Williams's homecoming was the same weekend as Clark Atlanta's should intensify her interest in all things homecoming related.

Mari couldn't wait to put her plan into action. She barely got her clothes on before she was on the phone with Dewayne, plotting to get her sister to not only the game, but the parties, too.

"It'll be cool," said Mari. "We'll just tell her that we heard through the grapevine that the other Fire contestants were going to be hanging out at the games this weekend, and she'll definitely want to go."

"That's the only way you're going to get her to go," agreed Dewayne. "I can barely get her to call me back or speak to me in school, she's so busy. You know she gave up one of the leads in chorale because of Fire?"

"Yeah, she told me," said Mari. "She also said that she's thinking about not trying out for the spring musical this year either because auditions are in the fall. Kalia has been in her school's musical since ninth grade. She's all about Fire."

"I know what you mean. She's always running from class to the practice studios, sipping on hot water with lemon and honey. She's so theatrical."

"What she is is serious," said Mari. "I came home tonight to find her asleep at the piano. Head down and everything."

"For real? Yeah, I guess it's time to take some action."

"She's not going to listen to me either. She thinks all I wanna do is party anyway."

"Well that's true, ain't it?"

"Shut up."

"You must not want me to help you talking to me like that," Dewayne threatened.

Silence.

"All right, all right," Mari said. "Look, I just need some backup, okay?"

"I got you, hot lips."

"Don't push it."

Mari didn't need much help at all. As soon as Kalia found out about Fire's involvement in Clark Atlanta's homecoming, she was primed and ready. She even decided she'd go to Williams High's homecoming to get herself prepared for Clark Atlanta's. Mari was so amped that her sister was finally showing an interest in Williams High activities besides school and vocal practice that she stayed up under Kalia. They spent the week before the homecomings combing the malls looking for something to wear to both games and Williams's party.

On homecoming Friday, Kalia, Mari, Shauntae and Colby all piled into the Camry and headed to the Williams game. When they arrived, Kalia met up with Dewayne, and they split off from Mari and her crew. The plan was to meet up later at the homecoming party in the gym.

It was an unusually warm early November in Atlanta, nearly eighty degrees, so Kalia was right on time in her cut-up Billie Holiday T-shirt (sliced by Mari), low-rider stretch bronze jeans and chocolate-brown stacked boots. After Mari teased up her normally conservative flip, threw some bronze sparkle on her face and shoulders and slid bronze gloss across her lips, Kalia's transition was complete. She was a little nervous about her new look until she got out of the car at the stadium and was treated like a hottie by several of her male classmates.

"Dang, girl," said Dewayne. "You've got these dogs around here dragging their tongues on the ground. What's up with the getup?"

"Just trying a little something new," she said, fluffing her hair. "Whadya think?"

"Well, it's sure a different you," said Dewayne, looking her up and down. "I've never seen you in anything tight before. I didn't even know you had all that."

"All what?"

"All that back there."

"You keep your eyes away from my back there," said Kalia, putting her hands on her behind.

"Girl, you can't wear second-skin glowing pants and think that a man ain't gonna look," said Dewayne, looking around at the men ogling his friend. "I'm gonna have to be your bodyguard tonight."

"Come on, fool. Let's go."

The next day for the Clark Atlanta game, Kalia had on another funky outfit. This time Mari had her in some psychedelic low-waisted jeans and a fuchsia baby T that read Play in metallic silver on the front and At Your Own Risk on the back. The boots were black and stacked. The makeup was shimmering and sexy.

"I guess the Chosen One is gonna have to escort you again tonight," said Dewayne when Kalia answered the door, looking like she'd stepped off the cover of *Vibe* magazine.

"You dig?" she asked, spinning around.

"I do," he said with a wink and a smile.

"All right, so let's be out," she said, bopping down the front steps and throwing over her shoulder, "Ladies, the car's leaving in thirty seconds with or without y'all in it."

Everybody was squeezed in the car, and they were just about to back out of the driveway when Elaine came running out the front door, yelling for them to wait.

"Damn. We almost got away clean," said Shauntae.

Kalia tried to avert her shimmering face as her mother closed in on the car.

"Ladies, ladies, ladies—and gentleman," she said, peering into the car, "where are we off to today? I thought homecoming was last night."

"It was, Ma," said Kalia, "but Clark Atlanta's is today."

"Ooh…so you guys are going to a college game? And that's it, right? No college parties for anybody because none of you are in college."

"Yes, ma'am," said everyone in the car.

"Oh, Ma, there's another like post-homecoming party that this guy from Williams High is having tonight. Can we go to that?" asked Kalia.

"Whose party is it?" said Elaine, looking closely at Kalia, who was fumbling in her purse for anything that would keep her from looking directly at her mother. "And where is it?"

"It's just this guy's party we heard about, but I can call you later and tell you where it is," said Mari.

"Do that," advised Elaine. "Kalia, what is that on you face? And what have you done to your hair?"

"I'm just trying out some new styles for the Fire contest," said Kalia, fingering her spiral-curled style.

"Okay, young lady. Just remember that. You're a young lady, not a grown woman."

"Oh my God." Shauntae moaned.

"Did you say something, Miss Washington?" asked Elaine, staring into the back of the car.

"No, ma'am," eked out Shauntae. "I just had something caught in my throat."

"Umm, hmm," said Elaine, moving away from the car and walking toward the house. "You kids have a good time. Be safe."

Backing out of the driveway, Kalia was too excited. She'd had to beat the guys off her at the Williams party, and now she was going to try her new look out on some college men. Much to everybody's surprise, she cranked up the crunk on Hot 103.5 and rolled out.

Mari, Shauntae and Colby were nowhere to be found.

"I don't know where they are, but I know they better show up soon," said Kalia. "We told them we'd meet them at Applebee's. That's where they said they were walking to."

"I told you we should have stayed with them," said Dewayne.

"Your self-righteousness is not doing me any good right now."

"Touchy-touchy. Look, let's just find them, okay?"

"That's what I'm trying to do, Dewayne," said Kalia, slamming her hand against the car door.

Neither said anything for a few minutes.

"Okay, let's think about it," said Kalia. "Where could they be? It's almost nine o'clock."

"Maybe they went somewhere with those dudes they were talking to."

"They better not have. They don't know those guys."

"Well, they did seem to be trying to get all of the information about that party they were talking about."

"What party?" said Kalia, looking intently at Dewayne.

"Oh, that's right, Miss Hottie, you wouldn't know. You were so caught up in that Phat Farm dude."

"Okay, he was fine, so what? You jealous?"

"Naw, that's not it," said Dewayne, looking out the passenger window to hide his hurt. "I'm just saying, he was like a junior in college, probably twenty-one, right?"

"I don't know, I guess. Look, what are you getting at, Dewayne? What does this have to do with finding Mari?"

"Nothing. Maybe they went to that party. They sure weren't going to a Williams's party tonight. They had that look in their eyes."

"Well, where is this party? Did you hear where it was?"

"Somewhere near the campus. I heard one of those dudes say it was off MLK. Some place called Atlanta Live or something like that. It can't be too far from the stadium 'cause I heard Shauntae tell Mari that she'd been before and that they could walk right over there."

"Okay, well let's find it."

An hour later after asking a bunch of college students about the club and standing in line for another half an hour, Dewayne and Kalia walked into Atlanta Live, which was literally underground. They paid ten dollars apiece and had blue bands affixed to their wrists, proving they were underage.

"I don't know how we're going to find them in here," said Kalia, looking back over her shoulder at Dewayne, who was squeezing between two beefy guys with huge beers in their hands.

"What?" said Dewayne, surveying the crowd of scantily clad women and hip-hop dressed guys. He was having a hard time hearing Kalia over the thumping baseline of T.I.'s latest hit.

Kalia stopped to wait for Dewayne, but the crowd kept pushing her and she found herself in the middle of the dance floor, which she noticed was bare concrete. She looked desperately for Dewayne, and everyone around was throwing their hands up to the beat. Suddenly she thought she saw the back of Colby's head. Making her way through the crowd toward the deejay booth in the front, she realized it was Colby. She'd almost made it to her when the deejay went old-school and so did the crowd.

Swept back to the dance floor by people wopping to Slick Rick's "Bedtime Story," Kalia craned her neck to see if she saw Mari in Colby's direction, but it was no use. When a guy with the smoothest skin she'd ever seen grabbed her hand and started dancing with her, Kalia gave in. The party was winning. She just had to go with it. Soon enough she had her hands around his neck, and he had his on her waist. They were dipping to the left and the right, she was sweating, he was sweating and neither cared. The deejay took them away in a mix of old-school hip-hop hits hot enough to make a tribute show for BET.

Twelve songs later, Kalia was still dancing with a dude whose name she didn't even know. The music was way too loud to even exchange "What's up?" She'd totally forgotten about her sister until she heard Mari's voice on the mic.

"I'd like to give a shout-out to my sister, Kalia. She's out there dancing with that fine-ass man. Kalia, you've got that fire, girl! Get it, girl."

"Hey, that's my sister," Kalia said to the guy with whom she was dancing.

He just nodded and kept dancing. She knew he didn't hear her. She looked hard at the deejay booth, trying to see Mari, but the nearly nonexistent lighting only allowed her to see a few feet in front of her. Deciding she needed to find her sister, she pointed toward the deejay booth and danced that way, pulling her cutie with her. By the time she got near enough to the booth to see inside, Mari was gone, but the music was pumping. She threw her hands up in the air, knowing the deejay was going to wear her out. He went from old-school to a reggae set and started blending dirty south booty shake. When he segued into some new Fire Records' crunk mixes thrown over a classic Biggie beat, Kalia went wild. She closed her eyes and didn't even see when her fine partner danced away.

She felt a set of strong hands grasp hers in the air. They moved together. When she opened her eyes, she was staring at a picture of Che Guevara against a barrel chest. The strong hands brought hers down to her hips and both sets rested there as she looked up into the face of her captor. Piercing brown eyes with the longest eyelashes she'd ever seen held her gaze.

She felt his well-lined beard graze her cheek as he bent down toward her ear.

"What's your name, queen?"

Every inch of her skin tingled at the sound of his baritone. She thought she said her name, but apparently he didn't hear it. Leading her off the dance floor, through the deejay booth and out the other side to a back room, he helped her sit in a chair near a desk.

"Whew," she said, pulling her hands through her sweated-out hair. Kalia didn't even realize how whipped she was until she was sitting. "I must look a mess."

"Not to me," said the guy. "You look happy, like you just had the best time of your life."

"What are you talking about? Wait. Who are you? What's your name?"

"I'm Malcolm, Miss Lady. What's yours?" he asked, stepping closer to her.

Looking at his short curly dreadlocks, gleaming white teeth and rippling arm muscles, Kalia felt a little warm, and it wasn't because she'd just finished dancing like she'd never hear music again. This brother was fine.

"Uh, I'm Kalia."

"Do you go to Clark?'

Kalia wished so much she could say yes.

"No. I, um, well, I'm still in high school."

"No kidding?" said Malcolm, moving back a few paces. "How old are you?"

"Eighteen."

"Oh, that's cool then. I'm twenty, so that's only a couple of years. Are you thirsty? Want something to drink?"

Kalia was just watching his beautiful lips move, not really hearing what he was saying. All of her answers were a beat behind, and his last question didn't even register.

"Wait here," he said. "I'll be right back, okay?"

Malcolm disappeared back through the deejay booth, which was being manned by a female deejay. Kalia had never seen a woman deejay before. She hadn't even considered that a woman could be one. Kalia looked around the small room she was in, noticing all the party flyers on the walls, many of them touting DJ Malcolm Lee. She was just putting it together when he walked in with two bottles of water.

"You're DJ Malcolm Lee?" she asked, taking a sip.

"The one and only." He bowed.

"So this is your party?"

"Well I'm one of the deejays for this homecoming gig. DJ Fly Girl is out there ripping it now. She's got some serious skills."

"I've never seen a woman deejay before. That's kinda cool."

"She's one of the best in Atlanta. People don't even know yet," said Malcolm. "So how do you feel? You looked like you were going to pass out there for a minute."

"Is that why you kidnapped me back here?"

"Well, I did want to get you alone," he said, stroking his chin, which barely hid his kilowatt smile. Kalia noticed an ankh ring on his ring finger.

"That's a nice ring," she said, purposely changing the subject. "That's an ankh right? Egyptian?"

"Smart girl, I see."

"Woman," Kalia corrected.

"Oh yes, woman," he said, hoisting himself on the desk next to her. She could smell the musky essential oil on his skin.

She looked up past his well-defined jawline into those lashed eyes again and quickly averted her face away from his intense gaze, hoping to avoid him seeing her blush. Her eyes landed on his watch, which, to her alarm, read 12:45.

"Oh my God." She jumped up, knocking over ledgers and papers on the desk. "Is it really almost one o'clock?"

"Yes, little lady. It is," said Malcolm, standing up.

"I've got to find my sister right now. We've got to go. We were supposed to be…" She cut herself off, not wanting to let Malcolm know about her curfew.

"Who's your sister? Oh wait, you said your name is Kalia, right? That was your sister on the mic. She gave you a shout-out."

"Yeah, that's her. Did you see her when you went to get the water?" she asked, dialing Mari's cell phone, which went directly to voice mail.

"No, but I saw her and her girls talking to these two dudes in the poolroom about an hour ago. You want me to show you where it is?"

"Please," said Kalia, walking out of the room.

The rush of hot-bodied air almost knocked Kalia over as they reentered the party, which was in full homecoming-night rage. People were wilding out. Arms and behinds were flying everywhere in a frenetic crunkfest. There were some funny smells in the air, which Kalia decided came from marijuana, liquor and sweat. Holding her around the waist, Malcolm steered her from behind, his body heat making the scene that much hotter. Kalia didn't mind the extra warmth at all. When they got to the poolroom, Mari and her girls were nowhere to be found, but they did see Dewayne with a cue stick in his hand, holding court with several mature-looking ladies.

"Hey, where've you been all night?" she asked Dewayne, tapping him on the shoulder.

Turning around to see a guy holding her hand, Dewayne grimaced and said, "Well, where have *you* been?"

Kalia looked from Dewayne to Malcolm and back to Dewayne.

"Dewayne, this is Malcolm. Malcolm, this is my neighbor Dewayne," she said.

"What's up?" and pounds were exchanged.

Dewayne leaned over to Kalia. "I see you've made a new friend."

"I see you've made several," Kalia shot back, eyeing his tipsy-looking female friends who seemed to be splitting one outfit between them. "Look, have you seen Mari? We need to be getting out of here."

"Last time I saw her she and her gang were across the room. That was at least an hour ago. I think they were headed outside or something. I heard Shauntae talking about going somewhere with some dude."

"And you let them go?" demanded Kalia.

"Well, the Chosen One was kinda tied up rescuing distressed damsels, ahight?" he whispered, nodding to his lady friends.

"Well if the Chosen One doesn't help me find Mari, he's gonna be walking his butt home tonight."

"All right. All right," said Dewayne. After saying goodbye to his groupies, he followed Malcolm and Kalia to the front of the club.

"There she is," said Dewayne, pointing toward the glass door. Kalia could see her sister arguing with Shauntae, who was being held from behind by a huge guy. He was rubbing his hands up and down her sides.

"Something is going on," said Kalia. They were trying to make their way to the door, but the crowd was thick and their going was slow. They saw Shauntae pointing her finger at Mari and Mari with her hands on her hips. Their mouths were moving so fast, it was clear they were pissed with each other. Then all of the sudden, Shauntae flipped her hand in the air at Mari, turned and said something in the ear of guy who was mauling her, and walked off with him. As they burst through the door, Mari was just standing there looking after them.

"Hey, is everything okay?" asked Kalia, running up to her sister.

Mari turned and looked at Kalia to say something, then changed her mind when she saw Dewayne and Malcolm. "I guess. No. Whatever."

"Where's Shauntae going?"

"Off with that guy," said Mari, motioning to the couple, who'd just made it to his truck.

"Oh, that's Rafael King," said Malcolm. "She'd better watch out. He's kinda rough."

"I could tell," said Mari, "and I tried to tell her. He was high and drunk and everything. Talking about how he wanted to give her a taste of something."

They watched Rafael kiss Shauntae really hard, then pick her up like a rag doll and deposit her in the passenger seat of his black chromed-out Ford Explorer.

"Was she drinking, too?" asked Kalia.

"Yeah. She had a couple of something he bought her. She wouldn't listen to me. I told her that I saw him earlier grinding on some other chick, but she didn't care. She's just stupid. I mean how can you leave with a dude you just met?"

"Hey, where's Colby?" Dewayne asked.

"Oh, you won't believe this, but Sean showed up, and they left like two hours ago. She probably called him. I think that girl got a man," said Mari.

"Well, good for her," said Kalia. "Look, we gotta break out. It's like one in the morning."

"For real?" said Mari. "Ooh, we better call home. You call."

"I already did."

"And?"

"We're in trouble," Kalia whispered in her sister's ear before slowing up to walk with Malcolm.

"Oh well, whatcha gonna do?" Mari shrugged, walking with Dewayne toward the car. She looked back over her shoulder at her sister smiling up at the deejay.

"What's going on with them?" she asked, nudging Dewayne.

"I don't know. I'm not back there in their conversation," said Dewayne, a bit annoyed.

"Ooh wee, somebody is jealous," sang Mari.

"Well, at least I got some play tonight. It seems that everybody else did, too. Can you say the same?" spit Dewayne, speeding up, leaving Mari to walk by herself just as Kalia caught up to her. She turned to see Malcolm heading back toward the club.

"I know you didn't pull the deejay," she teased. "My sister came to the party and kicked it to the deejay! You're like my idol."

"Shut up, silly," said Kalia, a bit embarrassed.

"I won't," Mari protested. "I really needed a camera phone

tonight. You need to see how you looked grinding all up on the deejay."

"I was not grinding." Kalia chuckled.

"So, did you get the digits?"

"Absolutely." Kalia grinned.

"You got his, or did he get yours?"

"I gave him my cell number. Why?"

Mari stopped in her tracks. "Whaaat? Not my sister, giving out the cell number. Now you're joining the rest of us in the twenty-first century." She giggled. "I'ma have to teach you how to text message pretty soon."

"I know how to text message. Shut up," Kalia said. "Listen, I'm really glad that you're okay. I mean, I can't believe that Shauntae left with that guy. He looked kinda hard."

"Yeah. I think he's a real thug, and I'm scared for her, but I did what I could. She just wouldn't listen. I'll call her when we get in the car. Maybe she'll answer her cell," said Mari, rubbing her eyes. "Really though, I'm sick of her. She's getting on my last nerve."

"I hope she's all right."

They'd reached the corner of the street on which the Camry was parked. "Look at that fool," said Mari. Dewayne was leaning against the car, arms folded across his chest, scowl etched on his face.

"What's wrong with him?" Kalia asked.

"What do you mean? He saw you and Malcolm, duh."

"Oh, please. You can't be serious."

"K, you know that Dewayne has liked you since forever, and you've never given him the time of day."

"Well, if he ever got out of that damned fantasy world—"

"You wouldn't pay him any attention then, either."

"I don't know what to do about Dewayne," said Kalia.

"I know what you're about to do."

"What?"

"Break his heart."

chapter 7

Mari was sick of being on punishment. It had been almost two weeks since her father dropped the hammer on the sisters—no telephone, no television, no going out with friends, no nothing. He'd all but nixed letting her drive anywhere with him.

I'll never get enough hours to drive by myself now, she thought, lying in her bed. Thank God for cross-country, or else she'd never get out of the house except for school. She stared at the clock as she had for the past few nights. Once again it was only a little after midnight, and she couldn't get back to sleep. She'd been going to bed at 9:30 every night because after she ate and finished her homework, there was nothing left for her to do but chores, and she'd finished those up early in the week. Sitting up on the edge of the bed, Mari surveyed her room. It was clean as a whistle. Not one item of clothing was on the floor. She'd gotten so bored that she'd even cleaned up. This was ridiculous, she thought, but then she remembered how much fun she'd had homecoming weekend and decided two weeks of severe restriction was worth it.

Not going back to sleep, she walked out of her room to go downstairs for a midnight snack. She passed by her sister's room and heard the radio playing softly, but she thought she heard some stirring as she walked by the guest room. Standing in the doorway,

Mari was surprised to find her father sleeping soundly. Something drew her into the room. On the dresser lay his keys, his brush, his cologne and his wedding ring. Some of his underwear and T-shirts peeked out of an open drawer. Turning to look in the closet, she saw several of her father's suits, shirts, pants and ties. Four pairs of shoes were lined across the closet floor. He even had a couple belts hanging behind the door.

Her father turned over, and Mari froze like a cat burglar. As soon as he stopped moving, she tiptoed out of the room and padded downstairs to the kitchen. What the hell was going on? she wondered, staring into the refrigerator. Why did it look like her father had moved into the guest room? She decided on cookies and milk. Not even dipping Oreos into ice-cold milk helped stave off the fear that something was very, very wrong in the Jefferson household.

The next day Mari spotted Colby and Shauntae rolling up to East Moreland as she was walking from her last class to the gym for cross-country practice.

"What's happening?" said Shauntae, slamming the car door.

"What are y'all doing up here?" Mari said to Colby. She was still a bit sore at Shauntae for her homecoming shenanigans. *Everybody knows the rules,* she thought. *You leave the club with the same people you came with.*

"We hadn't seen your butt in so long," said Colby, "we had to come up here to make sure you were still alive."

Mari noticed something different about Colby. She was glowing or something.

"Well, what's up with you, Miss Thang? You're looking all happy."

"Not too much," said Colby. "Just Sean. Girl, he's great. I love me some Sean."

"Oh, Lord, young love," Mari teased. "I'm so happy for you, Colby. You deserve it."

Shauntae rolled her eyes, sucked her teeth and sat down on the steps.

"What is your problem?" Mari asked Shauntae as she and Colby joined their salty friend on the steps.

"Nobody wants to hear about that corny love shit," said Shauntae. She turned to Colby. "Has that fool given you anything yet? Some gear? Some jewelry? Have you met anybody famous at Fire?"

"He doesn't have to do any of that stuff," said Colby. "We just spend time with each other and have great conversations."

"I bet that's not all y'all have. He's around all those video girls at Fire. I know if you ain't givin' him some, he's getting it from somewhere," said Shauntae.

"It's none of your business what Colby and Sean are doing," said Mari, jumping in.

"Was I talking to you?" Shauntae threw at Mari.

"You don't have to for me to answer," Mari shot right back.

"Shut up."

"You shut up."

"Both of you shut up," said Colby, turning to Mari. "We're supposed to be cool. We came up here to see how you were doing."

"I'm surprised you even care," said Mari directly to Shauntae. "The last time I saw you, King Kong was putting you in his truck, and you weren't giving me one thought. You just left me alone at the club."

"I knew your sister was there. You were fine, right? I see you made it home all right."

"The question is, did you make it home at all?" Mari smirked. "I hope you and Rafael had a good ole time."

"How did you know his name?" Shauntae demanded.

"Don't you worry about it. I heard a lot about Mr. King. Could you handle it?"

"I'm grown," assured Shauntae. "I can handle anything, and let me tell you, Rafael was not disappointed."

"I'm sure," said Mari. "Have you seen him again?"

"Yeah. I've been to his dorm room a couple of times. You don't know nuthin' about this college thing. It's all that."

"You don't know anything either, except what a dorm bed feels like," said Mari.

"What are you trying to say?" said Shauntae, glaring at Mari.

"All right, ladies," Colby broke in. "We didn't come here to discuss our sex lives. Like I said, Mari, we came here to see what was up with you. We haven't seen you in a minute. When do you get off punishment?"

"Just a few more days."

"They were serious this time, huh?" said Colby. "No time off for good behavior?"

"I'll be lucky if they don't extend it. I haven't seen my daddy that mad in a minute."

"I just don't understand this punishment deal," said Shauntae. "How can they keep you from going anywhere?"

"What are you talking about?" asked Mari.

"You can drive. You're sharing a car with your sister. If you wanted to, you could get in the car right now and roll out with us."

"But Mari wouldn't do that," said Colby.

"You're right about that," added Mari. "I can't imagine what they would do to me if I like just broke out while I was on punishment. I probably wouldn't see daylight until I graduated."

"Girl, my mama tried that punishment mess on me a couple of years ago, and I just walked out of the house," said Shauntae.

Mari and Colby looked at her like she was crazy.

Shauntae continued, "They can't really do anything to you. They love you, so they're not going to keep food from you or kick you out the house, and if they try to, you can just call social services on 'em. They have to take care of you until you're like eighteen. That's the law."

Mari and Colby were still looking at Shauntae as if she was someone they didn't know.

"What?" she said, looking back at them. "Y'all better get with the program. Old heads always think they know what's better for you. They don't know shit. They just wish they were young like you. They're really jealous that you can go out, party and kick it like they used to. They have to go to work and are always complaining about bills and stupid stuff like that. I ain't got time for their sad asses. I'm young. I got my life to live, and my mama gotta take care of me until I graduate."

"Well, what are you gonna do when you graduate?" asked Mari.

"Shoot, I don't know," Shauntae said, leaning back, looking at the sky, then she sat straight up and grinned, an idea hitting her like a lightning bolt. "By that time I'm gonna have me a college all-star, like Carmelo Anthony, who's gonna go pro early."

"Well, what's gonna happen if some other chick has the same groupie plan as you and gets your man?" asked Colby.

"Girl, my man is only gonna have eyes for me. How can he have all this," she asked, smiling and rubbing her hands across her breasts, "and want anything else?"

"You better get another plan, in case those things start drooping." Mari laughed. "You know gravity is gonna take control of those babies soon, and those of us with perky small ones are gonna rule the world."

Colby giggled and Shauntae frowned, looking down at her chest like the thought had never occurred to her.

"I think I wanna be a nurse or go to medical school when I graduate," said Colby quietly, playing with a piece of grass.

"You wanna wipe people's butts and put Band-Aids on their boo-boos?" asked Shauntae. "I don't know how you could want to be around sick people all the time."

"Well, I don't know," said Colby. "I just know that I want to help people."

"I think that's great, Colby," said Mari. "What made you want to be a nurse?"

"Well, you know my grandparents are kinda old, and they're always complaining about some aches and pains and stuff. So I started going on the Internet in the school library and looking up some of the stuff they were complaining about and kinda helping them to see what kind of conditions they could be suffering from."

"For real?" said Shauntae. "I've never seen you at no library."

"You probably don't even know where it is. We may go to the same school, but we ain't together all the time," said Colby.

"Whatever," said Shauntae, scraping one long nail back and forth against the cement.

"So were you able to help your grandparents?" asked Mari.

"I sorta helped my grandmother. One time we went to the clinic after she had a bad reaction to the new blood pressure pills she was taking, so I was able to describe to the nurse better what the symptoms of her reactions were, and it turned out they had been giving her the wrong type of medication."

"That is so cool," said Mari.

"Yeah, and when she got on the right medication, she was feeling so much better. She was able to get around better without feeling sick and dizzy and everything," said Colby. "I felt great, like I had really helped somebody, made their life a little better."

"Sounds like you've found your calling, Dr. Gresham."

"So what? You think you and Sean are gonna have that bourgeois life?" asked Shauntae. "He's gonna be like P. Diddy in the Hamptons and you're gonna be some big-time doctor on *Oprah* or something? Plueeeeeze."

"Well, why can't she be a doctor?" asked Mari.

"Yeah, why can't I? At least I won't be dependent on someone else to take care of me. I can do it for myself," said Colby.

"Whatever. Go on, be a big-time doctor. Cure AIDS or cancer or something. I don't give a damn," said Shauntae, standing up and dusting off the back of her black stretch pants and walking toward the car.

"I think it's great you have a plan, Colby," said Mari. "I still don't know what I wanna do. I've been looking at college Web sites since last year, and with Kalia going off next year, there's been a lot of college talk in the house."

"Don't worry. Something will come to you," said Colby.

"I know, I know. I'm good at public speaking, and I like writing. I was really thinking of joining the debate team or the school newspaper or something to help me figure out my real interests."

"See, you're on your way already," said Colby, getting up and slowly following Shauntae. "I guess we're outta here. We'll check you later."

Mari watched Colby jog toward the car. Shauntae cranked up the crunk and moved the car forward every time Colby put her hand on the handle of the passenger door. She did it so many times that Colby just stood still with her arms folded across her chest waiting for Shauntae to stop playing. She was finally able to get in the car, and they sped off, leaving a trail of exhaust from Shauntae's hooptie.

Mari headed toward the gym, thinking about the differences between herself, Colby and Shauntae. In the past couple of months, she'd really begun feeling closer to Colby. She liked where her head was, especially in terms of the future. Shauntae didn't seem to have a clue, plus, she had the worst attitude, and she was prone to making really stupid and dangerous choices. *One of those bad decisions could affect me one day,* Mari thought. *What if I'm with her somewhere, and she decides to just leave me, or she's smoking and we get pulled over by the police?* At that moment, Mari decided it was time to put some distance between Shauntae and herself. She wasn't sure for how long, but she knew it was the right decision—one she felt so good about that she went to cross-country practice and beat Asha by a full two minutes on the horse trails.

Kalia couldn't believe she was going to go out on a date with a college guy. Shuffling through the four half-completed applications on her desk, she thought about how she'd been agonizing for weeks over where she was going to college, and that night she had a date with someone who'd made that decision. If the opportunity arose, she was definitely going to ask him how he decided to go to Morris Brown College. Having made it into the top twenty finalists in the Fire contest, Kalia was really feeling like she wanted to pursue her music career. She picked up the application for Juilliard, the most prestigious performing arts learning institution in the nation. Just holding the application made her nervous, but now she was sure she wanted to go.

Flipping through the several other applications, one for Clark Atlanta, another for Howard University in Washington, D. C., and one more for the University of Pennsylvania, she thought about what her father wanted for her. They'd had another wicked argument several nights ago about where she should go to college. He was of the get-a-business-degree-so-you'll-have-something-to-fall-back-on mindset. Her mother, lamenting her dance career, was on her side. That didn't bode well for either of them in the conversation. Her father launched into a diatribe about how because he had a degree in business, he could always get a job and had some skills that could be used in a variety of industries. What was she going to do if she ever lost her vocal ability or if she couldn't play for some reason?

Kalia, not really having thought of that, was taken aback at first, then she became livid. It was the first time in her life she could remember raising her voice at either of her parents, but she did go off on her father. How could he not be more supportive of her talent and her dreams of becoming a professional performer? When her mother stepped in to try to explain that her father just wanted her to have security, Kalia shouted her down, too, telling them both they didn't believe she was talented enough to succeed and storming out of the room.

She remembered the ugly scene now, sitting at her desk and crafting her answers to the essay questions for the applications, and wondered if she was too hard on her parents. She knew they only wanted the best for her, but she also knew she'd never forgive herself if she didn't at least apply to Juilliard. As soon as she finished the applications she could concentrate on what to wear on her date. She wrote furiously, promising herself that she'd reread and make corrections the next day so she could mail them off the following week.

Hours later, Malcolm was holding her hand as they walked through Piedmont Park. He'd taken her to the movies and out to dinner at a nice Italian restaurant with white tablecloths and candles and now they were having a stroll in a park. No guy had ever treated her like this much of an adult before, she thought, looking down at his large brown hand covering hers. Of course she'd only been on a few dates anyway, she admitted to herself, but they all should have been like this.

She and Malcolm had talked about everything that night: parents (he was raised by a single father), college (he had two more years), even the three first date no-no's: relationships, religion and politics, which she knew little about, but to her surprise he was well versed in. Where they really connected was their shared dream of getting a record deal. Malcolm was a very driven young man who was well on his way. As they sat on a bench under a streetlamp on one of Atlanta's strangely pleasant November evenings, Malcolm laid out his plan to her.

"These CDs of my mixes that I've been burning, they're selling out. I can't burn them fast enough," he said, "so I think I'm going to talk to this guy over at Soul Soundz about selling them at his spot. You ever been up to Soul Soundz?"

Kalia shook her head, playing with the puffy-ended ties on her fuchsia pullover shawl.

"That's cool, baby. I'll have to take you up there. It's in Little Five Points. They've got some really funky stores over there. I bet you'll like it. The guy who owns it is this cat who is really knowledgeable about independent artists. He imports music from all over the world. He's got hip-hop from all these different places like Paris, Cuba and even some places in Africa."

"Do they rap in English?" she asked, trying not to stare at his perfectly groomed locks. *How does he sleep and keep them so neat?* she wondered, not paying any attention to Malcolm's answers to her questions.

She tuned back in to hear him saying, "…a lot of it is in whatever language they speak, but the music, the beats are unbelievable. They're spitting lyrics over their styles of music, like house music, drum and base, Soca, all kinds," said Malcolm, rubbing her hand between both of his.

Kalia was extremely interested in what he was saying, but everything about him was so attractive—his Sean John style, the way he looked directly in her eyes when he spoke to her, his impeccable manners and his cultured attitude—that she could barely take his touch. She heard what he was saying, but it was like in a dream. She couldn't even speak.

"Yeah, so anyway I'm going to talk to him, and maybe he'll stock my CDs, you know. What I really want to do is get one to the Nite Bandit on Hot 103.5. You know he plays local deejay mixes on his show on Saturday nights?"

Kalia shook her head again. She'd never even heard of the Nite Bandit's show. Malcolm smiled down at her and put his arm around her shoulders.

"That's cool, baby," he said again. "I guess I'm going to have to turn you on to some things."

Kalia wanted to tell him that she was already turned on, but her voice was continuing to be uncooperative.

"Come on. Let me take you home. I don't want to get you in any trouble that's going to keep me from seeing you again," he said, standing and pulling her up off the bench. Unready for the motion, she tripped a bit in her bone high-heeled boots and fell right into his arms. His closeness rushed to her head.

"If you wanted a hug, all you had to do was ask." He chuckled, hugging her and steadying her at the same time.

"Oh I—I…didn't mean to do that," she stammered, pulling away from him.

"So you don't wanna hug me?" he teased, folding his arms across his chest.

"No…I mean, yes…but not right now…but…" Kalia was so flustered and embarrassed that she didn't know what she was saying. "So do you wanna tour and stuff?" she asked, desperate to change the subject.

"Well, yes," he said, grabbing her hand and leading her down the path toward his car, "but I don't really want to get into all that groupie type stuff. The industry is so whack now. You really don't hear good lyricists; one company controls all the radio stations, so you hear the same playlists. I miss the creativity back in the midnineties. When I was a kid, my cousin used to play Tribe and De La Soul and KRS-1. Even Tupac and Biggie had something to say, but today it seems to be all about who's got the spinning rims and the phattest cribs and stuff—not that I don't want those things, but you know what I'm saying, right?"

"Umm, hmm," Kalia nodded. "Yeah, I don't like those popcorn singers—you know the ones, the studio artists. When you see them live, they sound like somebody's killing a cat or something."

"Yeah, yeah, we're on the same page, but I saw you getting wicked on the dance floor."

"You were spinning what I was dancing to—and it wasn't some conscious Lauryn Hill stuff either. You were killing the crunk."

"All right, you got me," he said. "It's the beats though, you know. Those booming beats are so fire sometimes that I don't even care what they're saying."

"I feel ya."

"So what about you? What do you wanna do? Do you wanna tour and stuff?" he asked.

"I'd love to do something like the Alicia Keys thing," whispered Kalia.

"Why are you whispering?" Malcolm asked.

"Because it's a secret. I've never told anybody really what I wanted to do."

"Ooh, I feel special."

"You should," said Kalia. "I think I want to go to Juilliard and really study voice and the piano. I want to be able to perform all kinds of music."

"That sounds real cool. So when are you going to let me hear some of these skills you've got?"

"I don't know," said Kalia, not sure if she was ready to let Malcolm that far into her life. "But I bet you didn't know that I'm one of the finalists for Who's Got That Fire?"

"For real?"

"Yep. We have our first competition in a few weeks," she said.

"Oh, I'm gonna have to come and check you out."

Walking along, holding hands with Malcolm, Kalia was in a dream world. What if she and Malcolm got married? They could be a power couple like Will Smith and Jada Pinkett Smith. They'd have a maid and a mansion, and they'd spend all their time in their in-home studio, he producing and she composing.

"What are you smiling at?" he asked, opening the car door for her.

Snapping back to reality, she said, "Nothing. Just the future."

"What do you see in your crystal ball?"

"That's for me to know and for you to find out."

"Well, if I'm gonna find out," he said, sliding into the driver's seat, "at least that means I'm there."

"We'll see," said Kalia, glad he couldn't read her mind since she'd already married him in her head.

"Umm, hmm… We sure will," he said. With that, Malcolm drove all the way to her house with one hand holding hers and one hand on the wheel.

Kalia was hooked.

Mari wondered what time Kalia was coming home. She'd spent hours helping her sister get ready for her first date with Malcolm, and she was dying to hear how it went. She'd watched several hours of television, listened to Colby go on and on about Sean for an hour on the phone and even worked on a newspaper story she'd been assigned by an editor at the *East Moreland Review*. She was bored silly, sitting on her bed, wishing she had a guy to pay her some attention, when the doorbell rang.

"I'll get it," she shouted, almost breaking her neck running down the steps.

She peered through the peephole to see Dewayne.

"Oh, it's you," she said, opening the door. "Kalia's not here."

"She's not?" he asked, looking at his watch. "It's like ten-thirty on a Friday night. Where is she?"

"Out," Mari said, standing in the doorway with one hand on her hip.

"Oh," said Dewayne, not moving.

"Okay, so you want me to tell her you came by, or you wanna come in and wait or something?"

"Yeah."

Dewayne threw his shoulder bag on the floor, and they plopped down on opposite ends of the sofa in front of the television. Mari flipped on BET. Five minutes into the video countdown, Dewayne announced he was going upstairs to check his e-mail and he'd be right back.

Getting up to get some ice cream, Mari noticed Dewayne's bag had come unzipped and his sketchbook had fallen out. Picking it up and flipping through the pages and pages of illustrations, she forgot about the ice cream altogether. "He's really got skills," she said out loud. She sat back down on the couch and curled up with his sketchbook, when she heard a car pull up in the driveway. She ran to the entryway and pulled back the curtains from the front window so she could see the end of her sister's date.

She heard Dewayne coming down the stairs and remembered she didn't put his sketchbook back. Cursing her forgetfulness, she sprinted into the living room intending to slip his book back into his bag before he noticed, but by the time she got there, it was too late. She had the book in her hands as he entered the room.

"What are you doing with my sketchbook?" he demanded.

"Nothing," she said. "It fell out of your bag, and I was just putting it back."

"You looked at it, didn't you?"

"Well…" she said, handing him the book. "It was open when I found it on the floor, so I didn't mean to, but yeah, I looked at it. Actually your stuff isn't bad."

"How would you know?" he said, stuffing the book back in his satchel. "What do you know about illustration?"

"Nothing really, except that my sister probably doesn't give you enough credit for your drawings."

Dewayne got a strange look on his face. He was about to say something, when they heard the front door open,

"You want something to drink?" they heard Kalia say.

"Yeah, baby. That's cool," said Malcolm.

Dewayne's strange look changed to a perplexed one. He looked toward the entryway and back at Mari, then back toward the entryway. At that very moment, Mari realized what a bad idea it was for her to have asked Dewayne if he wanted to wait for Kalia. Watching his face drop as Kalia and Malcolm entered the room, she felt sorry for him.

"Oh, hey," said Kalia, seeing Mari and Dewayne. "Malcolm, you remember my sister Mari and, uh, my friend Dewayne, right?"

"Fah sho," said Malcolm. "What's happening?"

"Ain't nuthin'," said Mari.

"What's up, man?" said Malcolm, giving Dewayne a pound.

"It's all good," fronted Dewayne. "I was just getting out of here, K. I left my book in your room."

"Okay, cool. We're about to get something to drink. You want something before you go?" Kalia asked Dewayne, oblivious to his smashed feelings.

"Naw, that's all right," he said, sliding around the back of the sofa and into the entryway.

"I'll lock the door," said Mari, following Dewayne. "It was nice seeing you, Malcolm." She looked back over her shoulder to see Malcolm taking Kalia's hand.

By the time she got to the front door, Dewayne was down the steps and loping across the front yard. She'd wanted to apologize to him for looking at his sketchbook and for putting him in a situation where he'd see Kalia with Malcolm, but he was gone. She stood in the doorway for a long time looking out into the night, wondering how bad Dewayne was feeling and wishing just as much that she could make it go away.

"So how was it?" Mari asked her sister on the way to school Monday morning. "I waited all weekend for you to tell me about it. So, how was it?"

"How was what?" Kalia smirked.

"Okay, stop with the games, missy. How was it with Malcolm, a college man?"

"You say that like he's a hundred years old or something."

"Well, he sure ain't no boy."

"He sure ain't," Kalia agreed.

"What does that mean?" Mari giggled, pulling down her visor to roll on some ChapStick.

"Nothing. Just that he's got plans for the future, you know? He's a grown-up."

"Are you included in these future plans?"

"I don't know, Mari. Get out of my business." Kalia was trying hard not to smile, but just the thought of Malcolm made her heart jump.

"Ooh wee, girl. You're in love," Mari teased, tightening her ponytail.

"What? What are you talking about? How can I be in love after only one date? You're really exaggerating."

"Umm, hmm, so why can't you stop smiling?"

"It's a lovely morning," said Kalia. "Just look at the sun shining. Listen to the birds singing."

"It could be a hurricane outside and you'd think it was a great day," said Mari as they drove by a park where their parents used to take them to play when they were children. Mari remembered her parents sharing an ice cream as she and Kalia hung upside down on the monkey bars.

"Hey," she said, "do you think that Ma and Daddy were giddy like you are after their first date?"

"I don't know. Probably not," said Kalia. "Didn't Ma say that her brother had to go with them as a chaperone?"

"Oh yeah, I think she did. You're right. Grandma would have never let Ma go anywhere without Uncle Fred. I know we complain about them, but I sure am glad our parents aren't as strict as Grandma was. They couldn't go anywhere or do anything."

"I know that's right."

"Well, do you think they were happy when they first got married?"

Stopping at a light, Kalia turned and looked intently at her sister. "Why do you ask?"

"I really didn't want to tell you this," started Mari, then she just turned and looked out of the window.

Kalia braced herself for the worse. She had no idea what her sister was going to say. "But?"

"K, the other night, I saw Daddy sleeping in the guest room."

Kalia immediately turned back to the road, hoping Mari didn't see the worried look on her face.

"Maybe he was sick or something," she said weakly. "It's getting chilly outside."

"No. He wasn't sick. He had moved like his clothes and shoes in there and stuff. I think he's staying in there."

"Umm, hmm." Kalia had no idea what to say. She'd known her father was sleeping in the guest room for several weeks. Mari sat up in her seat and looked at Kalia.

"Did you know about this already?"

"Well, yeah."

"Oh my God. Why didn't you tell me? How long has this been going on?" Mari's voice was raised.

"Just calm down, Mari. I don't really know. Maybe a couple of weeks or so."

"A couple of weeks?" Mari screeched. "Oh my God. They're getting a divorce, aren't they?"

"I don't know," Kalia shouted. "I don't know what's going on. I'm just as in the dark as you."

Mari flopped back in her seat and looked back out the window. Neither said anything for several minutes.

"How come people don't stay together anymore?" asked Mari. "Everybody's parents are divorced or were never married or something."

"I wish I could tell you."

"Does it even make sense to like a guy? I mean what's the point?"

"I don't know, Mari, but you know, maybe they won't get a divorce. Maybe they're just going through something and it's gonna work out."

"It didn't work out for anybody else's parents. I don't want to live with Ma and have to go and visit Daddy in some crummy apartment somewhere. I've seen too many people go through that."

"Mari, just slow up. We don't really know what's going on," said Kalia, pulling up to East Moreland.

"So, how do you suggest we find out? 'Hey, Ma. Hey, Daddy. Are you guys splitting up? If so I wanna stay with you, Daddy, 'cause you always bring home the popcorn shrimp from the Fish Fry.'"

"Look, I don't know what we're going to do, but getting all mad at me isn't going to help."

Mari threw an evil look at Kalia and got out of the car, slamming the door so hard Kalia was surprised the window didn't break. As she watched Mari jog up the steps and down a cobble-stone path toward one of the massive buildings on East Moreland's campus, she hoped her sister's day got better. In her heart though, she knew it wouldn't, because the rest of her day was filled with thoughts of visiting her parents in two different households. Skipping her first period, she knew the only thing that would make her feel better was locking herself in one of the practice rooms and belting out whatever came to mind. By the time she made it to her second period, psychology, she thought she'd sang and played all of the emotion out of her, but when the class dis-cussion turned to one of the most successful therapy practices, marriage counseling, she felt a tear roll down her cheek.

chapter 8

Kalia was worried about her sister. She'd been acting strange for several weeks, wearing more makeup and clothes that showed a bit more skin. One day she caught her in heels. Mari never wore heels. She'd peeked in her room late at night and a few times, Mari wasn't even there. She'd tried to ask her if everything was all right, but every time she did, Mari would brush her off with an "I'm fine, why don't you go somewhere and find Malcolm?" She was just impossible to talk to.

When Kalia was invited to Colby's surprise birthday party, which Shauntae was throwing, she was encouraged. At least maybe she could see what Mari was up to. As she and Malcolm drove into the mixed-income apartment complex where Shauntae lived, Kalia said a silent prayer that she would be able to get her sister to talk to her that night. They walked into the community center and surveyed the crowd. There were about a hundred teens, dancing and kicking it to hip-hop too loud to be heard over.

"I'm gonna hit the food," Malcolm shouted. "You want something?"

"Uh, not right now. I'ma try to find Colby and Mari."

"All right. I'll catch up to you," he said, dipping off.

Kalia stood on the edge of the party, looking for her sister. Feeling a hand on her shoulder, she turned to see a very mellow Shauntae.

"Happy birthday to Colby," she sang, throwing her arms around Kalia's neck. Half holding her up, Kalia wondered what was up with Shauntae. Pulling back and looking at her bloodred eyes, she knew.

"Are you all right?" she asked Shauntae, leaning her back against a wall.

"I'm cool as polar bear's toenail," slurred Shauntae, flinging one hand in the air.

"Umm, hmm. I think you need to sit down."

"What I need is to get my sip on. Let me find my hookup," said Shauntae, taking careful steps toward the dance floor.

"Hey, wait. Where's Colby? And have you seen my sister?"

"The birthday girl is probably getting her birthday present from Sean. I saw them in the car a few minutes ago and um, um, um." Shauntae giggled uncontrollably.

"Okay," said Kalia, "but where's Mari?"

"Where there's a Qwon, there's a Mari," sang Shauntae and disappeared into the throng of sweating bodies.

Malcolm walked up, handing Kalia a soda. "It's a lot going on here at this party. Three dudes tried to sell me some smoke on the way back over here."

"Yeah. Shauntae is high and probably drunk. I really want to find Mari," said Kalia, looking around and dialing Mari's cell number, which went to voice mail. "I hate caller ID. She never answers when I call her."

She and Malcolm went walking through the dance floor, looking at every couple, but were unable to locate her sister. He motioned for them to go out back. There was a haze of smoke behind the center. Kalia saw Qwon pushing up on a girl who had her back against the wall. The closer she got, the more she dreaded finding out the girl's identity, especially when she saw Qwon slide his hand underneath the girl's jacket. Sure enough, it was her sister.

"What should I do?" she asked Malcolm, her eyes fixed on Mari, who was locking lips with Qwon.

"I don't really know, babe. I mean she's just getting her kiss on."

"Yeah, but it's behind a building at a smoked-out party. What if the police show up?"

"Good point. This isn't the best 'hood," he said. "I think you've got yourself an excuse to break it up."

Kalia walked slowly toward Qwon and Mari, hoping that her sister would see her before she had to say something. No such luck.

"Mari," she whispered.

They kept kissing, and Qwon's hands were inching down Mari's back.

"Mari!"

Her sister broke from Qwon and looked around his shoulder. "What the hell are you doing here?"

Kalia was startled by red lipstick smeared all across Mari's face and chin. "Uh…I was invited," she said sheepishly.

"Well, what do you want? Can't you see I'm busy here?" she said, rubbing Qwon's chest. Qwon had his face buried in Mari's neck.

"I think we need to get out of here."

"Why? I'm chillin'. If you wanna leave, be out." She turned back to Qwon.

"Mari, everybody's smoked out here. What if the police show up? You know they'll be over here."

Mari stopped nuzzling Qwon and thought for a second.

"You wanna have to call Elaine and Ronald from a cell tonight?" asked Kalia.

"All right, all right," Mari said, trying to disengage herself from Qwon, but he wasn't letting go.

"Aw, baby," he said, "don't let your sister tell you what to do. Stay here with me." He was kissing her on her neck and holding her tight.

"Naw, Qwon. I gotta jet," said Mari, pushing against his chest.

"I ain't letting you go," Qwon said, getting a firmer grip on her. He turned to Kalia with burning anger to go with his burning eyes. His face was covered in red lipstick, too. "You need to get the hell on. Me and your sister got some unfinished business."

"I think you're done for the night," said Malcolm, stepping to Qwon. "Let her go, man."

"Who the fuck are you?" said Qwon, letting Mari go and eyeing Malcolm, who was a bit shorter than him, but much more built.

"You don't need to know all that. Come on, Mari," said Malcolm, turning around and walking toward the community center.

All of the sudden Qwon ran up on Malcolm and grabbed him behind the neck.

"Oh my God," yelled Kalia.

"Qwon, get off him," screamed Mari.

Malcolm flipped Qwon over his shoulder from the back, and they both went tumbling down a grass hill behind the center. By the time Mari, Kalia and a dozen other people made it down the hill, Malcolm was on top of Qwon pummeling his face.

"*Daamn,*" said one drunken girl, weaving back and forth. "Qwon gettin' hiss aaass whooped." Oohs and cheers emanated from the growing crowd. People were grimacing, pointing and putting their fists to their mouths like they were watching a Mike Tyson fight.

"Malcolm, stop. Let's go," Kalia said, trying to grab his arm midpunch. The next thing she knew, she was laying on her back in the grass and her head was throbbing.

"Kalia," screamed Mari, running over to her sister.

"Aw shit," said Malcolm, dropping a bloody, punch-drunk Qwon in a dirt patch and rushing to Kalia. He picked her up, started kissing her face and apologizing for hitting her.

"That's okay, baby. I know you didn't mean it," said Kalia, putting one arm behind his neck and her other hand over her right eye.

"I'm so sorry, Kalia. I didn't mean for this to happen," said Mari, even though she was looking back over her shoulder at Qwon.

"Let's just go home," said Kalia.

"Okay. I'll let Colby know we're leaving," she said, running up the hill.

By the time Malcolm got Kalia into the car, Mari was back, and Shauntae was following her. She leaned up to the passenger window making faces at Kalia.

"Your man knocked the shit out of you, huh?" She laughed. "That'll teach your prissy ass."

"Mari, let's go," said Malcolm, getting in the driver's seat.

"Shauntae, move out the way," said Mari, opening the back door.

"Why you leaving, girl? It's 'bout to get good now. My boy is bringing the real fire."

"I'm out," said Mari, slamming the door and rolling down the window. "If you see Colby, tell her I said happy birthday."

Dancing in the street by herself, Shauntae didn't even answer her. Her blue jean micro-miniskirt was twisted all the way around, and her tight green sweater was hanging off one shoulder. Watching Shauntae stumbling and dancing back toward the party as they drove off, Mari swore to herself that she'd never party so hard that she ended up looking that much of a mess.

It had been a few days since Kalia practiced what she was going to sing for the preliminary round of Who's Got That Fire? and she had a rehearsal that day. Her head had been hurting so bad since Malcolm had accidentally hit her that she'd been unable to study for her upcoming finals or sing, but she really wanted to that day. For the last couple of days, the twenty constants had been scheduled to rehearse with the stage band that was going to back them during their performance in a few weeks.

Arriving at Fire Records for her session, she said a silent prayer that God would free her from her headache, so she'd be able to rehearse. She signed in and was ushered into a waiting room. She'd just picked up an *Upscale* magazine when a striking woman floated into the room and sat down, gracefully crossing her legs. Holding up the magazine in front of her face, Kalia peeped over it to see the woman dialing a number on her cell phone. She had on an ocean-blue kimono-type top that split right above her navel and flowed to the floor. Her low-waisted, wide-legged jeans revealed a silver belly chain and black pointy-toe boots with stiletto silver heels. Chatting on the phone in low tones, she flipped her long jet-black, bone-straight hair out of her furry maroon scarf and fake-smiled at Kalia who smiled back and pretended to be all up in the *Upscale*.

The woman hung up the phone, looked at her fingernails, brushed off her jeans and seemed annoyed that she had to wait. Without even a hello, she asked Kalia, "Have you been waiting long?"

"Uh, well, about twenty minutes," she said, wondering if she was a stylist or a singer already signed to Fire.

"Well, they need to come on. I can't be here all day. My trainer's waiting," the woman said to nobody in particular. She turned back to Kalia. "Are you here for the contest? Do you have your rehearsal session scheduled today?"

Kalia hoped the shock didn't register on her face. She couldn't believe this well-put-together woman was in high school. "Are you a contestant?" she asked.

"Yes, I am," she said curtly. "Sooo…you're here for the rehearsal, right? What time was yours supposed to start?"

"I think five-thirty," said Kalia, "but they did say they were running late. I guess that's the business, you know?"

"Umm, hmm," said the girl, dialing her phone again. Kalia went back to pretend reading her *Upscale*. "Pierce, this is Asha. I'm going to be late," she heard as she watched her competition get up and walk into the hallway.

Asha, she thought. *That must be Mari's classmate Asha.* A strange resolve came over Kalia. Initially she'd felt outmatched when she first saw how together Asha's style was, but she also remembered that Mari had been bragging about beating her lately in cross-country.

When Asha came back in, Kalia struck up a conversation.

"So do you go to East Moreland?"

"Well, yes. How did you know that?" asked Asha.

"I heard you say your name on the phone, and my sister goes there."

Asha looked at Kalia intently. "Oh, you're Mari's sister, huh?" She looked down her nose at Kalia again from head to toe.

Kalia didn't know how to take this immediate hostility. She hadn't done anything to this girl. She was just about to say something—she didn't know what—when her name was called from outside the door.

"Break a leg, puleeze," she said on her way out the door.

"Not if you trip first," said Asha, twisting her mouth and crossing her legs.

Walking down the hall behind yet another thin, but well-endowed video girl assistant, Kalia was determined not to let Asha throw her off her game. She strolled through the door and onto the stage like she owned it. Realizing her headache was gone, she made her rehearsal count.

Kalia was a nervous wreck. It was noon, and she was supposed to be at Fire at 6:30. For the rest of the day, she needed to concentrate on relaxing her mind, and she knew just who could help her get in the right mood. Kalia peered around the half-open door into her parents' room and saw her mother in the bed, her head half covered by the bedding. Hoping her mother was finished napping, she knocked softly.

"Come in," said Elaine sleepily, stirring a bit.

"Are you sleeping?" Kalia asked quietly, crawling into bed next to her mother.

"Umm, not really."

"So how are the plans for the yoga studio coming?"

"Fine," said Elaine, pulling her head from under the covers to look at her daughter. "I've found a location, and I hope to be starting classes in the next few months. I've even come up with a name, the Studio of Love, Peace and Soul. What do you think?"

Kalia smiled at her mother. She loved seeing her in the creative mode.

"I love it, Ma," she said, wrapping herself around the pillow she hadn't seen her daddy sleep on in weeks. "Speaking of peace, I need to relax."

"Why? What's wrong? Are you nervous about tonight?"

"No… Well, yes, kind of. I just need to really let everything go. I don't want to be all stressed out trying to perform."

Elaine rubbed her eyes and yawned. "How about a nap? That always makes me feel better."

"Well, I was thinking more like some of those breathing exercises or some type of yoga you were telling me about earlier."

"Ah, the ulterior motive comes to light. So *now* you wanna try yoga?" Elaine asked, her left eyebrow raised. "I couldn't even get you to do any stretching with me last week. Oh, how the mighty have fallen."

"Are you gonna make this difficult for me, or what? I need to do whatever it is that you did before you had big dance performances. Come on, Ma. Hook me up."

"Okay, okay. I want you to be at your best tonight, darling, and you're right, a little bit of yoga and some meditation will certainly do you some good," said Elaine, getting out of bed. "Look in the closet and get out those two yoga mats."

Kalia let her mother help her get in a groove. For the next

forty-five minutes, she moved slowly and gently into and out of easy positions, each time following her mother's directions to release all of the tension in every part of her body. She totally forgot about everything else but her peace of mind. When she left her parents' room, her mother was sitting in the middle of the floor, meditating. As she closed the door, she wondered why she hadn't done any yoga since the classes her mom put her and her sister in when they were kids. She was certainly happy she did that day. She was totally relaxed, and there was no way she was going to let anyone disturb her mood.

It was going to be her night, Kalia thought, looking into the bathroom mirror. She couldn't be any more prepared. Everybody she loved and cared about had promised to be there, except her father, but she wasn't going to let the possibility of him not showing up get to her. Trying on different eye shadows and lip-sticks, she got excited. She thought about her outfit. She and Mari had been to every boutique in Atlanta putting together a unique look that no one else was going to have. Now all she had to do was get her hair done, and she'd be straight. She pulled her fingers through her flip and let her excitement build.

"I'm gonna make the finals," she said, giving herself a pep talk in the mirror. "I'm gonna be one of the eight. I'm talented, I've practiced hard. I'm gonna do my best, and I'm gonna make it."

Mari loved Atlanta in December. It was never that cold this time of year, with the average temperature usually hovering in the fifties. Stuffing her hands in the pockets of her navy pea coat, she breathed in the crisp air as she stood outside the Fox Theater looking at all the holiday decorations lining Peachtree Street. She turned her head left and right, keeping watch for Colby and Shauntae, who were supposed to be meeting her out front at 7:15. She was so excited about her sister's performance she'd rushed her mother to make sure they were on time. They were a half an hour early, so Elaine wanted to check out a few boutiques, but Mari decided to hang out in front of the Fox to make sure she wouldn't miss her girls.

After sending them a text message that she was already at the theater, she looked at all the different people dipping in and out of stores, arms filled with bags and packages. She wondered what

Christmas was going to be like in the Jefferson house that year, with her parents sleeping in separate rooms. She doubted they'd be drinking eggnog and singing carols around the tree like they did when she was younger. Warm memories of all of her immediate family members sitting around their gigantic dining room table grubbing down on her mother's Christmas feast almost brought tears to Mari's eyes. She must have been ten or eleven the last time the family Christmas celebration was at the Jefferson house. Christmas had moved to Auntie Cheryl's house ever since her mother's sister had married Uncle James and they had two children. It had always been a rule in her mother's family that Christmas celebrations were held at the family's house that had the youngest children, so the babies and toddlers and their parents wouldn't have to be uprooted on that hectic day.

The rule worked out well for us, thought Mari, straining to see if her girls were coming down the street. Because Elaine was nine years older than Auntie Cheryl, Mari and Kalia were the youngest children on her mother's side of the family for years. Christmas had been at their house for more than a decade before the big change. Mari watched a man help his elderly father across the street and wondered like she did every Christmas what her father must be feeling since he grew up an orphan, being shuffled from one foster home to another until he went into the Army at age eighteen. He never talked about his childhood, and even though he usually started out Christmas in the spirit, it was too much of the spirits that had him just sober enough to drive home from Auntie Cheryl's house.

Mari shook her head to rid herself of the image of her inebriated father slumped down in a Lay-Z-Boy quietly cursing at a football game as the rest of the family fellowshipped all around him. She hoped something would catapult him out of ending the holiday in a funk that year. Seeing her mother approaching, she didn't have much hope.

"Your friends aren't here yet, sweetie?" said Elaine, bending down to consolidate the several bags she was carrying.

"Nope. I see you did well in thirty minutes," said Mari, trying to look in the packages.

"No peeping, you silly girl. Do you wanna spoil your Christmas? I'll tell Santa to leave coal in your stocking."

"If I catch a big fat man in our house on Christmas Eve, I'm calling the police."

"Ha-ha. Look who's not in the Christmas spirit," said Elaine, unbuttoning her coat.

Mari didn't want to tell her mother that thoughts of her daddy were driving her to feel a little like the Grinch.

"I'm in the spirit, Ma," she assured her mother, looking around at the number of people starting to enter the theater. She didn't want to get caught up in any lines or thick crowds and end up getting to her seat late. "I just wish Shauntae and Colby would come on."

"Did you call them?"

"Shauntae just sent me a text message that they were on their way. I bet they ran into traffic."

"Well here's one of Santa's little helpers now," said Elaine, motioning to Dewayne, who'd just turned the corner. "Oh, and there's Cheryl. I'm gonna go on in with your aunt. I'll see you inside."

"Okay, Ma," said Mari, waving at Dewayne. She noticed his clothes weren't wrinkled and his hair was freshly cut. He really wasn't half-bad looking, she thought.

"What it be like?" said Dewayne.

"It's like late and Shauntae and Colby ain't here yet."

"Well, what time did you tell them to get here?"

"Seven-fifteen."

"Aww, give 'em a break. They're just a few minutes late," said Dewayne, looking at his watch.

"I don't know why black folks can't ever be on time."

"'Cause we know the party don't get crunk until two hours after it starts," said Dewayne, bouncing his shoulders in some lame imitation of Lil Jon.

"Well, I'm about to leave them, and they're going to be hot because I've got their tickets," said Mari, turning toward the theater. "They've got two minutes."

"They don't need 'em," said Dewayne, pointing at Colby, Shauntae and Sean coming up the street.

"Hey, Mari," said Colby.

"What's going on, y'all?" said Sean, giving Dewayne a pound.

"What's up?" said Mari, looking at her watch. "It's like seven twenty-five. Come on. Let's go on inside."

"Man, I don't want to go to this mess," said Shauntae, twisting up her mouth.

"What? What are you talking about?" asked Mari, annoyed.

"I heard there was this hot party going on down by the black colleges. I'm trying to hit that," said Shauntae, untying the belt on her black three-quarter-length leather jacket.

"We've been trying to convince her that no college party is going to get started until after eleven, so she might as well come on with us to the show and then we can go downtown," said Colby.

"I'm really not trying to sit up there and look at a bunch of kids who can't sing," said Shauntae.

"Then why did you come down here?" asked Mari.

"I thought if I told y'all about this college joint, you'd dump this kid stuff and come kick it with the big boys and girls." Shauntae smirked. "Plus, I'm hungry, too. Let's go get something to eat, then it'll be time to hit the party."

"I am not going anywhere. My sister is performing tonight, and I'm going to see her," said Mari, glancing at her watch again.

"Well, go on. Watch your damned sister try to win a fake *American Idol*," said Shauntae, turning to Sean, Colby and Dewayne. "So whatcha'll gon' do? You gon' see this talent show mess, or are you gon' step up your game and come with me? You see I broke out the big guns for them college guys. It's gonna be on tonight."

She turned around, modeling the shortest, lowest-cut red sweater dress that Mari thought she'd ever seen. Men passing by were stopping in their tracks looking at Shauntae's breasts, which were much more than just on display. They were the main event.

"Dang, girl," said Dewayne, trying not to stare at Shauntae.

"You need to put those away, girl, before some cop gives you a ticket for indecent exposure," said Sean.

"Pleeeze," she said, moving closer to Sean. "You had your chance, but you went with Miss Straight and Narrow."

"And I'm happy I did," he said, hugging Colby from behind.

"Whatever. I don't want no high school cat anyway. I'ma get me a college man. That's what's up."

Impatient and bored with the whole scene, Mari breathed hard, rolling her eyes to the heavens.

"Look, you all can do whatever you want, but I'm out," said Mari, walking toward the theater.

"Hold up, Mari. We're coming," said Colby, pulling Sean with her. Dewayne followed.

"Y'all so young acting. You need to leave that high school mess alone," Shauntae shouted after them, her hands on her hips. Mari didn't even turn around. She knew the only reason Shauntae was yelling at them was to bring more attention to herself.

"Why did you even bring her down here?" Mari asked Colby as they gave their tickets to the usher at the front door.

Colby shrugged. "She said she wanted to come, and when we got in the car she started talking about that college party."

"She really gets on my last nerve."

"Well, she's outta here," said Sean, closing the subject. "What's up with your sister? You wanna try to go backstage real quick and tell her good luck?"

"You can really hook that up, Sean?" asked Mari.

"You know I got skills, baby," said Sean, flashing a kilowatt smile and patting down his wavy fro with one hand. Colby grinned up into his freckly face.

"Thanks, man. This is so cool," said Mari as she, Colby and Dewayne followed him through a side door.

After navigating a maze of nondescript corridors and security guards at every door, they finally got to the area where the contestants were preparing. There was chaos going on backstage. All kinds of music was playing, both live and recorded. It was hard to tell who the contestants were, there were so many people, friends and family, musicians, technicians and stagehands milling around. People were shouting and singing and running around frantically trying to find everything under the sun—a safety pin, eye liner, even deodorant. Mari saw one girl, who she knew was a contestant by the ridiculous amount of makeup she had on, crying so badly that she had to sit down.

She just knew she'd never find Kalia in all of the insanity, but as she neared the back of the dressing room, she saw her sister sitting in front of a mirror with her eyes closed, her head leaning in her hands. Colby, Sean and Dewayne started toward Kalia, but Mari held up her hand for them to wait. She looked at her sister for a minute, not really wanting to disturb her peace. Suddenly as if she knew she was being watched, Kalia opened her eyes and turned to see her friends looking at her. When Mari saw the calm, confident smile spread across her sister's face as she waved them over, she knew Kalia was going to make it into the finals.

I would have to go after Asha, Kalia thought, standing in the stage wings watching the excellent performance of the girl who'd been crying so hard earlier that she'd almost hyperventilated.

"That's just her routine," her mother had told several people before the show started. "She has to get that emotion all worked up and moving around, and she uses that when she sings."

At the time Kalia thought that was a whole lot to go through to have a good performance, but when she heard the girl wear out some old-school Mary J. Blige and saw the audience jump to their feet and applaud crazily before she could even finish, she began to think differently. After the three *American Idol*-style judges all praised her, even Carter LeGrand, the wannabe Simon Cowell, Kalia wished she had some kind of emotional routine.

But she didn't. All she felt was afraid. She was trying to turn that fear into positive anticipation, but she was having a hard time. It helped a great deal that her sister came backstage with her friends, but getting into the finals was really up to her and only her. The pressure was on, and she was literally shaking. One minute she wished her mother had come backstage, and the next she was glad she hadn't. To stop herself from pacing, she went back over to the wall where the performance order was listed. She was eleventh, right behind Asha. At least an intermission separated them.

Why couldn't I have been first? At least it would have been over with, she thought, walking back to the stage wing to watch the sixth performer, a blond-haired, blue-eyed stacked Jessica Simpson look-alike, who had the audacity to wear a short dress that accentuated her knock-knees. Her voice cracked so much, Kalia knew it had to be nerves because she would have never been able to make it through the auditions unless she had some talent. While Lola Sanchez, the celebrity makeup artist-turned-judge tried to give the knocked-kneed girl some constructive criticism, Carter ripped her apart for everything from her style to her weak performance. The last judge, a pudgy washed-up b-boy from the eighties who still went by Big Spinner, just shook his head and gave her a thumbs down. And the audience just oohed and aahed through the judges' comments.

Kalia watched the girl come off stage to be embraced by her boyfriend and wondered where Malcolm was. They'd been spending so much time together and he'd been so giving and attentive, she just knew he'd show up backstage with roses or something, but he was missing in action when she really needed him. Just like her father, who was probably still at one of his restaurants, she thought, holding onto the curtain in the wings. Her mind was jumping around. She needed to calm down. After watching the blond girl get reamed by Carter, she decided she didn't need to see any more singers.

She walked back toward the dressing room, which was still buzzing, longing for some quiet place to get her mind together. Strolling through the hallways, she remembered her mother bringing her and her sister to see productions like *The Wiz* and *A Raisin in the Sun* when they were children. She'd wanted to be onstage even back then, and now that she was getting her chance, she found herself trying to get as far away from it as possible. Finally at the end of a long corridor, she discovered an empty dressing room and deposited herself there and closed the door. At least there was a monitor in the room, so she'd be able to know when intermission started. She fiddled with the remote, trying to take the TV off mute, but was unsuccessful, so she spent the next three singers' performances dabbing the sweat off her carefully applied makeup, picking imaginary lint off her outfit and trying not to watch the monitor.

Kalia couldn't help but look at Asha's performance. Striking in a white haltered backless fitted jumpsuit with wide-leg pants, white ribbon-strapped stilettos and a huge white flower behind her ear, she strolled out on stage as if she'd sang for crowds of thousands millions of times. There was still no sound, but Kalia could tell by Asha's expressions and the audience's reactions panned by the cameras that Asha was blowing them away. As she moved back and forth, her wavy waist-length hair swung this way and that, giving her what Kalia thought was real star appeal.

Wishing she could tear herself away from the monitor, Kalia stood transfixed as the cameras showed large smiles on the faces of Lola and Big Spinner. Even Carter was looking entertained.

Asha bowed at the judges professionally and waved at the standing, applauding and whistling audience as she walked offstage. It was only then that Kalia could move, but it was in a daze. She opened the door and made her way to the dressing room.

Chaos was going on all around her, but she didn't hear much. The fog didn't even lift when Sean brought her mother and her aunt backstage during intermission. She accepted their hugs and well wishes, but she couldn't remember what they said. Her eyes were focused on the large ticker in the front of the dressing room that counted down the minutes and seconds for intermission. When it reached five minutes, she heard her name called by the stage manager. Her mother gave her one last squeeze and she, Sean and her sister rushed off to their seats. Kalia stood in the wings, clasping her hands together tightly. She prayed to the Creator for a good performance as the announcer boomed her name.

Kalia had no idea how she made it to the middle of the stage or from where the cordless microphone came that she was clutching for dear life. As the lights focused on her, she was blinded and couldn't see the audience or the judges to her left, but she knew they were out there. She was at war with herself. *You've performed in at least fifty concerts,* said the confidant Kalia. *But that was just junior high and high school,* said her alter ego. *Oh God, I'm going insane,* thought yet a third Kalia. *Relax and get it together,* a fourth Kalia scolded. Hearing the intro to "Fallin'," she decided she'd better listen to the last Kalia, who seemed to have the best grip on herself.

She held the mic with both hands, bent her head down, took a deep breath and let out the first note. A little fluttery at first, she improved rapidly. She felt the lyrics soar out of her, and by the time she finished, she just knew she'd knocked it out because she heard the audience clapping. When the house lights were brought up, the audience wasn't on their feet as they were at the end of Asha's performance. Kalia held her hand above her head, shielding her eyes from the lights to see if she could find her family in the audience. Still searching, she heard someone calling her name and realized it was Big Spinner.

As she turned to face the judges, she heard several loud claps and "Woo-hoo, Kalia" and knew it was her family and friends, but her mind wasn't eased. Kalia couldn't understand why the audience wasn't giving her a standing ovation, but the judges did.

"Kalia, Kalia, Kalia, such a pretty name for such an uptight performance," sang Big Spinner. "We thought you were going to choke that mic to death."

The audience joined Big Spinner and Carter, snickering and laughing.

Lola looked at Kalia pityingly. "Well maybe she was just a little nervous. She wouldn't be the first," said Lola. If there was one thing Kalia didn't want, it was someone to have to come to her rescue. She stood silently nodding, a plastic tight-lipped smile plastered on her face. She wanted to accept her criticism gracefully, but felt she'd burst into tears any minute—either that or storm across the stage and knock every one of those judges in the head with the mic.

"Were you nervous, sweetie?" asked Lola.

"A little bit," she managed to get out, gripping the mic so tightly in her left hand that she knew her fingernails were drawing blood in her palm.

"Well, lots of people are, and we could only tell for the first couple of lines. After you got yourself together, you were terrific. You captured the emotions in the song very well," said Lola.

Kalia was feeling a little better, but she knew that Carter hadn't spoken yet. Big Spinner and Lola were tenderizing her, she thought, and Carter was waiting to swoop in at the end for the kill.

"Yeah, the end was great, like Lola said, but you might want to try some tai chi, some hot tea, something to relax before you perform next time." Big Spinner chuckled. "What do you think, Carter?"

Carter crossed his arms over his chest, leaned back in his chair and cocked his head to one side, looking intently at Kalia.

"I think the girl's got some talent. You can sing, you can sing," he said finally. Kalia let out the breath that she'd been holding for at least a minute. "But, I also think that Fire's gonna want someone who is cool under pressure, and you're just not there. That's something you need to work on. No one wants to sign someone who looks like she might run off stage if her mommy's not there to clap for her. Are you feeling me, Kalia?"

He then turned to the audience. "We don't want any scared little girls, do we, folks?"

The long, loud, collective "No," nearly knocked Kalia back a few feet.

"Oh, I think you're being a little hard on her," said Lola.

Carter continued staring at Kalia with raised eyebrows. "Well?" he said.

"Thank you for your honesty. I'm sure it will help me in the future," she said clearly, praying they didn't hear the attitude in her voice.

"I hope so. Thank you very much. Good luck and God bless," Carter said, waving her off.

As she walked off the stage, waving and fake-smiling at the audience, she heard Big Spinner saying, "If she'd just moved around a little bit. I mean I thought she'd caught her heel in a rut or something. She didn't move an inch."

Lola replied, "Oh, everybody has a little bit of stage fright sometimes."

"Frightened singers don't get signed," dismissed Carter. "All right, who's next? I can't hang out here all night. Let's get a real powerhouse out here. Isn't someone going to give that Asha some competition?"

Backstage, people were patting Kalia on her shoulder and telling her "It's okay," and "Good job," as she passed through what felt like a gauntlet of pity. Nodding left and right, she kept her strained smile and walked straight to the dressing room. Others continued to come by and congratulate her on how well she took Big Spinner's jabs and Carter's critique.

She was wiping off her makeup in the mirror when she saw Mari come in the dressing room behind her. Their eyes met, and Kalia thought she would cry—until she saw Sean and Malcolm with her. All of the sudden her sockets were dry. For some reason, she didn't want Malcolm to see her come undone.

"Hey, babe. You did great," he said, walking up to her and kissing her on the back of the neck.

"How would you know? You just got here five minutes ago," said Mari.

Kalia still hadn't turned around. She looked in the mirror from Mari to Malcolm, more hurt registering on her face.

"I saw almost all of it," said Malcolm, glaring at Mari in the mirror.

"You didn't sit down until Carter was doing his thing," said

Mari. Seeing Kalia's face, she added, "Sorry, K. I didn't mean to bring that up. I thought you did great."

"Yeah. You were really good," said Sean. "I'm sure hardly anybody noticed that you didn't move around too much."

"Shut up, man," said Mari, reaching up to slap Sean in the back of the head.

Then it was quiet in their little corner, everyone realizing that Kalia hadn't said a word.

"What's up, K?" said Mari, pushing Malcolm out of the way to hug her sister from behind. "You did good. For real. You know I wouldn't tell you so if I didn't really mean it."

Kalia spun around, almost knocking her sister over. "Well, why is everybody trying so hard to convince me then?" she asked, looking from Mari to Sean and finally to Malcolm.

"Look, so you had a little case of the nerves, baby? That happens to everybody," said Malcolm, taking her hand.

She snatched it back. "How would you know? You weren't even here to see me sing."

"I said I saw the whole thing. I was standing in the back while you sang," Malcolm swore.

Kalia just looked at him.

"I mean I may have missed like the first verse or something," he said, turning his back on her and looking around the dressing room. "See, I had this big meeting with this guy who said he could hook me up with a deal. We were in the studio, just making these beats, right, and…"

Malcolm stopped talking when he saw tears well up in Kalia's eyes.

"You knew how important this was to me," she said, standing up, "and you promised you'd be here."

"You don't understand, K," said Malcolm. "You don't know who this guy is. He's really connected."

"So what?" said Mari, coming to her sister's aid. "You should have been here."

Malcolm tried to explain. "Kalia, you'll understand when you're good enough to get your deal. People will just start hooking you up with other people and—"

"He is kinda right," Sean agreed. "When you tighten your skills up, the right people just kind of appear, especially if you've got your vocals, your performance and all that."

"Shut up, both of you. Just shut up," shouted Mari. "This isn't helping Kalia. Can't you see she's upset?"

"So neither one of you thinks I'm ready?" Kalia asked Sean and Malcolm. "You don't think I can win, do you?"

"Truth?" asked Sean.

Kalia nodded.

"Well, one day, but not right now," he said. "You had stage fright pretty bad, and that's something most performers have worked out at this stage."

Kalia looked at Malcolm.

"Baby, I don't know what to say," he said, looking into her eyes.

"I do," said Mari. "Get out. Just leave. Both of you."

She pushed them both in their chests. Tiny as she was, neither moved an inch. Kalia just turned and sat down in the chair and looked back in the mirror. Sean mumbled an apology and walked toward the exit. Malcolm put his hand on Kalia's shoulder, but she shrugged it off, looking away. He looked to Mari, who pursed her lips and shook her head. Looking around like he was lost, Malcolm gave up and walked out of the dressing room, too.

Mari sat in the chair beside her sister and reached over to smooth her hair back.

"Do you want me to stay back here with you? I can. No problem."

Kalia looked at Mari, thinking how great it was to have a sister who was there for her, but she really wanted to be alone.

"No, Mari," she squeaked. "Go ahead. Go on back out there. I'll be fine. The show's almost over anyway." She looked back in the mirror. "Yep, it's almost over, then we can go home, and I can forget I ever entered this mess."

"What if you make the finals though?"

"You gotta be kidding me," said Kalia, turning to face her sister. "There is no way in hell I'm going to be chosen as one of the final eight."

"K, it was your physical performance that was just okay. Your vocals were on. You shut it down vocally."

"Well, you need the whole package to win."

"I guess, but there were lots of other contestants who couldn't sing as well as you even if they had great stage presence. Plus, it's easier to teach a person stage presence than it is how to sing," said Mari, standing.

"I guess."

"Look, don't worry about it. You're gonna make it to the finals, and we're gonna use all the time between now and the big show in March to get you some help with your presentation."

"What are you talking about?" asked Kalia, eyeing her sister. "It will be a miracle if I happen to make it to the finals."

"Quit it. Just quit it," she demanded. "You're gonna make the finals, so put that makeup back on and get ready to go out there so we can clap for you. G'on brush your shoulders off, K. Okay?"

Kalia nodded.

"Naw, I wanna see it. Brush your shoulders off."

Kalia wiped her hand across her shoulder.

"Good," said Mari, getting up and starting toward the exit. "And promise me you're going to put that makeup back on."

Kalia almost smiled at her sister. "So who's bossy now?" she said.

"I knew if I hung around you long enough I'd pick up some of your bad habits," said Mari.

Kalia did smile this time. Mari grinned back and left the dressing room.

Forty-five minutes later, Kalia felt her armpits moisten as she listened to the host call the name of the sixth contestant who'd made the finals. There were only two spots left. She was in the wings with fourteen other contestants who were in varying states of emotional distress. She crumpled the red crushed velvet curtain in one hand behind her back. Somehow squishing something made her feel slightly better.

"The seventh contestant who will perform in the Who's Got That Fire? final iiisss…Miss Asha Wright," announced the host.

Cool as a cucumber, Asha floated on stage and stood next to the sixth contestant who Kalia thought was grinning so wide she could have swallowed her ears. This was it, she thought, squeezing the curtain with the other hand. She looked at the other contestants around her. Some were pacing, others were crying and holding hands. Kalia realized at that moment that she wanted to become a finalist more than anything else in the world.

"And the last contestant who will perform in the Who's Got That Fire? final iiisss…Miss Kalia Jefferson."

Kalia didn't move. She stood in the wings, clutching the

curtain. A stagehand ripped her hands from the curtain and shoved her onto the stage. Nearly stumbling, she recovered just in time to miss bumping Asha, who looked over at her like she was a minor annoyance. This time Kalia's smile was real, and it was brighter than all the stage lights in the theater.

chapter 9

After the show, Mari insisted on everybody going to Houston's for a celebratory dinner. Everybody was game, except Malcolm, who told Kalia he'd promised to hook back up with his record label connection after he'd dipped out of the studio earlier to see her performance. Kalia was in such a good mood about winning that it really didn't hit her until she and Mari were in her room around one in the morning how angry she was with Malcolm.

"How could he just squeeze me in like that? This was like the most important night of my life," said Kalia, lying across her bed.

"I know, right?" agreed Mari. "Men can be so stupid."

"They sure can."

"I mean they're either lying or selfish or cheating or something."

"Yep, yep," said Kalia, getting up. "I'm going downstairs to get something to drink."

Mari followed her, continuing her tirade.

"What gives them the right to think that they can treat us any old way?"

"Most of them are just conceited for no good reason. I mean Malcolm really isn't all that," said Kalia, staring into the refrigerator. She stuck her head all the way in. "I have no idea what I want."

"Neither is Qwon," said Mari, staring in the refrigerator, too.

"You know what I think," she said, turning to Kalia.

"What?"

"I think we should have a beer."

Kalia looked at Mari.

"Look, you had a long, hard exciting day. You're almost grown, and everybody else in the world drinks. One beer isn't going to hurt us," said Mari. "It'll probably make us feel a whole lot better. Plus, Ma and Daddy are knocked out. We could drink a whole six-pack and Daddy would never know. We'll just replace what we drink. He's got a ton out in the pantry."

"I am not drinking a six pack of beer, Mari," said Kalia sternly.

"Oh, but you'll drink at least one, huh?" asked Mari, leaning over and grabbing a cold one from inside the refrigerator door. "Shoot. We gotta celebrate you getting into the finals, too."

That last excuse did it for Kalia. "Yeah, I guess one is cool. I probably need one to calm my nerves," she said, getting herself a beer, too. "I'm all hyped up over getting into the finals. Can you believe I made it in?"

"Of course I can—I predicted it, remember?" said Mari, popping open her beer and then Kalia's. They stood in the middle of the kitchen, toasted to her success and took sips.

"Not bad," said Mari, smacking her lips.

"Stop acting like you've had a beer before." Kalia smirked.

"I have."

"Where? No, when?" asked Kalia, taking another swallow.

"Don't you worry about it."

"I won't."

"So what's up with this Malcolm guy? Do you really like him or what?" Mari asked, leaning against the counter.

"I did until he turned into a selfish asshole tonight."

"Well, that's dudes for ya. If you want to be with a man, then you've got to get used to the crap that comes with them."

"How do you know?" asked Kalia.

"I just know," said Mari, gulping down her beer.

"Well, I liked Malcolm at first. He was mature, cool and creative. I mean his knowledge of music is incredible, but now, I just don't know."

"It must be cool dating a college man, though."

"I guess," said Kalia, finishing her beer. "Right now I just wish he would pay me some more attention."

"I'm almost finished with this one," said Mari, turning up her can. "Let's split another one."

"Okay, and that's it," Kalia said, reaching into the refrigerator and popping open another beer.

By the time Kalia had finished telling Mari all of the things that had attracted her to Malcolm, they'd downed that beer and opened another. Mari telling Kalia about her hurt feelings over Qwon had them finishing a fourth beer, so they decided to knock their father's six-pack out with one more apiece.

"Yeah, men are just dogs," said Mari, trying to make a jump shot in the wastebasket with one of her cans. She wobbled a bit.

"But why?" asked Kalia, slumping over on the kitchen table. "Why do they have to be such animals? Why can't they act like human beings?"

"You answered your own question, silly," slurred Mari, shaking Kalia by the shoulders.

"I'm no sillier than you, and you're drunk."

"Not by myself," said Mari. "I bet you can't stand up and walk a straight line."

"I can so," said Kalia, rising quickly and knocking two cans to the floor. They clashed loudly against each other.

"Shh, shh, shh." Mari giggled, pushing her index finger to her lips.

Kalia flopped to her hands and knees and tried to reach the cans under the table.

"You look like the dog now," said Mari, continuing to giggle.

"Shut up and help me get these damn cans."

"Why should I? You dropped them," sang Mari, exaggerating a tiptoe dance across the kitchen.

Kalia had both the cans and was getting up when she bumped her head underneath the table, knocking the whole thing over and causing such a commotion that Mari ran into the dining room.

"Woo-wee," she said, peeping around the corner. "You are gonna get it. I know Daddy heard that."

"You're drinking, too," said Kalia, sprawled out on the floor. She wanted to get up, but her head was banging and the room was spinning.

By the time their father appeared in the kitchen, Kalia had dragged herself back into a chair, and Mari was still peeping in from the dining room.

"Mari, get in here," he said. "I can't believe you all are drinking my beer. Get upstairs to bed. I'll deal with you tomorrow."

Kalia stood and swayed toward the steps. Mari kept up her exaggerated tiptoeing until her father's stern face made her walk upright.

The next thing Kalia knew, the sun was shining brightly on her face and someone was talking loudly. She groaned and turned over, covering her head with the sheets.

"Get up, girl," said Mari, flopping onto her sister's bed. "I'm trying to see what my punishment is going to be before I make any plans for the day."

"Mmmmmmh," said Kalia. "Go away."

"Daddy said he wanted to see us downstairs right now, so I'll just tell him you said to go away."

"Mmmmmmh," said Kalia, rolling over. "Close those curtains."

"Nope," said Mari, walking out of the room.

Kalia dragged herself to the bathroom, wondering how Mari could be so alert when they'd both had the same amount of beer. Face washed and teeth brushed, she appeared in the kitchen to find Mari sitting across from her parents. Her mother was stirring a cup of tea, and her father had his arms folded, waiting. Nobody was speaking. She pulled up a chair and assumed the about-to-receive-a-lecture position she hadn't sat in in months.

"So?" said Ronald, looking from one to the other.

Mari looked out the window. Kalia fidgeted with her sleeve. No one said anything.

"If someone doesn't speak up and tell me why a sixteen-year-old and an eighteen-year-old think they can drink alcohol in my house, then you're both going to be on punishment so long, I'll be in a nursing home when you get off."

Sensing their father was serious, Mari and Kalia started talking nonsensically at once.

"See, Daddy, I'd had a long day, and we just wanted to cool out and celebrate a bit. We were at home, and it wasn't like we were drinking and driving or anything," said Kalia.

"Yeah, we were safe and sound, drinking at home. Nothing could happen to us here," echoed Mari.

Elaine got up and slammed her mug in the sink. The sisters jumped.

"Do you think that makes it better? You think it's okay for you to drink because you were doing it at home?" growled their mother. She walked over to Kalia, bent over and put her nose a hair's length away from her daughter's.

"You're the big sister. You're supposed to set an example for Mari." Kalia could smell the tea on her mother's breath. "Who's idea was this anyway?" asked Elaine, shifting her attention to Mari.

"I…well…see… It was my suggestion…but," said Mari, her eyes growing big as her father stood and moved closer to her.

"You girls aren't old enough to drink—that's it," said Ronald, staring down at Mari. "I don't care whose idea it was. If I catch either of you ever drinking again—ever—you will be grounded until I die."

"You aren't to leave this house for anything but school for two weeks," said Elaine, "and don't think you're going to be getting on the phone and chatting your friends up. There's no phone, no television, no anything that has to be plugged in—that includes the Internet, unless it's homework related. And believe me, I'm gonna be on you."

Kalia thought about practicing for the Fire final. "But, Ma, what about the Fire contest? We might have practice or meetings or something."

Her father turned to her. "Well, I guess you should have thought about that before you turned into Boozing Betty."

Mari had been stewing in her seat. She thought about the Christmas parties she'd surely miss and blew up. "Daddy, you come home every day and have three beers before you even take your coat off. How are a couple going to hurt us one time?" Mari stood.

Ronald froze for a second and started toward his younger daughter. Elaine blocked his charge. *Thank God,* Mari thought.

"Girl, don't you ever question me in my house again," said Ronald over Elaine's head. "When you start paying the bills here, then you can have some say. I don't know who you think you are."

Ronald walked out of the kitchen. Elaine looked after him.

"You're lucky I didn't let him knock you into next week," she said to Mari. "You know what? I want this house to be as clean as the day we moved in."

Kalia and Mari stood still.

"Didn't you hear what I said?" Elaine shouted. "You're not going to just sit in your room and read and do homework. These two weeks are going to be productive. You're cleaning this house from top to bottom. Get to it."

Shaking her head and throwing them both an exasperated look, she walked up the back stairs.

"You and your bright ideas," said Kalia, turning to her sister.

"I didn't have to twist your arm."

"Well, now we can't do anything."

"You don't do anything, anyway," said Mari, pushing the chairs underneath the kitchen table.

"Shut up."

"You shut up."

"Both of you shut up," said Elaine from upstairs. "And get to cleaning. Don't make me have to come back down there."

Kalia and Mari looked at each other and began two weeks of the most intense cleaning they'd ever done.

About a week later, Kalia had three finals in one day, including one where she had to play a piece by Mozart, and the chorale had a Christmas performance at the end of the week. She was stressed and really needed to relax. Luckily her parents had let up enough to allow her to practice for at least an hour after school. She was on her way to a practice room when she spotted a familiar-looking guy in the hallway. As she approached him, it became clear that it was Malcolm. She stopped for a second, trying to decide what to do. They hadn't spoken or seen each other since the night of the Fire preliminary show.

Malcolm started walking toward her. She just stood in the middle of the hallway, watching his features get clearer the closer he came. She loved his confident, laid-back stride. By the time he was close enough for her to see the words on his T-shirt, If It Ain't Real, It Ain't Right, she'd sworn to herself five times that she wasn't going to let him apologize his way back into her good graces—and she certainly wasn't going to hug him, even though he looked good enough to eat.

To her surprise, Malcolm didn't say anything. He walked straight up to her, grabbed her by the waist, pulled her to him and hugged her so tightly, she thought she was going to faint, then he took her hand and escorted her to her favorite practice room. He led her to the piano, sat her down and walked over to the corner, sitting down in a chair. Kalia didn't really know what to do. She put her hands on the keys, but nothing happened.

Malcolm got up and kissed her once, very softly on the lips. He walked back over and sat down in the corner. Kalia started slowly playing a tune she'd never played before—something she hadn't heard before. New lyrics of love, patience, forgiveness and under-standing spilled out of her mouth. Malcolm came over to the piano, whipped out a notebook and started writing down the lyrics.

"You've got something here, baby," he said. "That's real emotion there. Go with it." Kalia looked up at Malcolm and felt a surge of creativity. They spent nearly an hour writing what ended up being, "Just Us." She'd never really written a song before. She'd flirted with lyrics and had ideas about songs, but she'd never put them down on paper.

When they were done, Malcolm told her he'd hold on to the song and maybe one day she could record it for her debut album. Kalia almost jumped his bones. Just like that, he was forgiven and they were back together. They never spoke of the night he left her per-formance and ran off to meet with his record company connection.

Kalia drove home in a daze, only to find Mari meeting her at the door. "Dewayne has stopped by here like three times looking for you," she said. "Are you not dealing with him anymore or something? If so, I wish you'd tell him. He's driving me crazy."

"Have you forgotten that we're on punishment?" asked Kalia. "That means no company."

"Now you know Ronald and Elaine don't care about Dewayne. He ain't nobody anyway," said Mari, following Kalia into her room. "And what are you all smiley about?"

"Nunyah."

"What?"

"Nunyah bizness." Kalia smirked, kicking her shoes into her closet.

"Ha ha. Very funny. Is that the type of thing you learn from a college man?"

"Umm, umm," said Kalia dreamily. "He's got more important lessons to teach."

"So you saw him, huh?"

"What?" said Kalia, snapping back into reality. "What are you talking about?"

"Kalia, I know you," said Mari, sitting in her sister's computer chair. "So y'all back together. Well, that's good 'cause I'm trying to meet some of his friends."

"Absolutely not," said Kalia. "Your little drinking idea already got me grounded for at least another week. If the parents found out I introduced you to some college guys, I'd be in prison until I went to college."

"Well, how about a brother? Does he have a younger brother?"

"No, and even if he did I wouldn't subject him to your craziness," said Kalia, changing into a pair of shorts.

"What are you talking about? I'm just as sane as everyone else in this house," said Mari, swinging her legs back and forth under the chair. "So does he have any sisters?"

"What, are you a lesbian now?"

"No, silly. You just really haven't told me anything about him, and I can tell you really like him. Give me the lowdown on Mr. Malcolm. I don't even know his last name."

Being that she really wasn't the girlfriend type and talking to Dewayne about Malcolm seemed a bit weird, Kalia hadn't really talked to anybody about her new love, so she sat down on her bed and told her sister about her boyfriend. She recounted the time she and Malcolm had gone to his father's house, which was right down Martin Luther King Jr. Drive, not too far from the Atlanta University Center. Ten years ago, when he'd relocated himself and his only child from Oakland, California, to Atlanta after the sudden death of his wife, Tyrone Lee let his activist orientation lead him to living in the heart of a community that could certainly use his conscientious initiatives.

"That's his daddy? Tyrone 'Get It On' Lee? The one who was down there protesting the close of the first Paschals? Remember Daddy was all up in that drama because it was about a black-owned restaurant?" asked Mari.

"Yep, that's him," said Kalia, "and actually he's real cool. We had dinner over there a couple of times. His house has all this

African art and more books about black people and African people and just people of color all over the world. He's really intelligent."

"Every time you see him on TV, he's got on those African shirts. What do you call them?"

"Dashikis. He's got a kazillion of them, too."

"So is Malcolm all black power and everything?"

"Well, he knows a lot about black people, but he's really more into music. You should see how many albums he has. It's like thousands."

"For real? Dang," said Mari. "Well, how old is he? What year is he at Morris Brown?"

"He's twenty and technically a sophomore, but he's not in school right now."

"Why not?"

"Well, you remember all that stuff on the news when Morris Brown lost their accreditation? He decided not to register for classes. He was thinking about trying to transfer to Clark Atlanta or Georgia State, but he owes some money to Morris Brown and well, there's just some drama going on with his college stuff."

"Sooooo what? Is he just deejaying?"

"Yep. He's deejaying all over the place. He's playing somewhere like every night, and he's actually trying to get a deal. You know how deejays get record deals for their mixed CDs?"

"Ooh yeah, like um, DJ Kid Capri. That means he might be meeting all those stars like Snoop, Nelly and Ludacris."

"I guess," said Kalia, getting up and straightening up her dresser.

"Well, if he doesn't have a brother and you won't let him hook me up with some of his college boys, the least I can get is an introduction to T.I. or Young Jeezy or somebody."

"Uh, no," said Kalia.

"Aw come on. I can't even meet the Nite Bandit? He's just got a radio show."

"Okay, I've had enough of you. Get out," said Kalia.

"But…"

Kalia pointed to the door. Mari stuck out her tongue at her sister as she skipped out. She was on her way to her room when she spotted Dewayne through her parents' window coming up the driveway. She knew Kalia was going to give him the brush-off, and for some reason she didn't want Dewayne to get his feelings hurt, so she bounded down the stairs and opened the door before he could even make it to the front steps.

"So how many times are you going to come over here today?" she said, leaning against the door.

Dewayne stood at the bottom of the stairs, looking up at her. "I just wanted to talk to her about something. I know she's home, so just tell her I'm here, okay?"

"Man, she just got here, and she's getting ready to do some homework and stuff. I'll just tell her to call you."

"Mari, what's up? Don't make me have to come up in there."

"All right," said Mari, turning around. "Come on in."

Dewayne followed her into the kitchen and sat at the table. She walked slowly up the stairs and dipped her head into Kalia's doorway.

"K, Dewayne is downstairs."

"What does he want?"

"I don't know. That's your friend," said Mari, walking to her room. She heard Kalia saying, "I really don't feel like dealing with him right now," then she heard her sister walking downstairs. Mari had barely gotten started studying for her psychology final when she heard the front door close and Kalia walk back into her room. She went to her parents' room and looked out the window to see Dewayne standing in their front yard, looking at the house across the street, she guessed. She grabbed her jacket, rushed downstairs, threw open the front door and ran down the front steps. She slowed her pace, approaching him.

"So what's going on? What's your deal?" she asked him, checking to see if there was mail in the mailbox as an excuse to be outside.

"Huh?"

"What was all the rush-rush to see Kalia?"

"Oh, it was nothing."

"Nothing didn't bring you over here four times in two hours. You could have at least called a couple of those times," she said, sifting through the mail.

Dewayne ignored her, sitting down on the front steps. Mari stood in front of him.

"Hey," she said, "I've got this idea that I need you to help me with."

Dewayne said nothing. He just stared out toward the street.

"I think that Kalia's major competition in the Fire contest is going to be this girl who goes to my school—Asha Wright. We've got to do something about her."

"Do something? Like what?" Dewayne asked, looking at the ground and zipping up his jacket against the early December chill.

"You know, find some way to get to her. Maybe find out what song she's singing and tell Kalia, or I don't know, find some way to freak her out right before she goes on. Shake her up or something before the show. She's just too...too sumthin'...like arrogant. She really gets on my nerves."

"Sounds like a personal problem to me."

"You don't have to get smart about it," said Mari, rolling her eyes. "I thought you'd want to help me help Kalia, seeing as that's your friend and all."

"Is she? Is she really my friend?" asked Dewayne.

The angst in his voice really caught Mari off guard.

"What—what are you talking about?"

Dewayne shook his head. "I don't know." He turned to Mari. "So is it really serious between her and this guy?"

Mari didn't know how to answer. She didn't want Dewayne to be hurt any further. He already looked like someone had stepped on his heart.

"I guess. I don't know," she lied. "I mean you know we've been on lockdown. Neither one of us is getting out much, so she can't be really seeing him too tough."

"But you know, we haven't really kicked it in a while, and she's always telling me she's got something to do, and she never calls me back."

"Dewayne, I thought you and K were, you know, just friends?"

"I guess we are. I guess that's all we are," he said, getting up. He started to cross their driveway.

"Don't be a stranger, man," Mari called out after him.

Not even turning around, Dewayne walked into his house, leaving Mari sitting on her front porch feeling sorry for him.

When Mari woke up on Christmas morning, she wasn't even excited. For one thing, she'd hated the third page, below-the-fold placement that her story about a visiting African professor had gotten in the *East Moreland Review*. She was also still slightly annoyed that, although she'd finished her first semester of tenth grade with four As, she had gotten one B in, of all things, Early World Literature. She'd studied especially hard for that final, and when her grades came in the mail a few days ago, she literally had to sit down when she saw her B.

She rolled over, really not wanting to go over to Auntie Cheryl's. Sleeping late and getting her Christmas money a few hours later would have been just fine with her. That was all her parents had given them for the last two Christmases anyway, so the thrill was gone. Her father didn't even put up the fake Christmas tree that year. Taking a quick shower, she remembered the big deal her parents, especially her mother, used to make about Christmas, even after the big dinner had moved over to Auntie Cheryl's. The preparations began early—really early. Although they didn't go to church all year round, her mother would start getting the guilts right after Halloween, so by the time Christmas came, the whole family would have made it to at least five or six Sunday services so that they could celebrate the birth of Jesus in good conscience.

A few weeks before Christmas, her daddy would string a million lights around the house and surprise them with a live tree one night. That evening was almost better than Christmas Day because her mother would cook a big meal, after which they'd put up a ton of other decorations—wreaths, angels, poinsettias, candles and anything else of which they could think—until they'd almost fall asleep hanging all of the ornaments, garlands and their favorite, the silvery icicles, on the tree. Right before the girls went to bed, their father would affix a lighted star on top of the tree and make a big production of plugging the whole thing in.

Drying off, Mari could almost taste the gingerbread men and milk on which she and Kalia would snack while dreamily watching the lights on the tree flash off and on. She missed waking up Christmas morning smelling her mother's famous pecan pancakes and sausage. She missed them all sitting around the tree, opening gifts before they went to Auntie Cheryl's. Putting on a pullover and some stretch jeans, she padded down to the kitchen to find her mother mixing something in a bowl.

"Merry Christmas, darling," said Elaine, turning around to greet her daughter.

"Ma, what are you doing?" asked Mari, surveying the ingredients of what looked like Christmas breakfast of yesteryear on the counter. "I know those aren't pecans."

"Surprise," said Elaine, grinning. "Wanna help?"

"Woo-hoo," sang Mari, grabbing an apron from a drawer. "What's got into you? You haven't made this breakfast in years."

"I don't know. Things have been kind of strange around here, so I thought a good Christmas breakfast could get us started off right today."

"I am *so* not mad at that," said Kalia, coming into the kitchen. "I'll make the sausage."

Mari went into the family room and turned the stereo on to Hot 103.5, just in time to hear Kalia's favorite Christmas song, James Brown's "Santa Goes Straight to the Ghetto." They were deep into cooking and dancing around the kitchen when Ronald appeared, fully dressed.

"Wow," he said. "What's going on in here? Something smells good."

"We thought we'd have a real Christmas breakfast this morning," said Elaine. "Would you like some coffee?"

"No...uhh...no thanks," he said, grabbing his keys off the rack. "Elaine, can I talk to you for a minute?"

Kalia and Mari watched their mother wipe her hands on her apron, following their father into the entryway. They stood still, trying to make out their parents' urgent whispers over the Temptations' "Silent Night" blaring on the radio. When they heard the front door slam, they quickly resumed their cooking activities. A moment later Elaine came back into the kitchen. She stood in front of the sink washing utensils silently.

"So, Ma," said Mari warily, "are we putting the pecans in the mix or are we just going to sprinkle them on top?"

"Do them however you like, Mari," Elaine said quietly.

Mari looked at Kalia for help.

"Ma, where did Daddy go?" Kalia asked, taking the pan of sausage off the stove.

"To work," said Elaine.

"But it's Christmas," protested Mari.

"That it is," said Elaine.

"Is he coming back soon?" asked Kalia.

"I don't know. He didn't say," said Elaine. She wasn't doing anything, just looking out of the kitchen window.

"Well, what did he say? The Frys aren't even open on Christmas, are they? I mean we're up here cooking breakfast, and he's gonna miss it," shouted Mari.

"Oh, who gives a damn about this mess," Elaine said, grabbing the pancake mix from Mari and emptying it into the sink. "Your daddy would rather be at his precious Fish Frys than he would here with his family on Christmas Day."

Stunned, Kalia was still holding the pan with the sausage. She put it back on the stove and walked over to her mother.

"Ma, it's okay," she said, motioning Mari over.

"It is not okay," shouted Mari. "What the hell is going on in this house?" She looked at her mother. "How come Daddy's sleeping in the guest room, Ma?"

Kalia looked at her sister, horrified.

"What are you talking about?" asked Elaine, her eyes growing wide.

"Okay, let's stop the pretending. Everybody in this house knows that Daddy has been sleeping in the guest room since this summer."

"Mari," Kalia hissed through clenched teeth.

"What?" shouted Mari, looking at her sister. "You're trying to tell me you haven't seen Daddy sleeping in the guest room?"

Kalia didn't say a word. She just stood against the counter holding her sobbing mother around the waist.

"So what's up, Ma? Are you and Daddy separated? Are you getting a divorce? Is that why he's going to work on Christmas Day, because he can't stand to be around you?"

Elaine stood up straight, walked over to Mari and slapped her in the face. Mari slumped down into a chair. Elaine looked down at her and seemed at a loss for what to do next. Kalia burst into tears, then Mari started whimpering. Seconds later all three Jefferson women were crying their eyes out. Kalia walked over to her mother and gave her a hug, then Mari joined in for a group hug, and they all leaned on one another.

"I didn't mean any of that, Ma," said Mari, drying her eyes on the back of her sleeve.

"I know, sweetie," said Elaine, giving Mari an extra squeeze.

"You don't have to talk about anything that you don't want to," said Kalia, eyeing Mari.

"Yeah, Ma. You don't have to tell us what's going on between you and Daddy," said Mari.

"Well, no, girls, we should have said something to you earlier," said Elaine, sitting down. "You live in this house, and you're old enough to notice when something isn't right."

Kalia turned the radio down and both she and Mari sat at the table across from their mother. Elaine reached out across the table, taking one of each of her daughters' hands.

"Listen, your daddy and I have been going through a very rough period," said Elaine. "You know I've told you before that a married couple is just two people who decided they have enough in common and love each other enough to want to spend their lives together, but they're still different people who are always growing and changing."

Kalia and Mari both nodded.

"Well, your father and I have been wanting different things for some time now, and we're trying to figure out how to work out what each of us wants, and it's hard."

"Can we help?" asked Mari.

Elaine smiled at her younger daughter. "I wish you could, but it's really up to me and your daddy to figure this one out."

"So you are going to figure it out, right?" asked Kalia, squeezing her mother's hand.

"I hope so, baby." Elaine let their hands go and stood. "Go turn up the radio. We're going to have our Christmas breakfast, then we're going over to your aunt Cheryl's and help them open their gifts. Oh, that reminds me," she added, hurrying into the dining room. "I've got something special for you girls."

Mari turned up BoyZ II Men singing "Let It Snow" on the radio and came back into the kitchen. Elaine returned with beautifully wrapped gifts in both hands.

"I know that we've been just giving you girls money for the last few years, but I wanted you to have some real gifts this year," she said, handing them both packages. "Kalia, with you graduating, we don't know what's going to be going on this time next year. Christmas might not be the same."

As they opened their presents—mp3 players, digital cameras and gift cards to their favorite stores—both Kalia and Mari couldn't help but think that the reason Christmas might be different next year had nothing to do with them. Neither said a word about their parents' strained relationship, but it stayed in the back of all three of their minds for the rest of the day.

chapter 10

Kalia stood on her front porch waiting for Malcolm to come pick her up. It was nearly eleven, and she was afraid the new year was going to get there with her sitting at home if he didn't hurry up. She stamped her feet to keep warm. Wondering why she was standing outside in the first place, she stepped back in the entryway, but didn't close the front door all of the way. She took in her outfit for the one thousandth time in the large mirror in the hallway. More than satisfied with her blue asymmetrical strapless dress and her blue heels, she picked up the black fitted shearling her mother was letting her borrow and slung it around her shoulders. *If this outfit gets wasted, I'll kill him,* she thought, just as she heard a car door slam.

She grabbed her keys and her purse and hurried outside. Instead of seeing Malcolm, she saw Dewayne getting out of his mother's beige Lincoln. For a split second she thought about ducking back inside, but her indecisiveness got her caught out there. Before she knew it, Dewayne was in the front yard and at the bottom of the steps trying to act like he wasn't pressed.

"What's up, K?" he said, looking up the steps at her. "Long time, no see."

"Hey, Dewayne," she said, trying to muster as much enthusiasm into her voice as was humanly possible.

"So whatcha been up to? Practicing?"

"Yep," Kalia said, checking her watch and pulling out her cell to send Malcolm a text message.

"Oh, happy new year, you know, early," Dewayne said, moving up a step.

"Yeah, same to you." She was eyeing Dewayne's approach, text messaging and straining her neck, looking back and forth up the street.

"So, I guess you're going out. I mean you sure are dressed…kinda…you know…nice."

"Umm, hmm…thanks…I guess." She wasn't sure if she was thanking him for the compliment or answering him about going out.

"Well, if he stands you up, I can step in if you'd like…it would be cool…like friends just hanging out," he said.

"Oh, he'll be here," Kalia said quickly enough to hurt Dewayne's feelings. She wanted to take it back, but it was already out there. She needed to cut this conversation short because Malcolm might drive up any minute.

"Hey, I left something in my room. Can I catch up with you later?" she said, stepping back into the house.

"Yeah, yeah, yeah," said Dewayne, stepping down and starting across the driveway. "Cool. I'll just get up with you later. It's all good. Have a great time tonight."

"Okay, you, too," she said, but he was already on his doorstep. Walking back toward the kitchen to get something to drink, she wondered if Dewayne was embarrassed. She'd just opened the refrigerator when she heard another car drive up.

This had to be Malcolm, she thought, abandoning her thirst. She stepped outside, and there he was. Malcolm stood next to a silver BMW 6-series, looking unbelievable, she thought, in black slacks, a black large-collared shirt and a tan camel-hair coat. He walked up to the steps and escorted her down.

"I'm sorry, baby," he explained, kissing her on the cheek, "but I just had to pick up the car. I got your message just now, but I was right up the street."

"That's okay. You're fine. I just got ready anyway," she lied, walking around the car.

"Damn you look *good*. Hold on. I have got to get a picture of you," he said, pulling his camera phone out of his pocket.

"Thanks, baby. You look pretty good yourself." Kalia grinned, posing for a few shots by the BMW, then letting him help her into the passenger side.

Kalia rubbed her hand along the wood-grain dashboard. "Where did you get this?"

"You won't believe this but Jimmy let me hold it for tonight."

"Jimmy? The guy who owns Atlanta Live?"

"Yep. Ain't it sweet?"

"It sure is," she said, adjusting her seat and looking into the back of the car. "He must really trust you. Hey, my butt is hot. What's that?"

"Oh." He laughed. "That's the seat warmer. You know I can't let your fine ass freeze tonight."

Kalia laughed and moved her behind around in the seat. "I love it. Everyone should have one of these."

"Drop eighty grand and you can have one of these babies fully loaded, including the warmers."

Kalia pulled down the lighted rearview mirror and puckered her lips. "Maybe after my first album drops, you know, I can have my assistant pick me up one of these to go with my Jag and my six other cars at my mansion."

"Oh, so you're gonna be doing it like that? Can a brutha get a ride?"

"Sure, baby. I'll hook you up with a ten speed or something." Kalia grinned.

"That's all right. When the Feds come and take all your cars away for not paying your taxes, at least I'll have something to get me back and forth to the store."

"What are you talking about? I'm not going broke."

"It's inevitable, baby. Just like Mike Tyson and MC Hammer, the more you make, the more you spend, and the less likely it is that you're going to want to pay those taxes," said Malcolm, grabbing her hand in his. She noticed his watch. The diamonds in it almost blinded her.

"Hey, where did you get this?" she said, lifting his arm to get a closer look. "Don't tell me Jimmy loaned you this, too."

"Nope. That was a gift."

"From who? Jay-Z?"

"Naw, baby. Just someone who's taking an interest in my career."

Kalia dropped his hand and looked at him. "So who? How come you're not telling me this person's name?"

"Oh, no reason. You just don't know them."

"Is it a girl?"

"Well, yes it is," said Malcolm, stroking his chin. Kalia could swear that he was enjoying telling her that the watch came from another woman.

"*Okay...*" she said.

"Okay what?"

"Do I have to ask?" said Kalia, folding her arms across her chest. "If a dude had given me a watch like that, wouldn't you wanna know who he was?"

"Nope."

"Umm, hmm. Well, I wanna know who gave you that watch and why."

"Her name is Sasha, and she works at Fire."

"Fire Records? What does she do there, and why is she giving you a watch like that?"

"It ain't really no big deal," said Malcolm, flipping open his cell. "She's like one of the VP's cousins, and she does some production and other stuff."

Kalia just looked at Malcolm, wondering what he gave this Sasha for Christmas. She had yet to receive even a card from him.

"What? I'm trying to get signed, and she says she can help me get hooked up."

"I bet she can."

"Look, I'm here with you, ain't I? I'm taking you to the hottest party in the city because she got us in, okay? Gimme a break."

"So she's gonna be there?"

"Uh, *yeah,*" said Malcolm sarcastically. "Didn't I just say she's the reason we're getting in? God."

Kalia wanted to jump out of the car, but they were already at the Swissotel where the party was happening. They left the car with the valet and walked into the lobby, looking almost like they weren't together. Malcolm was walking so fast in front of Kalia that she was having a hard time keeping up. Annoyed, she slowed down to a stroll and smirked at him, having to wait longer than he wanted holding the elevator doors open. The ride to the penthouse was a long one in the glass elevator. Standing on the other side of the elevator, Kalia took in the hotel's opulence as they climbed.

"Look, I don't want to argue tonight," said Malcolm, looking at his watch. "It's like eleven-thirty, and I really want to have a good time."

Kalia didn't want to fight either, but she wasn't going to make it easy for him. She didn't say anything. He reached in his coat pocket and handed her a small box.

"I was saving this for later on tonight, but I think I need it now," he said, walking over to her side of the elevator, just as they reached the penthouse. He hit the stop button.

Kalia's hand trembled as she took the black velvet box from his hands. No man had ever given her a gift in a jewelry box before. When she opened it, her name spelled out in crushed diamonds gleamed back at her. "Oh my God," she said.

"Let me help you put it on," said Malcolm, taking the name chain from its case. Fastening it around her neck, he kissed her deeply. Her hands went around his neck, and she forgot where she was. The elevator buzzed, scaring them both. Laughing, Malcolm hit the stop button again, and the doors slowly began opening.

Kalia was still looking into Malcolm's eyes when the thundering sounds of JD's new song snatched her attention. She turned to see what looked like the scenes in every over-the-top Diddy video ever made—and she and Malcolm were the center of attention, since the elevator opened directly into the suite.

"Come on, baby. We're on blast in here," said Malcolm, shielding his eyes from the light, taking her hand and leading her into the beautiful crowd. Holding Malcolm's hand, Kalia tried not to stare at everyone and everything around her. Every woman was statuesque and striking in what had to be designer clothes. Their shoes—Dolce & Gabbana, Jimmy Choo and Gucci—made her gasp. Every man was clean and suited down. Kalia had never seen so many ears, necks, wrists and fingers weighted down with carats and carats of diamonds.

It took a minute for her eyes to become adjusted to the dim light of the corner Malcolm had steered them into. She sat on a bar stool and took in the scene—the hundreds of guests milling and dancing, talking on cell phones and two-waying; the ice sculpture of a phoenix rising from flames in the center of the floor; the huge spread of sushi and decadent desserts in one corner; the numerous waitstaff passing through the crowd with champagne-filled glasses; and DJ Fly Girl working it out in the front.

Malcolm had taken their coats and disappeared for a moment, but returned before she even knew he was gone with two flutes of champagne. She took one and put it on the bar, not sure if she was up for any alcoholic beverages.

"It's eleven-fifty," Malcolm said in her ear. "Do you wanna go out on the balcony?"

Not even having noticed there was a balcony, she nodded and grabbed her glass. They stepped out into what she expected to be brisk night air, but found she was warmed from above. Looking up she saw ornate fire-shaped heat-producing lights were warming her bare shoulders.

"You look beautiful tonight," Malcolm said, kissing her neck. He put their champagne on a tall table to their left and led her to the balcony's edge. Looking out over the lights of the city, Kalia knew she was dreaming.

"This is incredible," she said, taking Malcolm's hand. "Thanks so much for bringing me tonight." She turned to him. "I'm sorry about how I was acting earlier."

"Please," he said. "It ain't no thang."

The music stopped, and DJ Fly Girl started the countdown. Malcolm grabbed their champagne, and they counted down together.

"Happy New Year," they said to each other, followed by a kiss and a quick sip of champagne. After hugging for what seemed like an eternity, they heard the deejay get the party started again, and Malcolm dragged her onto the dance floor where they stayed for the next thirty minutes.

Kalia excused herself to go to the ladies' room, telling Malcolm she'd meet him back on the balcony. The ladies' room was crowded with women adjusting their dresses, filling in their lip liner and fixing their hair. A woman who Kalia guessed worked at the hotel showed her to a little room, which turned out to be where the actual toilet was. Kalia marveled at all the products lining the counter as she approached the sink to wash her hands. Before she even got there the bathroom attendant squirted liquid soap in her hands and was waiting with the softest paper towels she'd ever used when she was done. She took a peppermint and was about to leave when she noticed women leaving money in a tip basket. She smiled at the attendant and took a dollar from her bag and dropped it in the basket, too. The attendant nodded at her in the mirror.

She turned to leave and collided with an extremely tall woman who was so well endowed, Kalia bounced off her breasts.

"Damn, watch where you're going," said the woman.

"Oh, I'm so sorry," said Kalia. "Are you all right?"

"I would be if you hadn't stepped on my Manolos."

"Oh, I'm *so* sorry," Kalia said again, looking down at the woman's silver open-toed stilettos and not knowing what else to say.

"Aw, girl, you're okay. Leave her alone," said another svelte woman in a tight gold number that had shimmering beads all over it. She turned to Kalia. "She's got like four hundred pairs of shoes in her closet. She probably wasn't ever going to wear those again anyway."

"Oh, okay," said Kalia. "I'm still sorry."

"Hey, sweetie, can you hook me up back here?" asked the woman in the gold dress, turning around and pointing one long manicured nail down her back.

"Uh, sure." Kalia fastened the woman's dress.

"So what's your name, anyway? You don't look like one of the usual industry suspects."

"She sure don't," said the big-breasted woman, adjusting herself in the black super-low-cut, nearly sheer top she was wearing. She looked Kalia up and down.

"Shut up, Sasha," said the woman in the gold dress.

"Sasha?" said Kalia, taking in the gaudy false eyelashes, matte-finished skin and glossy glittery lips pursing at her.

"Yeah, you know me or something?" asked Sasha, sucking her teeth and looking in the mirror at herself. She flipped her ash-blond Beyoncé-styled wig and bent over to perfectly position the diamond-encrusted S pendant hanging from a platinum chain between her breasts. Her numerous platinum bangles clattered noisily.

"No, we've never met," said Kalia, wishing she'd dug her heel into Sasha's foot. There was no way in the world this could be the Sasha that gave Malcolm that watch, she hoped.

"Well, we're meeting now. I'm Chi Chi and you've already met Sasha," said Chi Chi, blinking incessantly from the ill-fitting blue contacts she was wearing and finger-combing the bangs of her bone-straight blond weave to cover her coarse black new growth. Kalia looked at herself in the mirror standing between two mountains of video sophistication and felt very plain in her flip and her simple blue strapless dress. A strange desire came over her to show a little more skin. She wished her dress was a micromini.

"So are you here with somebody? If not, there's a lot of bodies out there, girl." Chi Chi smirked in the mirror. "You need to hook up with one 'cause they're out there throwing bills around like money ain't a thang."

"It's my thang, girl," said Sasha, "and I'm 'bout to work it out. Excuse me." With a roll of her eyes at Kalia, Sasha sashayed out of the ladies' room. Chi Chi did a little wiggle with her fingers and followed.

By the time Kalia made it back to the balcony, she knew she was going to have to figure out a way to see if she'd met Malcolm's Sasha in the bathroom. If she didn't find out, she'd go crazy. Malcolm was engaged in a heated discussion with several very wealthy-looking men when she returned.

"Now who is this young lady?" asked one of them as Malcolm broke away to kiss her on the cheek.

"Oh, this is my girl Kalia," said Malcolm. "Baby, this is Gene Grady, Lawrence Mathis, Ken 'Big Dog' Murphy and Cool Mike. Gene's with Fire, Lawrence is with Shine and Big Dog has the hottest producers around and well, you know how Cool Mike does his thang on Hot 103.5."

"Nice to meet you," said Kalia, eyeing Malcolm as he gestured to each man he was introducing with a tumbler filled with dark liquor. He was acting a little different from when she'd left him.

"Naw, baby. It's nice to meet you," said Lawrence, looking at her in a way that made her skin crawl. "Malcolm, why didn't you tell me you had a little something like that?" Lawrence puffed on a cigar and looked back and forth between Kalia and Malcolm, who just laughed along with Gene, Big Dog and Cool Mike.

"Yeah, girl, you're a little young, but if Malcolm hadn't gotten to you first, I could have shown you a few thangs." Gene sneered, giving Cool Mike a pound.

Again, Kalia watched as all the men around her snickered. She waited for Malcolm to speak up about the obvious way she was being disrespected, but all she got from him was a pat on the behind, which she found incredibly inappropriate. They started their conversation again, with Malcolm jockeying to join in like a junior high kid who was really too young to hang with the high schoolers. As they joked about the big butts on female celebrities and what rappers had the whackest lyrics, Malcolm paid little attention to Kalia besides squeezing her hand or grabbing her arm to hold himself up when he was doubled over laughing at some weak joke one of the fellas made. All of his pandering to them, not to mention his disrespect of her, annoyed Kalia.

She excused herself again and walked toward the inside of the party. Looking back over her shoulder at Malcolm and his crew, she knew they were talking about her by the way they laughed and cut their eyes at her. Inside, the party had kicked up a notch, and so had the crowd. Kalia made her way through the throng of high-profiling people, catching snatches of conversation about all kinds of drama along the way.

Kalia was having information overload. She sat down on a plush plum sofa next to a cool-looking lady who was tapping her fingers on one of the cushions and looking around the room. The lady looked at her briefly and smiled.

"This is a wild scene, ain't it?" she said to Kalia.

"Sure is."

The lady turned toward Kalia. "I bet you don't come to these parties often, do you?"

"No. This is actually my first one," admitted Kalia, thinking she must have a sign on her forehead that read First Time Partyer. She did admire the lady's style though, especially her dark brown curly pageboy. She dug her mauve feathered top and matching leather skirt with fringed edges and the black fitted knee-high stiletto boots that capped off her funky look.

"I'll let you in on a little secret," she said, leaning over, but still looking at the crowd. "If you've been to one of these little shindigs, you've been to them all." Then she chuckled to herself at her own joke.

"So I guess you've been to a lot of these, huh?"

"I feel like I live at these damn parties," she said, stopping a waiter who was passing by. "Can I get some water, please? Make that two."

"Thanks," she said, assuming the second water was for her.

"No problem. So why are you over here sitting by yourself? It's New Year's. You should be out there shaking it up."

"Well, why aren't you?" asked Kalia.

"I'm over it. This is just another day's work for me."

"Oh."

The lady turned to Kalia. "You'll see. When you get in this industry, as I'm sure you want to do, you'll do these all over the country—all over the world—for a few years then all this will be just a job to you, too," she said, waving her hand in a sweeping arc over the crowd.

"So how long have you been doing this?" Kalia asked, guestimating the lady was in her late twenties. She had no idea what this lady did, but she didn't want to let on how clueless she was.

"My daddy has been an exec at like every major label. I grew up in this," she said, lighting a slim cigarette and staring at Kalia. "What do you do? You sing, huh?"

"How did you know that?"

"I can spot them a mile away. You can probably really sing, too. You shouldn't be out this late and around all this smoke," she said, blowing her smoke away from Kalia. "You're not drinking, are you? I know you're not old enough to drink."

"No. No, not really," said Kalia.

"Good 'cause it will ruin your voice," she said, flicking her cigarette into an ashtray. "I'm quitting…really."

Kalia just nodded and smiled. She had heard before that drinking too much, staying out too late and smoking were all bad for singers, but for some reason she believed it more when this woman was warning her. An hour later they were still talking, the woman chain smoking and downing water like there was no tomorrow and Kalia mentally taking notes of all of the music industry insider information she was getting. She hadn't even thought about Malcolm until she saw Sasha and Chi Chi walking toward him at the bar. Kalia flinched when Sasha grabbed his waist from behind and he leaned over and said something in her ear that made her laugh and push her body against him. Chi Chi dragged Sasha away, pointing in the direction of some tall basketball player, and Malcolm leaned unsteadily against the bar. As he ordered another drink and sloppily fumbled around in his wallet to pay for it, Kalia wished she had another way home.

"I think I need to get out of here," she said, fishing around in her purse for their valet claim ticket.

"Okay, cool," said the lady, throwing up the peace sign. "I hope you have a good night, and remember what I said."

"I will. I appreciate all the knowledge," said Kalia, locating her ticket and walking toward Malcolm. She tapped him on the shoulder. "Hey. I'm kinda ready to go."

When he turned and looked at her, she thought it took too long for him to recognize who she was.

"Come on. Let's go," she said.

"I think I'm going to hang a little more," he said, grabbing her wrists. "I wanna dance some more. Come on."

"No, really," Kalia said, breaking his grasp. When she jerked him, he seemed to wake up from a daze and really look at her.

"Okay. Let me take you home," he said, straightening up.

When the valet brought the car around, Kalia spoke up. "I know a quick way to get home. You should just go ahead and let me drive."

"Aw, you just wanna push this Beamer. It's all good. I'll let you drive it, baby. I needs me a chauffeur," he said, beating his chest with one hand.

Kalia couldn't believe he was disrespecting her like that, but she let it slide because she wanted to get home safely, and the only way she was going to be able to do that was if she figured out some way to not let him drive.

When she pulled up to her driveway, she didn't even wait for him to come around to her side of the car for him to open her door.

"Dang, baby, you sure are moving fast. Don't I get a happy new year's kiss?" asked Malcolm, walking around to the driver's side.

"I gave you one at the party," she said.

"Ha-ha. Come here, girl," he said, grabbing her waist. He hugged her tight, and she could smell the whiskey on his breath as he tried to kiss her good-night. She kissed him on his cheek, maneuvered out of his grasp and popped up the steps.

"Hey, do you want some coffee or something?" she asked over her shoulder.

"No. I guess I better take it to the crib."

"Well, if you want, you can give me a call when you get home," she said, opening her front door.

Malcolm sat in the car and pointed a finger at Kalia. "Oh, you just want to see if I can make it home."

"Yes," Kalia turned to admit. "I do want you to make it home okay."

"Don't worry about me. I'll be fine." Malcolm slammed the car door abruptly and sped out of the driveway, and he kept her up all night, too. Not only did he not call her when he got home, he didn't answer his home phone or his cell phone either. When he finally called her on her cell the next day, she was happy to have caller ID. Whatever message he left, she knew she wasn't going to feel like checking it until she stopped wanting to slap the mess out of him.

Kalia took a frantic phone call a few days later though from Colby. When she tried to tell her that Mari wasn't there, she couldn't hang up. Colby was sobbing, saying she didn't have Mari's cell number programmed in her new phone and really needed to talk with her. Normally she didn't give out Mari's cell number, but Colby sounded so distraught, she reeled off the digits.

When Mari got home from working out in her school's weight room about an hour or so later, Kalia gave her the urgent message in the kitchen, hoping Mari would call her friend right there, so she could find out why Colby was crying, but she didn't. She went upstairs to her room. About a half an hour later, Mari walked into Kalia's room and plopped down on the bed.

"What would you do if one of your friends called and told you she was pregnant?" she asked her sister.

Kalia was taken aback for a moment. She didn't expect that.

"I don't know…I guess I would tell her that I was there for whatever she needed help with."

"Then I'm glad that's what I told Colby," Mari said, lying back across her bed.

Kalia didn't want to be any nosier than she already was, but she really wanted to know if the baby's father was Sean.

"She's more nervous about her grandparents finding out than she is about having a baby," Mari continued.

"Oh yeah, her grandparents are so religious, they're probably going to freak out," said Kalia.

"Probably."

"Wait. How does she know she's pregnant?"

"She's like two months late and she took three of those tests."

"Hmm. She really needs to go a doctor to make sure," said Kalia, "but three tests probably aren't wrong. Well, what's she going to do? She can't hide it but for so long."

"I don't know," said Mari, rolling over. "She's about two months along, so she's only got a little while before she starts showing. She said something about coming over here."

"Oh, is she thinking of hiding out or something?"

"I think she was just upset. Plus, I can't imagine Ron and Elaine wanting yet another daughter. I think that we're killing them as it is."

"Right, right," said Kalia. "Well, I hope she starts taking care of herself—you know eating right and stuff."

"I don't even know if she's going to have it."

"For real?" Kalia sat down on the bed next to Mari. "I hadn't even thought about that. Wow."

"I guess I just gotta be there for her."

"Yep. That's what friends do."

Later on that evening, Mari got another frantic phone call from Colby. She was at the bus station, and it was midnight.

"Girl, your grandparents have probably put an APB out on you. I'm surprised they haven't called me yet," said Mari.

"I don't think they have your phone number." Colby sniffed. "They don't have any of my friends' numbers."

"So what are you doing at the bus station?"

Colby detailed her whole plan—how she was going to catch the bus to her cousin's place in Memphis, so she could decide what to do. She just couldn't bear being in the house with her grandparents in her condition. Every time they came around, she said she felt like a big sinner.

"But your grandparents love you. They'll understand," said Mari hopefully. "Look, I'll go with you when you tell them if you want me to."

"You will?"

"Of course. Now, what about Sean?"

"I haven't talked to Sean in a week or so. I can't talk to him right now."

"He does know, doesn't he?"

"He knows something is wrong with me, but not what. I know I've been acting a little crazy lately," she said. Her voice was thin, like she was far away. The weakness in her voice made Mari speak more calmly.

"So is that what's really going on here? That you don't want to tell him?" she asked.

"I guess."

"Don't you think he deserves to know?"

"I guess," Colby repeated.

"Well, whatever you want to do, I'm cool with, but if you were him, wouldn't you want to know?"

"I guess."

Mari was silent for a minute. She knew they'd hit a brick wall. When Colby started talking again, it was about her relationship with Sean and how she'd never felt the way about a person as she did about him. She talked about the way he held her hand and opened doors for her, the way he told her she was the most beautiful girl he'd ever seen all the time, the way he kissed her. She told Mari that one day their kissing just wasn't enough for him. She had been so afraid that he'd leave her that she'd decided the only way to keep him from being with another girl was to have sex with him, but after they'd done it, she'd immediately regretted it.

"Well, did you talk to him about it?" Mari asked.

"No. I was too embarrassed," said Colby.

"Yeah, I can understand that. I guess I'll be nervous my first time."

"It wasn't that bad really."

"What do you mean?" asked Mari, trying not to sound too eager.

"Well, you know, it kinda felt good. Good like weird, but good."

"Oh," said Mari, not sure exactly what Colby meant.

"So I guess I'll just have it," said Colby.

"What? What?" said Mari, tuning back to the conversation after drifting off. "You're going to have it?"

"I think so. I hadn't really thought of myself as a baby's mama before this, but I guess that's what I'm gonna be."

"Okay cool, if that's what you wanna do. As long as you feel like you've thought it through."

"I have," said Colby confidently. "I know that I have two more years of school and then I want to go to college, and I'm gonna do it."

"Okay good. So you're gonna tell Sean, right?"

"Yeah. I guess I will."

"Good, good. So you need to go home. Call your grandparents first though, okay?" said Mari.

When she hung up the phone, she lay in her bed wide awake, thinking about what it would be like to be a teenage mom. She had seen girls her age in the grocery store or at the bus stop holding a baby on one hip with another toddler by the hand. They just looked tired and frustrated. She made a vow to be there for Colby, whatever she needed. Praying that Sean would take the news well, Mari drifted off to sleep.

Colby told Sean the next day, and Mari's phone was blowing up again. She tried to talk to Colby early in the day, but she was running between classes. Thank God she went to a private school, where cell phones were allowed to be used during the day and nobody bothered you if you were sitting out on a bench on the grounds in the middle of the day. She took the beginning of her free period to talk to Colby, who did a poor job of communicating Sean's reaction to her news. Mari knew he wasn't jumping up and down like he'd won the lottery, but he wasn't entirely upset, Colby told her.

Mari went over to Colby's house the following Saturday and sat in the Greshams' parlor while Colby enlightened them about their coming great-grandchild. She watched Mrs. Gresham's face purse and Mr. Gresham stand up and walk out of the room. She saw no more of Mr. Gresham during that visit. Mrs. Gresham immediately started praying and told the girls that they needed to do the same. After a lengthy set of prayers, Mrs. Gresham got up, told them she was going to prepare dinner and after that they were going to have a scripture reading focusing on Mary, because she thought it was appropriate for the situation.

Mari saw things get better for Colby after everyone important in her life knew. Shauntae nearly flipped when she found out. Colby had already heard around school that Shauntae had been talking about Sean, saying she was going to get with him anyway, and that she didn't care that the dude from Fire was with that "old skinny bitch."

Colby and Mari stayed on the phone comparing notes about Shauntae. Mari had heard from Kalia that Shauntae was hanging with a group of senior girls who spent more time getting with college guys and dudes who worked at UPS than they did in school. She was probably trying to impress those girls telling them she had a man who worked for Fire, Mari told Colby, who didn't care. Sean was being extremely supportive of Colby. He'd even gone to the obstetrician with her. Everything was fine until Mari had to tell her that Kalia overheard one of the Shauntae's new friends saying that Shauntae had sex with Sean. They were sitting in her room when Colby lost it.

"I just know he didn't....I know he wouldn't do that to me," whimpered Colby, sitting on Mari's bed. Mari watched her shoulders shudder as she cried silently.

"Now you know that girl made that mess up," said Mari. "She just wanted to come between you and Sean. You can't let her."

"I know, I know. It's just that…"

"What?"

"Well, you know he kinda liked her at first." Colby blew her nose.

"So? He wouldn't be a guy if he didn't look at her double Ds," said Mari, rubbing Colby gently on her back. "That doesn't mean he likes her really, or that he got with her."

There was silence for a minute.

Mari continued, "Sean has been with you for like four whole months now. That's a long time, so he obviously likes you more than her. If he didn't, he wouldn't be going to the doctor with you and spending time with you."

"I guess."

"Don't pay that fool Shauntae any attention. Just focus on having a healthy baby, and being worried isn't going to help you."

"You're right."

Colby left feeling a little better, but Mari couldn't help but think about how she'd stretched the truth with her friend to cheer her up. She was stressed about Colby's condition and thought maybe some television would distract her. Mari had just gotten into an episode of *ER* when the doorbell rang. To her annoyance it was Dewayne, who she just knew was looking for Kalia.

"She ain't here, bruh," said Mari, leaning against the open door.

"How do you know I came here to see her?"

"Ha-ha. The Chosen One has chosen to pay me a visit?" she said sarcastically, jogging back down the hall and into the family room. "Umm, hmm... You can come in and wait for Kalia if you want."

"Whatcha watching?" Dewayne fell onto the couch.

"Shh...it's getting good," said Mari, punching him in the shoulder.

They watched the last half of *ER*, which turned out to be an episode where a pregnant woman was going into labor in a taxicab. Watching the pregnant woman get help from the black doctor, Mari couldn't help but think about Colby and Sean.

"Hey," she said as the credits were rolling, "do you have any friends who have ever gotten pregnant?"

Dewayne leaned away from her and looked at her skeptically. "No. I don't think so, do I?"

Mari rolled her eyes. "Number one, we ain't friends. And number two, I ain't pregnant."

"I wasn't talking about you, but thank God anyway 'cause I would hate to see what type of little monster you'd hatch."

"Whatever. And it's not Kalia either. You know what? Just forget it," she said, taking the TV off mute and flipping channels.

Dewayne grabbed the remote from her and hit the mute button.

"So what? You know someone who's pregnant? And..."

"I think the guy might be cheating on her, and I wish I could find out, you know, 'cause you know how y'all are." Mari tapped Dewayne on his shoulder, thinking he looked different in the half-darkened room, lights from the TV flickering across his face. He didn't move away.

"How are we?" he asked, sliding closer to her.

Whatever was happening, Mari found it strangely exciting. All of a sudden Dewayne leaned back on the sofa and grabbed her to him. His arm ended up around her shoulders and her head leaned into his chest.

"Tell big daddy what the problem is," he said in a strained, silly voice, patting her on the shoulder.

Not really knowing what to do, Mari told Dewayne all about Colby and what she was going through. He listened intently, not saying anything, just giving her a squeeze every now and then when she seemed especially emotional. As she was spilling the details, Mari wondered why she was telling Dewayne of all people and why on earth she was cuddled up with him on the sofa.

"Everything will be okay."

"I hope so," said Mari, nuzzling his chest. She liked his fresh smell. Looking up, she noticed that his hair was combed. She sat up a little and saw that he had on a nice crisp green Polo shirt and some Rocawear jeans, and his kicks were fresh.

"What? Do I look funny or something?" he asked.

"Naw." She shook her head, cracking a smile. "Actually you look all right today. Who took you shopping? Better yet, who introduced you to an iron?"

Dewayne chuckled. "Oh, you've got jokes now. Don't let me have to get on that parallel parking I saw you trying to do the other day. How many cars did you bump?"

"Aww, now why you gotta go there?" Mari asked.

"Why you gotta talk about me?"

"'Cause I wouldn't be Mariama Jefferson if I didn't."

"You're right about that," he said, turning her toward him. They were staring into each other's eyes. "Are you sure you're going to be all right?"

Mari shuddered. *He really cares,* she thought.

"Sure, I'm fine. I'm good."

"Cool, because you know if there's anything I can do to make you feel better," he said, bending down to kiss her on her forehead, "you know I will, okay?"

She nodded and put her head back on Dewayne's chest and let him hug her.

chapter 11

It had been almost ten days since Kalia had spoken to Malcolm. She stopped being angry with him for his New Year's Eve performance a few days after it happened. Now she was in full-on game-playing mode, wanting to call him, but refusing to because she wanted to make him come to her. He'd called her once New Year's Day and only one time since then, and neither time did she feel he'd left an apology that was satisfactory enough for her. She'd been holding out now five days since the last time he'd dialed any of her numbers, and she was getting antsy. He hadn't even sent a text message to say "What's up?" Finally, after school one day, she skipped practice and came straight home to dial him up as soon has she got in her room. *Of course he won't answer*, she thought, listening to his voice mail message over Jay-Z's "Song Cry" in the background.

"Leave me a message or call me back, but either way, we'll get up. Peace."

She hesitated, but then remembered he had caller ID like everyone else.

"Uh, hey, Malcolm. It's Kalia," she said, wincing at identifying herself to her boyfriend. "I was just calling to say what's up, see how you were doing." She paused again, searching frantically for something to say that would convey just the right balance of casual concern. "We haven't talked in a while." She winced again. That sounded desperate. Then it hit her. "I wanted to get with you about this industry chick I met at the New Year's Eve party. She let me in on a few things that, you know, you might help me understand better." *That's it,* she thought. *Now wrap it up.* "Okay, give me a shout when you get a chance." *Bye? Or Peace? Bye or peace?* she wondered. "Bye." Bye was better, she analyzed. Peace would have been too this-is-one-wannabe-industry-person-calling-another instead of I-really-wanna-talk-so-call-me.

While she waited for Malcolm to call, Kalia decided to change into something to wear for later when she and Mari were going to her mother's new studio to help get the place ready for the following week's grand opening. That took her about ten minutes. She wondered what was taking Malcolm so long. She considered working on her paper for her advanced music theory class, but decided she wouldn't be able to concentrate enough to focus.

For the next hour she meticulously rearranged her closet, trying to distract herself from thinking about when Malcolm was going to call. She didn't turn on the radio or the television or anything electronic, for fear of not hearing the phone ring. After the first fifteen minutes she called her cell phone from her home phone and vice versa to see if the ringers were working. She had to fool herself into not looking at the clock every ten minutes, trying to guess when he was going to call. When the phone finally did ring, she jumped on it, answering before the first ring stopped, then she held the phone away from her for a second, took a deep breath and spoke.

"Hello."

"What's up?"

"Nothing much. How are you doing?" she asked, fingering the name chain around her neck that she hadn't taken off since he'd given it to her on New Year's Eve.

"I'm cool. So who, uh…who is this chick you met?"

Kalia was kinda surprised that Malcolm jumped straight into wanting to know about her connection at the party. *What about me?* she thought.

"Oh, um, she was this lady who, you know, said she had been in the business for a minute."

"Who was she? What's her name? Who'd she work for?"

"I don't know all that. I just know she knew a lot about the music business and she gave me lot of good tips and stuff," said Kalia, annoyed at his barrage of questions, especially since she was wishing she had gotten the lady's name because she may have been somebody she could have continued talking to about music industry inside information. She had been so disgusted by Malcolm that night and so ready to leave she had probably missed out on a good opportunity. Should she blame that on him? she wondered.

"You know when you go to these type of parties you should always get the name of anybody you talk to and who they work for or at least who they know," advised Malcolm. "So what'd this chick tell you?"

Kalia was really burnt up. He certainly didn't have to point out to her something she already knew, but she played it cool because he might drop some more little nuggets of information, something the lady at the party didn't tell her. She remembered he did get them into that fabulous party.

"She just gave me some advice about how to keep the audience really interested in my performance. They're like techniques that artists use, even those who are really good singers. They're just to make the performance more engaging to people who are watching and listening."

"Umm, hmm," said Malcolm. Kalia couldn't tell whether he was even listening or really interested at all, but she kept talking.

"She also told me about studying other artists, especially those who I admire—you know, study their performances, album releases, tour schedule, how their careers developed, all that. She even told me to watch my competitors' performances and learn what works for them. She encouraged me to have my own style, of course, but not to have a problem incorporating some things that work for others if they'll work for me."

"Sounds like she does know a little something. Are you gonna take her advice?" he asked.

"Yeah, I guess," said Kalia, confused because this wasn't how she'd wanted the conversation to go. She really wanted it to be more about him apologizing to her about New Year's Eve then him suggesting he make it up to her by taking her out.

"All right, I gotta go," he said abruptly. "I'm on my way to a meeting with some people about some big thangs."

Kalia was outdone. This was the first time they'd spoken in ten days and he had to go? Scrambling to figure out how she could keep him on the phone, she realized she missed him and really wanted to see him.

"Oh, is this what you've been so hush-hush about?"

"Well, you know, I don't want to jinx myself."

"Come on. Now you know I won't tell anybody," she coaxed. "Let me in on your secret."

"Naw, Kalia," Malcolm refused. "I gotta keep this one to myself, and I gotta go. I'ma hit you up later."

And with that Kalia heard a dial tone. *He didn't even wait for me to say goodbye or anything,* she thought, looking at the receiver. She spent the next two hours in her room, straightening, cleaning and organizing until she could have won the Martha Stewart Living Award for Cleanest Room of a Frustrated Girlfriend.

She promised herself she was going to stop stressing over Malcolm as she and Mari walked into their mother's new yoga studio that evening. There were Hispanic workmen painting several different rooms in soothing shades of lavender, mint green and a warm burnt orange, which Mari liked the best. Kalia preferred the lavender room. They worked hard the next week or so hanging up decorations and signs and cleaning the place from top to bottom, all the while saying silent prayers for their mother that her studio would be successful. Unfortunately the first couple of weeks proved to be very difficult for the Studio of Peace, Love and Soul.

One day near the end of January, they sat in the middle of the floor with their mother in the lavender room brainstorming about why the studio had only attracted a handful of people to sign up for classes since they'd been open nearly two weeks.

"Well, do people know about it?" asked Mari. "Do they know the studio is here and open?"

"They should. We're in a great location, in the same area as a bookstore and a grocery store and a coffee shop. There's foot traffic from all of those new apartments they're building around here," said Elaine.

"Maybe we should go and see if we can put some flyers in the lobbies of those buildings, then people would really know we're here," suggested Kalia. "We could probably post some in the stores, too."

"Oh, and have some coupons on the flyers," added Elaine.

"Yeah, that's great," said Kalia.

"But you don't want to give your service away, Ma," Mari cautioned. "I mean you gotta make some money."

"Yeah, but we gotta get a clientele first," said Elaine.

"Right, right," Mari admitted.

"And you know the coupons could just be like fifteen percent," said Kalia. "Fifteen percent of like a hundred dollars is only fifteen dollars, and it could be for only the first three classes."

"Yeah," said Elaine. "That's really good. I'm so glad you girls are here to help me out. I don't know what I'd do without you."

"Ma, you know we've got your back," said Mari. She stood and walked up to the mirror, braiding her ponytail.

"I know. I know," said Elaine, sitting in the lotus position. "You know I talked to this marketing person that I happened to meet at the Small Business Association the other day, and she told me that one mistake I made was deciding to open a business right after Christmas. She said that people are broke after Christmas and really can't afford to do anything in the first couple of months."

"That sounds like something out of my economics class. I would have never thought about that," admitted Kalia, trying to mimic her mother's lotus position, but she couldn't get her knees to touch the floor. Elaine reached over and gently pushed her knees downward.

"The woman also said that it was probably going to be a tough couple of months for me, but that one good thing I had going for me was that I was kind of in a healthy mindset-oriented industry," Elaine explained, getting excited. "See, the other big thing people overdo during the holidays besides spending money is eating. She said even people with the best eating habits and exercise regimens relax during Thanksgiving and Christmas.

"She also said that a lot of people get on these New Year's resolution kicks, and even though only about ten percent keep them, that ten percent who make the serious commitment to improve their health keep the industry in business during the year. We just need to capture that wellness crowd that slipped up during the holidays."

"*And* some of people who just moved here into those new apartments may already be into yoga, but have moved like far away from the place where they used to take classes," Mari offered.

"Good one, sis," said Kalia through closed eyes, her arms stretched out to her sides. Elaine clapped her hands in delight.

"Thank ya very much." Mari bowed to herself in the mirror.

"You know," said Elaine, stretching over her right leg, "I don't think your father thinks I can do this, but you girls give me the confidence that I can, and I appreciate that."

"Oh, Ma, don't get all sappy. We're supposed to help you out," said Mari.

"Yeah, Ma. You know Daddy is so serious about the Frys. That's different. You need to enjoy your business. I wish Daddy enjoyed his," said Mari.

"Well, I think he does enjoy it, but you're right. My enjoyment has to be a different kind," said Elaine. She rose and stood on her toes, reaching for the ceiling. "One good thing about him doubting me is that at least he's leaving me alone and not down here trying to run things. Oh God, could you see that?"

"Yeah, I think his loud military hover-over-everybody style would kind of cramp the spiritual peace in this place," said Kalia.

"Like a drunk bull in a china store," joked Elaine.

They all burst out laughing.

Kalia hadn't really thought too deeply about the Fire contest in several weeks when she'd gotten a letter in the mail from the officials saying she needed to come down to the offices with her parents and sign some waivers because she was under twenty-one and the final contest was going to be televised on a local channel. Kalia had also not thought about being on TV because she hadn't really expected to make it to the finals. Now it was all she could think about during the drive down to Fire with her mother.

She was so happy that her mother gave her advice about how to forget the cameras and the hundreds of audience members and just concentrate on performing, but she wondered if she could follow it. Thank God there was nearly two months until the show, she thought, walking into Fire. Just as she and her mother had finished signing several documents, Kalia spotted Asha and her mother being escorted past the doorway to the waiting room.

All of the anxiety she hadn't allowed herself to feel in more than a month rushed back to her. She wished she'd been able to see what Asha was wearing. All she caught was some high-heeled cream boots and some kind of fitted leather cream coat. On the way out of Fire, she started planning her attack. She was going to study Asha at the upcoming rehearsals and find out what her opponent had that her own performance was lacking. Something about Asha made the audience give her a standing ovation. She'd study Asha's outfits, her vocal style, the way she spoke and carried herself—everything.

While Kalia was studying her opponent, Mari was setting her sights on her prey. She walked slowly to the mailbox. She had only seen Dewayne a couple of times since she'd spilled her guts to him a few weeks back, and it was always in passing. They'd caught each other in the driveway a couple of times. They really hadn't had a chance to talk at all. She thought maybe if she lingered enough around the mailbox, he'd come home or come outside for something. It would be nice if that something was her. She'd even considered calling him, but quickly changed her mind when she realized she couldn't remember having ever talked to him on the phone before.

Realizing she'd been outside for fifteen minutes checking the mail, Mari gave up, hoping nobody saw her dawdling so long at the mailbox. She walked inside, dropped the mail on the kitchen table and headed upstairs, intending to do some homework. She stopped as she approached Kalia's door and knocked. Maybe she'd seen Dewayne.

"Come in," said her sister.

"What's going on?"

"Not a thang. What's up?"

"Hey, have you seen Dewayne lately?"

"Yeah. I saw him a couple of days ago," said Kalia, bending down to plug in her keyboard. "He caught me in the yard. I tried to give him the slip, but I guess the Chosen One was just too quick for me. Oh my God, I'm starting to call him by that ridiculous name."

Mari chuckled.

"As a matter of fact, that's what he was trying to talk to me about," Kalia continued. "He'd found some school where he could major in computer animation, and there was some guy teaching there who'd been some big shot in Japanese animation and Internet comic strips or some nerdy techie mess he was talking about." She bumped her head and turned the whole set of keyboards over trying to get up off the floor.

"That does sound kind of interesting, though. You are so clumsy," said Mari, helping her sister set the keyboards back up.

"I know, right?" said Kalia, rubbing the top of her head. "I really wasn't trying to talk to Dewayne about that stuff. I had stuff to do myself, and he was holding me up."

"Well, it's kinda strange that he's not over here a lot anymore," said Mari.

Kalia looked at her sister. "I never expected to hear you say that," she said.

"Oh, I was just saying, you know, he's usually around here bugging you and stuff, but I guess you've cut him back 'cause you've got a man of your own now. So how's Mr. Malcolm?" she asked, praying Kalia would take her lead in changing the subject. All she needed was for her sister to think she had some kind of interest in Dewayne. She'd never live it down.

"Oh, Malcolm's cool. He's got some big secret he won't share with me or something, but you know it's all good," said Kalia coolly.

"Maybe he's going to take you to another one of those hot parties, like the one y'all went to New Year's Eve. I sure wouldn't mind you taking me with you next time," said Mari, dancing around.

"Hmm, I don't know if I want to go to another one of those with him," Kalia mumbled, hitting a couple of keys to see if the keyboard was damaged.

"Huh?"

"Nuthin'. Me and Malcolm are good," she said again.

"Okay," said Mari, making her way to the door, trying to escape before her sister started wondering why she was asking questions about Dewayne.

When Mari left the room, Kalia started humming a tune to herself that had been in her head since the girls and their mother had had their strategic planning meeting for the Studio of Peace, Love and Soul. She loved the creative energy and calm spirit in the lavender room that day. She had been playing some notes to go with the tune in her head and writing them down in a notebook for about twenty minutes when her cell phone rang.

"Baby, baby, baby, baby, baaabaaay," she heard Malcolm screaming into the phone.

"What?" she said, immediately lifted by his excitement and even more thrilled that he'd called.

"Guess what?"

"What? What?"

"I got it," he said triumphantly.

"Got what?" She thought she was going to die of anticipation.

"A deal. A deal. I signed with Fire today."

"For real?" screamed Kalia, standing. "Oh my God. I am so excited for you."

"Yeah, baby. I went down there with my lawyer and my agent, and we signed the contracts and everything today," said Malcolm exuberantly. "They want me to start going into the studio like next week."

Kalia almost jumped out of her skin as her door flung open and Mari rushed in the room.

"What happened? What happened?" she yelled at Kalia, who put her finger up, telling her sister to wait while she tried to get the whole story from Malcolm. She mouthed, "Malcolm signed to Fire."

Mari's eyes grew big. Kalia nodded.

"So when do you think you'll have a CD out?" she asked Malcolm.

"I don't know, maybe the fall or something," he said. "Right now I'm just happy I got the deal. But look…"

"I'm happy you got it, too, baby."

"So how much money did he get?" Mari asked. Kalia smashed her finger into her lips. Mari sat down and didn't say another word.

"I'm sorry I cut you off," she continued to Malcolm. "Now what were you about to say?"

"Well, things are gonna be a little different now. I know we haven't seen each other in a minute, but I've been kinda caught up in all these meetings and stuff."

"Oh, of course. I completely understand."

"And to tell you the truth, I don't really think it's going to get any better. I mean today they were telling me how I have to meet with a publicist and the marketing people, and I need to get an accountant and—"

Kalia cut him off again and turned away from Mari. "No, really, you don't have to explain," she said. "I know you've got a lot of stuff to do."

"I just want to be up-front with you, you know, and actually I kinda have to go right now," he said. Kalia heard a couple of women's voices in the background. One said, "Come on, sweetie. We've got to take you out to celebrate."

"Who was that?" Kalia asked.

"Oh, that's one of the people who works here at Fire.... Look, I gotta go for real...I'll call you back, okay?" He hung up without waiting for her to say goodbye.

Kalia stood with her back to her sister, trying to decide how she felt. "Okay," she said to the dial tone. "That's cool. I'll talk to you later. Bye, baby."

When she turned around, Mari was lying on the bed with a curious smile on her face.

"What?" she asked.

"So what happened? Is my sister's boyfriend about to blow up?"

"I guess," said Kalia, sitting in her desk chair. "He got a deal— a recording contract with Fire."

"You sound like you don't believe it."

"It's just very surprising. I didn't expect it. I didn't even really get a chance to get used to the idea that it might happen," she said. "And we've been kinda going through it lately. He's been acting strange."

"I guess you know why now. So?"

"So what?"

Mari sat up straight on the bed. "So how much money did he get? Didn't he tell you what his deal was worth? Are you about to get your neck and wrist blazed up? He needs to be getting you some baguettes."

"What? You're talking crazy. Get off my bed. You're wrinkling the spread." Kalia got up and nudged her sister in the back.

"Excuse me. Your boyfriend gets famous and you get the attitude," said Mari, sliding off the bed onto the floor.

"He's not famous. You're trippin'. He's not even going to the studio until next week."

"Ooh…can we go to the studio? I've always wanted to push all those buttons and stuff like you see when they interview Pharrell and Diddy in the studio."

Shaking her head, Kalia stepped over Mari to straighten up her bed. "Calm down, groupie. You hardly even know Malcolm, and you're turning into his stalker. You can't go to the studio. I probably can't even go."

"I'm not the type of groupie you need to worry about," said Mari, getting up off the floor and leaning against Kalia's closet. "I read this one story in *Vibe,* where a groupie showed up in one of those NBA player's bed."

"Okay, well that's sports." Kalia vigorously fluffed pillows.

"And do you think that the music industry is any better? All that touring, staying in different hotels, all those industry parties and clubs. Women are going to be throwing themselves at your man all over the world and you could be here in Atlanta in high school."

"Shut up, Mari," said Kalia, standing with her hands on her hips, looking for something else to straighten. "You don't know what you're talking about. Malcolm…he's not like that." The image of her boyfriend whispering in the ear of laughing Sasha the Breast Monster from New Year's Eve burned in her mind.

"Uh…all men are like that. They just don't act on it unless they get too much temptation. When you're in the entertainment business, women are throwing sex at you all the time. I don't know how long your deejay man is going to be able to resist."

Kalia really wanted Mari to stop talking. She didn't want to hear one more thing from her sister about Malcolm. "Mari, I said shut up." She walked over to her computer and turned it on, staring at it while it booted up.

Mari kept talking. "I'm just saying, Malcolm ain't really hard to look at, and they're probably going to give him a funky wardrobe and—ooh, ooh, ooh—he's gonna do a video with girls in bikinis and—"

Kalia whipped around in her chair, cutting her sister off. "You need to shut up because you don't even have a boyfriend!" she shouted at her sister.

Mari's jaw dropped, then she squinted, and a look of confusion crossed her face. The last look Kalia saw on her sister's face before she turned and left the room was one of complete hurt.

As the door closed, Kalia just stared at it. She couldn't believe what had just come out of her mouth. She wanted to get up and go to Mari, but something wouldn't let her. She sat there with her pride and her uneasiness about Malcolm's good news and surfed the Internet for the next three hours.

She didn't talk to Malcolm again for three more days, and it felt like their conversation lasted three minutes. By the time they'd said their what's ups and he told her what he was up to—meeting with his lawyer, talking with producers, dropping by the video shoot of another Fire artist—he had to get off the phone to go meet with his lawyer, talk to a producer and drop in on a video shoot.

And that's how the next couple of weeks went for Kalia and Malcolm. She'd wait as long as she could to call him and he'd talk to her for maybe five minutes.

After text messaging one day, she called and caught him. He said he had a few minutes to talk before he had to meet with his lawyer. After he began telling her that he was going to be working with Fire's hot new artist, JD, on some tracks for his album, Kalia just cut him off and asked him when they were going to see each other. He told her soon, but he'd need to check his schedule and get back to her. Two days later they decided to meet three days after that, and he had the nerve to leave her sitting in a restaurant, except she wasn't really by herself because she'd let Mari tag along after her sister had begged her to death.

They sat at a window table at the first white-tablecloth restaurant Mari had been to without her parents. Kalia was in a worked-hard-to-look-like-I-just-threw-this-on outfit, and so was Mari. They ordered fried calamari and water with lemon and patiently waited for Malcolm for forty-five minutes before Mari brought up that fact that they had been waiting too long and maybe they should call him. He didn't answer either of Kalia's next two calls, but made one of his own about ten minutes later.

"Baby, I'm so sorry. I just...I got a really late start this morning…probably because I had such a late night or should I say an early morning this morning…see we were at the Verve Lounge…oh, you don't know what that is, do you, sweetie? It's this after-hours spot where, you know, the industry people who can make shit happen, kick it. JD was there and Mike Nice and Rachel Anders, the chick who shoots those videos for Dap Records. You know, we had some Martell, fired up some stogies… Anyway, so yeah, we were there until…shiiiii… until…what time did we get out of there, Dub?… Naw, naw…it was much later than that…Teanna hadn't even shown up by then and she came ready, you know? Wooo. Anyway, baby, what was I sayin'? Look, the deal is that I'm really just getting to what I needed to get today, and it's about to be tonight, so I just…I can't make it, okay? You haven't left home yet, have you? I mean we said six, and it's like seven now. You know I'm always at least an hour off. Where are you? In the car? Kalia? K?"

Kalia looked at the phone like it was an alien. She didn't know what to say or how to feel. She heard Malcolm still calling her name, but she had absolutely no desire to hear anything else he had to say, so she hung up the phone.

"Well, what did he say?" asked Mari.

Kalia picked up her cloth napkin out of her lap, put her phone in her purse and got up from the table, leaving a twenty-dollar bill. "Come on." She walked right out of the restaurant before Mari even knew what was happening. In the car, she was silent, not saying anything, just playing Alicia Keys's "When You Really Love Someone" over and over, all the way home. When they pulled into the driveway, Dewayne was sitting on their front steps.

"I was just about to leave… Dang y'all lookin' good. Where are you coming from?" he said, rising and walking toward the car.

"Oh, we just went to dinner," said Mari, eyeing Kalia, who still wasn't talking.

"What's up, Kalia?" Dewayne said.

Kalia slammed her door and brushed passed Dewayne. "Hey. Bye," she threw over her shoulder as she trotted up the steps and into the house.

"Okay, what's up her butt?" he said, turning to Mari.

"Well, she just got…kinda…stood up."

"Oh…by that Malcolm dude?"

"Yeah. So now the way is probably getting clearer for you to roll up on her," said Mari, slightly annoyed. She walked around the car, passed Dewayne and was about to go up the steps when he grabbed her hand, stopping her.

"Look, I came here to see you."

Mari looked closely at Dewayne. "For what? Dewayne, you've been in love with my sister for, like, forever, so don't act." She yanked her hand out of his and walked up the steps.

"What is it with you Jefferson women? Why do y'all make it so difficult?" Dewayne asked, looking up at Mari with his arms outstretched.

"Oh, so now I'm difficult, just like Kalia? Well, I'm not Kalia. I'm Mari, and you need to recognize the difference or stop coming around here," she said. Not even waiting for him to respond, she stepped through the door and closed it behind her. She leaned against it and wondered why she had gotten so angry with Dewayne. He didn't do anything to her. Then she realized she was pissed with her sister for being mean to him, but she'd just done the same thing.

She flung open the door and ran down the steps, but he was gone. She was kind of relieved he was because had he still been standing outside, she wouldn't have had any idea what to say. It was clear that there was something going on between her and her sister's best friend. She felt something for Dewayne she'd never felt for a guy before, and she was scared to death for anyone to find out about it, especially him.

chapter 12

Mari danced around her room, talking to Colby on the phone while JD's new song was blaring on the radio.

"It's hot, ain't it?" she said.

"It's got that fire," said Colby.

"I've been singing it all week."

"Have you seen the video for it?"

"It's out already?" asked Mari.

"Yeah, and I heard it's *tight*. I think your sister's boyfriend is in it."

"What? Malcolm's in the video?"

"I think that's him I saw with this girl with a blond weave in his lap."

"Ooh, I wonder if Kalia knows," said Mari, lying on her bed. "He's been calling her, and he even sent her some roses, but she ain't really trying to hear it."

"She's that mad?"

"I guess. I know she still likes him though. I think she was just embarrassed that I was in the restaurant when she got stood up. It would have been different if she was there by herself and nobody had to find out, but you know at least it was me and not anybody else she knew, and you know you're sworn to secrecy. You can't tell anybody."

"Who am I gonna tell? Who do I know that she knows?" asked Colby.

"You never know who knows who around here. How are you feeling anyway?"

"I'm okay, I guess. I've got a little pouch now, and I get these cravings for the strangest things."

"Yeah, I heard that pregnant women want pickles and ice cream, like together," said Mari. "Are you eating that stuff?"

"Naw…I just really want meat. Like any kind of meat. Chicken, fish, beef…just meat, meat, meat. My doctor says it's just the baby wanting protein, but it's weird to wake up in the middle of the night craving a Checkers double cheeseburger."

"Does Sean go and get it for you."

"*Pfft*, Sean? He is getting on my last nerve. He don't know squat, and he isn't trying to learn anything either."

"What do you mean?"

"I think he thinks that babies are brought by a stork like in cartoons."

Mari burst out laughing.

"He doesn't understand my mood swings and my cravings. I tried to give him some pamphlets and stuff I got from the doctor about what I'm going through, and he won't read them. I told him about all the things we'll need in like six months, and he keeps talking about how he's gotta do this for Fire, that for Fire. Whatever…just Fire, Fire, Fire."

"Maybe he's in denial."

"He sure as hell is, but I really need him to get his head in the game. I mean my grandparents are helping, but it's not the same. I need my baby's daddy to be more involved."

"I thought he was going to the doctor with you and stuff. What happened? And why haven't you called me?"

"I didn't want to bother you. I mean I will. I'll call you. I don't know what happened with him. He just started trippin', but he's not in total denial 'cause let me tell you about Shauntae!"

Colby went on to tell Mari about how another friend of hers told her about Shauntae rolling up on Sean one day at Lenox when he was working backstage at a fashion show that featured a couple of Fire artists. Her friend said Shauntae was with her new friends, the skanky seniors, and they lied to the security guard, saying they were local models for the show. When they made it behind the curtains where Sean was helping to organize the models, Shauntae proceeded to try to hug up on him and loud-talk about some night they'd had together so all the contestants and other Fire employees would hear. Sean had to shove her off him. He kicked her and her girls out of the show and security escorted them out of the mall through the front door on a Saturday afternoon, when everybody and their grandmama was standing outside kicking it.

"The whole school was talking about it this week," said Colby, giggling. "She is so ashamed."

"That's what she gets. Why was she trying to push up on your man?"

"'Cause she's a tramp. I heard that her so-called new friends are dogging her out, too."

"But I thought they got kicked out of Lenox, too," said Mari.

"They did, but they're like putting the whole thing on her, you know, saying she is trifling and immature and desperate and just doesn't know how to handle a man. You know how those two-faced chicks are."

"Umm, hmm. They're probably gonna drop her, and then where's she gonna be?" said Mari.

"I know you aren't feeling sorry for her," said Colby.

"Naw, naw, I'm just saying…" lied Mari. She had no idea why she pitied Shauntae. "I wonder why Kalia didn't tell me about Shauntae getting kicked out of Lenox."

"I don't know. That's your sister. She's still hung up on that Malcolm dude, huh? So when is his album dropping? She needs to tighten that relationship up. He may come into some bank, and she needs to be around for that," said Colby.

"Girl, you sure have changed. Last year, you would have never said anything like that."

"What do you mean?" Colby asked.

"Well, you know, talking about getting with a dude for his money."

"I'm not saying that's the only reason she should get with him, but being pregnant and all and thinking about how much formula and Pampers and a crib and all this stuff is going to cost, I mean, you start to think about money, you know?"

"Yeah," said Mari, sympathizing with her friend. "I hear ya. Like I said, I got your back. I don't have much money. My parents are kind of tight, but I can go with you to your appointments or whatever."

"That's cool, Mari. I've got one this week, and Sean can't go because of some Fire mess, but he better hook up something for Valentine's Day."

"Oh yeah, it's next week, huh?"

"Yep. You got some plans?"

"Uhh, no. Do I have a man?" said Mari sarcastically.

"Well, I have one and that doesn't mean I have any plans, either."

"At least you've got a chance. The only dude in my life this year has been Qwon," said Mari, frowning at the image of Dewayne popping into her mind, "and you know I'm not feeling him at all."

"I guess not. All right, we'll think of something for you. I gotta jet now. Gotta go to the bathroom, yet again," said Colby.

"All right, Miss Mommy-to-Be. I'll holla."

Mari got off the phone with Colby and sat on her bed for a minute thinking about Dewayne, wondering where he was and what he was doing. She pictured his kind of crooked smile and the beginnings of a mustache on his upper lip. Thoughts of their special night floated through her mind, and she could almost smell the freshness of his shirt when he'd held her as they watched *ER*. All of a sudden she wanted to see him, but was embarrassed by her own desires. How could she want to hang out with the Chosen One? She laughed to herself and went across the hall to her sister's room for some much-needed distraction. She started talking as she knocked on the door. "Hey, how come you didn't tell me Shauntae was up at Lenox acting out?"

There was no answer, so Mari knocked again, harder. The door creaked open. Kalia wasn't in her room, and for some reason Mari went in. She stood in the middle of her sister's room looking around, for what, she didn't know. She knew she had no right to be in Kalia's room, but she was feeling a little mischievous.

She peeped into the closet and decided not to disturb anything there because of how insanely neat it was. She walked over to Kalia's desk and shuffled through some school papers and magazines and to her surprise a condom fell onto the floor. Bending down quickly, she picked it up, put it back among the papers and hurried out of the room.

Mari lay back down on her bed and wondered what in the world Kalia was doing with a condom. Her sister was wondering the same thing on Valentine's Day a week later as she sat in a booth in Justin's with Malcolm, a condom burning a hole in her purse. They'd been there for almost thirty minutes and had been unable to have more than a few sentences of conversation because he kept getting up to "holla at one of my pahtnahs" every five minutes, or some overdeveloped, underdressed video girl would stop by and leave her lipstick on his cheek in their industry kiss greetings.

Kalia was getting fed up by the minute. JD's song was playing on the speakers, and she was sick of hearing it. It was on every station. She'd seen the video at least half a dozen times that week, burning up every time Malcolm showed up on the screen throwing the peace sign with one hand and using the other to palm the behind of a video girl sitting in his lap. And now these straight sex objects were cruising past their table and waving from across the restaurant at her man, who was enjoying every minute of it—even though he'd promised her that night would be about them.

That promise had given her the extra bit of courage she thought she needed to consider going all the way with Malcolm. Before he'd acted a fool on New Year's Eve, she was sure he would be her first. At that time he was just the type of caring, sensitive guy to whom she'd always dreamed of losing her virginity. They'd even had a conversation about it. When he told her that he'd wait for her as long as she wanted him to, Kalia became even more ready to have sex with him. Even though she'd been feeling neglected by him recently, earlier in the evening, she found herself once again contemplating getting intimate with him, especially since it was Valentine's Day. He'd presented her with a dozen long-stemmed red roses when he'd picked her up, and he'd apologized for being so distant for the past several weeks.

Sitting in the booth across from her boyfriend, who was quickly becoming an egomaniac, she was back at war with herself about whether he deserved to be her first. She waved the waitress over and ordered the spinach artichoke dip and water with lemon. After taking her order, she turned to Malcolm, who immediately threw his finger in the air as he was finishing up a call from his lawyer. Kalia watched as the waitress started to walk away and Malcolm waved her back and ordered by pointing to what he wanted on the menu. He gave her the okay sign, and never missed a beat in his conversation on his Blackberry.

She folded her arms and decided to play a game. How long was it going to be before he could calm down, cut off all his stuff and ignore the rest of his wannabe acquaintances to say more than two words to her? It had already been nearly forty-five minutes. Watching him nod in conversation and throw his hand up in the air to another droopy-jeans, cornrowed associate, she guessed it could be another hour. She wished she could just get up from the table and leave him there with his Blackberry and the people all around him he thought he knew.

"Whew, baby," he said finally, pulling out his earplug and placing his Blackberry on the table. "I'm so sorry, but it had to be done. You know in this game, you gotta play the game. I mean Lenny's got me just trying to approve all this stuff they want at the label for a tight contract. I've never had so many things I had to do. Everybody's just getting at me. This girl sent me a text about how she wanted to get me in her jackets—some local chick, you know, wants a little publicity for her clothes and stuff. I don't even know how she got my number. Probably Dub. Yep 'cause he was trying to kick it to her at B.E.D. You gotta meet Dub, baby. That's my pahtnah, my nigga if I don't get no bigga."

Kalia was just going to let him ramble on forever, until he said *nigga*. She'd never heard him use the word before. She considered it derogatory, and they'd even had a discussion about it one time at his father's house.

Mr. Lee said he'd never said the word *nigger* and had taught his son the same thing. Kalia couldn't understand what had changed so much with Malcolm that he thought it was cool to use it.

"Hold up," she said, putting up her hand. "What did you just say?"

Malcolm looked at her, confused.

"What was the last thing you said?" Kalia clarified.

"I said that Dub is my nigga, if I don't get no bigga."

"So it's cool to say *nigger* now?"

"You just said it." He smirked.

"Only to make a point. Don't be a smart-ass," she said, moving back as the waitress placed the spinach dip in front of them. "I remember the story your father told about when your grandmother had your aunt and your grandfather got thrown out of the hospital because he went off when some white nurse called him that name. How could you use that word after you know how they treated your grandfather?"

"Aw, that was a long time ago. *Nigga* don't mean the same thing anymore," said Malcolm, waving his hand nonchalantly. "You know my father is just into all that black power stuff. He don't know what's up today. Even white people can say nigga. Didn't you hear Eminem?"

"You aren't Eminem, not that I like him saying it either. You never said it before you got your deal. You're changing," said Kalia, spooning some dip onto her plate.

"I hope so. Naw, I know I'm changing—for the better. I'm becoming a real artist," said Malcolm, leaning back as the waitress brought him a carnivore's delight—a plate piled high with ribs, steak and chicken wings. Kalia's eyes grew large as she watched Malcolm dig right in and start devouring it like a ravenous animal. "Mmm. This is good," he said, smacking on a rib. "This is even better than the ones I had at Daddy D's the other night. Dub was there, too, with Renisha and Stephon. You're never around when Dub is around. I gotta introduce y'all. You'll like him. Maybe we can hook up after one of my sessions next week. I don't know, I usually hang with one of the producers after we get out of the studio, but there are always women around…. Aw, damn. Who's calling me now?"

Kalia watched and listened to Malcolm check his Blackberry, then his cell phone, then go back to talking with his mouth full, shoveling more food in every time he was about to speak a clear sentence. He was disgusting. She was about to excuse herself from the table when a tall, shapely Hispanic girl walked up. She removed her Gucci shades and leaned over to kiss Malcolm on the cheek.

"Happy Valentine's Day, *papi*," she said through black cherry-colored pouted lips, eyeing Kalia.

"What's up, *mami*?" said Malcolm, cutting his eyes at Kalia and wiping the lipstick off his cheek.

"I don't know why you're wiping that off. You know my kisses are good luck," she said, looking at Malcolm like she wanted to eat him alive.

"*Heh, heh, heh*…girl, you so crazy." Malcolm laughed, slightly uncomfortable. "Jasmine, this is Kalia. Kalia, this is Jasmine. We do some work together."

"I thought we were all meeting up here later," said Jasmine, barely acknowledging Kalia with a thin-lipped smile. Kalia started to say hello, but lost her train of thought hearing Malcolm's reply.

"Oh well, I had some dead time on my hands, so I thought I'd hook up with my girl here and then we could all meet at the studio later. I told Dub to get with y'all. I knew I shouldn't have trusted him. You know how he is." Malcolm laughed.

Jasmine laughed along with him. Besides being angry that she was just Malcolm's dead-time filler, Kalia felt she was on the outside of an inside joke.

Jasmine waved at someone across the restaurant. "All right, I'm out, sweets. I'll catch you later," she said, blowing a fake kiss at Malcolm. "Oh, and that 'Just Us' track is so hot. Those lyrics are fire. You can write your ass off. Okay, *ciao*." She smiled at Kalia and tiptoed off in ridiculously high black suede boots, twirling her shades in her hand.

"Cool." Malcolm threw up the peace sign and resumed eating.

"I know she wasn't talking about the 'Just Us' that I wrote," said Kalia.

Malcolm kept his face in his plate.

"I know you hear me talking to you," Kalia said, raising her voice.

"Calm down, damn," he said, putting down his fork. "Look, I was gonna surprise you, but I sold your song, and one of the Fire artists is probably going to sing it."

Feeling mixed emotions, Kalia frowned. "*Okay*…thanks, I guess, but why did she say you wrote the lyrics?"

"Well, I didn't think they would even look at it if I told them that my girl wrote it," said Malcolm, getting exasperated. "Don't worry about it. You'll get your cut as soon as I get the check."

"Money is cool and all, but I want the credit. I wrote it."

"All right, fine. Damn. You don't know how things work in the music business."

"Well, if stealing is involved, I don't want to know."

"You're really getting on my nerves," he mumbled between bites.

"What did you say?" Kalia asked. Not getting an answer she went on to her next question. "So what kinda work do you and Jasmine do *together?*" asked Kalia, watching Jasmine leaning over another guy at another table with another pissed-off girl looking at them both.

"Aw, here we go. She just does some backup stuff. She's cool."

"I'm sure she is. Do all these women you're talking to do backup work, or are they just trying to work on you?"

"Give me a break, Kalia. Actually, it's a good thing that these women are coming up to me."

"What?"

"The label says it's good for my image if I'm kinda on the scene with a few different women—you know, the right kind of women. I mean you understand, don't you? It's just some image stuff. They want my fans to see me as—"

"Your fans? Who the hell knows you?" Kalia asked, cutting him off. "You don't even have a single out yet. All these people seem like fakers, and you're starting to seem like one, too. I mean you talk about being a real artist, and I haven't heard you one time say you were at home working on some mixes, putting together some new beats like you used to say. You used to be up all night working on your music. Now it's all about the lawyers, the label and these backup singers, I guess."

Malcolm put down his fork and wiped his mouth. "Kalia, you don't know what you're talking about. Wise up. The music business is a business, and all that creativity and stuff is cool, but that's not what really sells albums. It ain't just talent," he said. "Your talent might be what gets you in the door sometimes, but sometimes it's your look and what they can make you into."

"But why do you wanna be made into something? Why can't you just, you know, do you?"

"'Cause they can make me sound better, look better and sell more albums," said Malcolm, giving a nod to an executive-looking man with a diamond pinky ring.

"And that's what's important to you, selling albums?" said Kalia. "I thought it was about spinning some good music and using music to take people to a place in their soul that they couldn't reach any other way. That's what you told me when we first met."

"Well, K, I'm not the buster I was when we first met," said Malcolm. "I'm on the come-up, and I'm learning some things that I didn't know from some important people I didn't even know I needed to meet. If you win this Fire contest, you'll see. You'll see what I mean."

"What do you mean *if*? You don't think I can do it?"

"I do, but you know you gotta do something about that stage presence. I mean the dead fish act ain't gon' work."

"Shut up, Malcolm. When I tried to talk to you, get your advice about this weeks ago, you were too busy. Now you wanna give me some advice 'cause you think you know so much from being signed for a few weeks? Please."

"Go on then. Be a fool," he said. "Don't listen to me. I bet I know one thing. I know what a true artist is, and I know what it takes to go eight times platinum like Nelly, and that's where I'm going. Not back to Morris Brown, not back to deejaying in those hole-in-the-wall spots. I'm 'bout to release some albums and blow up."

"Right, right," said Kalia sarcastically. "You've really got the big head now."

"I know what I'm talking about. And you can roll with all that 'I'm talented' crap all you want. But that ain't gonna get you far 'cause it's a lot of talented people out there who never get past their church choir. It's the game you play that gets you in the right circle to meet the right people to get you to the next circle, and you gotta look the part," he said, pulling his earlobe, which she just noticed had a small stud in it. She wondered if what looked like diamonds in it were real.

"You're certainly not the same guy I met months ago," said Kalia, pushing her plate away, her appetite gone.

"Why do you keep saying that? I know that, and I'm happy about it. You should be, too. Hold up, is that?…That is Keith," said Malcolm, getting up from the table. "I'll be right back, baby."

Kalia sat at the table, cursing herself out. Feeling around in her purse for her cell phone, her hand brushed against the condom. *I must be an idiot,* she thought, scrolling through her cell phone book, wondering who she could call. *There's no way in the world*

Malcolm will ever get in these pants. How could he treat me like this on Valentine's Day of all days? Emotionally overloaded, she needed to talk to somebody, was ready to get out of there and felt as though she was going to burst into tears any minute. She needed a friend. She needed Dewayne.

Dialing his cell, Kalia prayed he answered. It had been weeks since they'd had a nice long chat. *He's probably not doing anything anyway,* she thought, *just working on those silly comic book drawings.* She was surprised when he didn't answer. She didn't bother leaving a message and dialed his home number as she saw Malcolm slide into a booth already filled with four women. Dewayne's home number was ringing, Malcolm was leaning into the ear of one of the women, and Kalia's anger and frustration were escalating toward uncontrollable.

Where the hell is he? she wondered, slamming her phone shut. She looked around the restaurant and realized no one was paying her one bit of attention, not Malcolm, not other diners—the waitress hadn't even bothered to come back to check and see if she needed something. Kalia threw her phone in her purse, got up from the table and walked quickly out the front door. Thank God she'd taken her mother's advice and always traveled with twenty dollars just in case she needed to catch a cab home. She walked to the hotel across the street and jumped in a taxi. It was her first time in one by herself, so she was a little nervous, but she told the driver her home address and gave him specific directions in the most authoritative voice she could muster.

"Isn't that your phone ringing?" Mari asked Dewayne.

"Yeah, it's just Kalia. I'll call her back later. Do you wanna finish watching this movie or what?" He leaned back on the sofa. They'd been watching *Drumline* at his house, which she wasn't really that excited about, since she'd seen it at least a dozen times.

"I guess," she said, getting up and walking around the living room, looking at pictures of his family. "Y'all look so much alike."

"Who?"

"Everybody in your family," she said, picking up a photo of Dewayne, his parents and his brother, Spencer, and sitting back down on the sofa. Dewayne took the picture from her and stared at it intently.

"Wow. I haven't really looked at this picture in a long time. It's gotta be about ten years old. See that scar on Spence's chin?" he asked, pointing to his deceased brother. "About two weeks before this was taken, he'd gotten in this big fight at school, really because of me and this kid named Victor."

"What happened?" Mari asked, curling up in the corner of the sofa.

"Okay, now, you can't laugh if I tell you," Dewayne said, putting the picture on the low table in front of them.

"I promise. I won't." She grinned.

Dewayne told her how much he loved Halloween as a kid because he was able to dress up like his favorite superhero, Blade. When he was in second grade, he won his classroom contest for best costume, and he thought that because all the kids loved him so much as Blade that he should be Blade every day, so the next day, he stuffed his costume in his book bag and changed into it in the school bathroom. The kids in his class were so excited about his costume that he lied to his teacher, telling her he didn't have any more clothes into which to change. Everything was going great until lunchtime. When he strutted into the lunch line in his tight black polyester shirt and faux leather pants, with the tails of his pleather trench coat flapping behind him, the older kids on the other side of the lunchroom burst into laughter. His brother, a sixth grader at the time, took him to his teacher and made him change his clothes, which were stuffed in the bottom of his book bag. The trouble came after school when all the kids were waiting for the bus and Victor, a classmate of Spence's, spotted Dewayne and started clowning him.

"I kept sticking my tongue out at him and of course Spence stood up for me," said Dewayne, smiling. "He probably wouldn't have gotten into a fight at all if I hadn't called Vic's mama an ugly crackhead."

"Woo-wee, no you didn't."

"I didn't even really know what a crackhead was. I'm sure it was just something I'd heard on *In Living Color* or something. You remember that show?"

"Yeah, yeah," said Mari, barely able to stifle her laughter.

"But he was really mad because his mama really was a crack-head. How was I supposed to know that?"

Mari laughed so hard she fell off the sofa and rolled on the floor.

"You said you weren't going to laugh." Dewayne chuckled, helping her up off the floor.

"Okay, now you know that was funny. You called somebody's mama a crackhead and she really was. How could I not laugh? Ooh, I'm sorry," said Mari, cracking up again. "So how did he get Spence into it?"

"Oh, Vic called me a faggot after I talked about his mama and Spence ran over and just jumped on him. That scar he got is nothing compared to how bad he beat up Vic. They both got suspended for like a week, but nobody ever messed with me again."

"How you gonna get your brother suspended like that? Over a Blade costume? So you've always been really into this comic book stuff, huh?" Mari asked.

"Yeah, I really have," said Dewayne. "I guess I've always kind of liked fantasy and mystery. Hey, you wanna see something?'

"Sure."

"Okay, well, you gotta come upstairs."

Stepping into Dewayne's room was like entering an alternative universe where all things fantastical and tech-oriented ruled. His space was harried. Clothes were just slung into the closet any kind of way; video games, CDs and comic books were heaped in towering stacks in several corners. His bed was unmade, and he had a bunch of computer, video game and gadget equipment with a million different wires and cords in a huge snaky mass on top of and around his twenty-seven-inch television.

Dewayne started picking up clothes, CDs and comic books as soon as he walked in the room, throwing everything in the closet and straightening up the bed as Mari surveyed the room with her hands on her hips.

"You need to get Mr. Clean up in here. This place is a mess," she said, sitting in the chair at his desk.

"I don't think you're going to win any awards for the most spotless room in America," said Dewayne, straining to close the door of his overstuffed closet. "Don't look at me like that. I've seen you do this a million times."

"Ah, shut up," she said, walking over to the window. "Let me see what kind of view you've got here. Hey, there's my mother." Mari watched her mother walk carefully down the front steps in a red dress coat and red heels.

"I wonder where she's going in all that red," she said. "Her hair's all done and she's got lipstick on."

"It *is* Valentine's Day, dummy," said Dewayne, turning on his computer.

"Yeah, but she and my daddy haven't been getting along too well for the last few months. As a matter of fact, he's at work right now."

"Well, maybe he called her and told her to meet him some-place, like a surprise or something."

"That would be great," Mari mumbled dreamily, watching her mother drive up the street. She turned back toward Dewayne, who was busy typing away on his computer. "I know you didn't bring me up here to ignore me."

"No, no, this is what I wanted to show you. Come here." He motioned her over, got up and let her sit at the computer as he sat on the floor. He spent the next half hour explaining how he wanted to develop his character the Chosen One into an online comic strip and possibly an animated film one day. Mari found herself strangely interested in his ideas and the Web sites he showed her and the entire complex life he'd created for his main charac-ter.

"It's like Batman and Gotham, but darker," she surmised, getting up to stretch her legs. "I'm really feeling this, Dewayne. I'm so proud of you for not listening to Kalia. You're really good. I can see this on the big screen."

"That's probably a long time away, if ever."

"What are you talking about?" she said, thumping Dewayne in the head. "Between my sister, who's going to be a famous singer, and you, a wealthy animation film producer, I'm gonna be set. I'll be kicking it in Hollywood with Jamie Foxx *and* Vivica Fox."

"Slow down, slow down. Before you trip on the red carpet, I need to get the animation down first. That's why I think I might want to go to film school."

"That's a cool idea. You've really got a plan. Where did you come up with the name the Chosen One, anyway?"

"Oh, that's kinda from my brother," he said, shutting down the computer. "You know, since he's not around, I'm literally the chosen one—the one chosen to remain here in this universe."

Mari walked over to a bulletin board that had several sketchings pinned to it. "You really miss him, huh?"

"Think about this," Dewayne said, lying back on his bed with his hands behind his head. "Imagine if all of the sudden Kalia were gone. You were never going to see her again. You'd never argue with her about whose turn it is in the bathroom, who gets the car, anything. She'd just be gone."

Mari sat next to Dewayne on the bed. "I've never even considered that, but I guess I'd miss her, even though she gets on my last nerve most of the time."

"I'm telling you, you would," he said, looking up at her.

Suddenly Mari felt warm. Dewayne's gaze and his closeness made her nervous. She got up quickly and walked back to the bulletin board and looked closely at one of the sketches. It looked familiar.

"Who's this? It looks kinda like Kalia, except I've never seen her in a ponytail," she said.

Dewayne bounced up off the bed and snatched the drawing down. "Oh, it's nuthin'," he said, trying to stuff it under his bed.

"Wait, let me see it." Mari giggled, grabbing it back. She huddled in a corner with it in front of her while he tried to tickle her.

"Give it to me," he said, spinning her around.

"This is me, isn't it?" She laughed and squirmed in his grasp. He stopped tickling her and rested his hands on her waist.

"Yes, it's you," he said. "I drew that the other night, you know when we were at your house."

"For real?" Mari was not used to feeling weak. She hoped her knees wouldn't give out as she stared at the drawing of herself, purposely avoiding looking up at Dewayne.

"For real," he said, lifting her chin with one of his fingers. Mari closed her eyes and accepted the sweetness of a first kiss. All of the blood rushed to her head as Dewayne pulled her closer into his chest and wrapped his arms around her. He picked her up and sat her on the desk as the kiss deepened. Mari wrapped her arms around his neck and kissed him back just as urgently as he was kissing her. When she felt his hands move down her sides, seemingly searching for somewhere else to go, her nerves got the best of her, and she broke his embrace and pushed him back away from her.

"What's wrong? Did I do something wrong?" Dewayne panted, wiping his hand down the full length of his face.

"No, no…it's just that…that," Mari stuttered, getting down off the desk and walking toward the window. "That was a lot…I didn't really expect…"

"Me neither, but…I'm glad it happened," Dewayne said, leaning on the desk.

Mari looked at the unmade bed and the image of the condom falling from Kalia's papers popped into her mind. "Hey, let's go back downstairs, okay?" she said, moving toward the door. "I want to see the end of *Drumline*. It's the best part."

"Cool, but come here. I want to tell you something," said Dewayne.

"Can't you tell me from where we are? I'm cool over here," said Mari, gripping the doorknob.

"Come here, girl. I ain't gonna do nuthin' to you."

Mari walked over to Dewayne. He took her hand and said, "Look, I want you to know that I really like you, and I respect you, so I'm not trying to do anything that you're uncomfortable with."

Those words and the peck he placed on her forehead were the best Valentine's Day Mari'd had since she'd gotten the most Valentine's Day cards in her second-grade class.

On the way to school the next morning, she chatted about everything in the world except Dewayne to Kalia, even though she was dying to tell her about their kiss. She had no idea what her sister's reaction was going to be, so instead she asked her about how her date went with Malcolm. That ended any conversation for the rest of the trip, so she guessed Kalia didn't have the best Valentine's Day. After school, she and Colby spent hours in her room, analyzing every detail of her night with Dewayne. Colby had a great Valentine's Day, too. Sean had come over with a basket of baby gifts and a big box of chocolates for her.

They were so caught up in their great dates that they didn't even hear Kalia sobbing in her pillow across the hall. Kalia walked around like a zombie for most of the week. She didn't sing or play one note. When her parents or Mari asked her what was wrong, she told them she'd caught a cold and just wanted to be left alone. What she really wanted was to talk to Dewayne about Malcolm. Dewayne came to the house a couple of times, but he and Mari were always watching movies or talking about some animation project. She sat stewing in her room, wondering why he was spending so much time with Mari—after all, he was her best friend.

One day she heard them laughing across the hall, and she couldn't take it anymore, so she marched right over to Mari's room and burst through the door.

"Not that we were in here doing anything, but you could have knocked," said Mari from the floor where she was sorting CDs.

"What's up, K? Is something wrong?" Dewayne asked.

Now that she'd made such a production of her entrance, Kalia was unsure of what to do next. "Uh no…well, I just wanted to talk to Dewayne for a minute," she said, fidgeting with the doorknob.

"There he is, the Great Chosen One. Speak your mind," said Mari with a grand sweeping gesture.

"Dewayne, can I talk to you in private?" Going back to her room and sitting on her bed waiting, Kalia heard her sister say, "You better go. It seems you've been summoned."

Dewayne answered, "I'll be right back. Don't go anywhere." He loped through the door, sat down at her desk and gave her his un-divided attention. "So what's the deal? What's wrong with you?"

"Oh, nothing really," she said, trying to play it off. Now that she had Dewayne all to herself, she wondered why she wasn't getting that same feel from him—like he really wanted to hear what she had to say, whatever it was.

"Then why did you want to talk to me? The only time you ever do is if something is wrong with you. So what's the deal? You can't figure out what you want to sing for the Fire show? You haven't told your parents you want to go to Juilliard? Malcolm did something? What is it?"

"Why are you talking to me like that? All hard," she asked, getting up and rearranging the makeup on her vanity.

"Look, I'm not trying to be hard." Dewayne softened. "What's up? Really? I really wanna know."

Kalia started tearing up. She spilled her whole Valentine's Day story to Dewayne, who patiently sat and listened. When she was done, he told her that he thought Malcolm was disrespecting her, but even worse, that she was disrespecting herself by staying with him.

"I know, I know, but he was so sweet when we met, and after he got his deal he just started trippin'."

"So you gotta let this punk go. You're about to do your thing in the contest, too, then you're going off to college somewhere. You really don't need to be thinking about some cat who's not treating you right," said Dewayne, standing up. "There's plenty of dudes out there who'll wanna get with you. You know love is in the air."

"Wait, where are you going, and what are you talking about love is in the air? For who?"

"Oh, I'm just talking," he said, smiling.

"Why are you so smiley? What do you have to be so happy about?"

"You don't really want to know 'cause it has to do with the Chosen One and how I hooked up with this guy who's a professional animator at this gallery I went to the other day."

"Oh, that's nice, but can we talk about that after we figure out what to do about Malcolm?" Kalia asked.

"See, it's always about you. Can't you ever ask anybody about what's going on with them? I'm going back to Mari's room. It's more fun over there, and she wants to hear about my stuff."

"Okay, okay, I'm sorry," Kalia said, patting the bed. "I wanna hear about this guy and your comic strip. Sit down. You don't want to hang out with me anymore?"

"That's not it, really," said Dewayne. "I just...well...Mari and I, we're kinda kicking it."

"So?" said Kalia, twisting up her face. "Y'all can kick it anytime. I really need you to help me figure this one out."

Dewayne walked toward the door. "Same old Kalia," he said, shaking his head. "There's nothing to figure out. Your man just got signed. He's probably 'bout to get buck wild. You need to make a clean break before he embarrasses you or you embarrass yourself. I'm out."

Kalia was stunned. She couldn't believe Dewayne, who she

knew had been secretly in love with her since they were kids, just left her to go and hang out with Mari. And what did he mean they were kicking it? She shook her head at the thought of her sister and her best friend dating. The way her life was going she couldn't take anything else. She ran down the steps and sat at the piano. Throwing herself into practicing always made her feel better. She let her fingers glide over the keys as she launched into a session of Bach's darker pieces.

Kalia played as if she were possessed, pounding the keys. She didn't even hear her father walk in. He'd been standing in the doorway for several minutes before she saw him and stopped midrun.

"Feeling dramatic, sweetie?" he asked, walking over to the piano and sitting down beside his daughter.

"Daddy," she whimpered, burying her face in his shoulder.

After a good hug, he lifted her tear-stained face. "What's got my baby so upset?"

"Daddy, why are guys such idiots?"

"At your age, it's usually because we don't know a good thing until it's gone."

"Do you ever grow out of it?"

"I'd like to hope we do, but if we don't, you can always live here forever. You can take care of me and your mother in our old age," he said, standing. "So what's this about? That deejay guy you're seeing?"

"Yeah, well he got a deal with Fire Records and now he's acting like a complete jerk," said Kalia, wiping her eyes. "I mean he goes for days without calling me, then he's always on his Blackberry or meeting with some lawyers or other people. I never get a chance to see him."

"Sounds like that brother needs some space, baby. It might not be the right time for you and him."

"What are you, on Dewayne's side now?" she shouted.

"Dewayne? I thought this was about what's his name? Martin, Melvin—"

"Malcolm, Daddy. Malcolm. And Dewayne, he thinks…oh, just forget it. Forget everybody and everything." Kalia ran through the kitchen and upstairs to her room. She slammed her door and did what she'd done many nights since Valentine's Day—cried herself to sleep.

chapter 13

Snatching the note from Coach Little off her locker, Mari wasn't ready for her lazy break to be over. Not only was track starting, but she was going to have to be outside running in the cold. Of course Coach Little wouldn't let them run inside because he wanted to toughen them up—they had to do the mile warm-up and warm-downs outside in the freezing temperatures. She shivered, thinking of the cutting wind she knew would be blowing across her face every afternoon until March.

"I got a note, too," said Asha, sauntering by. "You ready, scrub?" Mari watched Asha stroll off, arrogantly flipping her hair, and immediately got annoyed.

"The question is," she shouted after Asha, "are you ready for me—and my sister? You're gonna be really shamed when we both beat you down."

Asha stopped in her tracks, turned around and walked pointedly back to Mari, her plaid pleated miniskirt flapping around her thin legs.

"I'm gonna wear you *and* your sister out," she said, pointing a finger in Mari's face.

"You better get that finger out of my face before I break it," said Mari, rolling her neck, something she made a practice never to do at East Moreland. Another black girl, who'd "acted black" and held her open hand up in the face of another black girl when they were in the sixth grade was still getting made fun of by the white students even though she was in the tenth grade now. She knew she was repressing part of herself, but it was worth it just to be left alone about all things black.

"Whatever," said Asha, turning back around and walking off. "You'll see. You and your little scary sister. She'll be easy to beat 'cause she'll probably freeze up again."

Mari was fuming, wishing she had something smart to say back to Asha. She didn't calm down until she was accompanying Colby to her doctor's appointment after school and could spill her guts to her friend about how she was really beginning to hate Asha. With that off her chest, Mari was totally relaxed by the time she and Colby walked into the Studio of Peace, Love and Soul expecting to see the same half-empty place they'd been coming to for the last couple of months. To their surprise, the lobby was full. A class was going on in the lavender room and about a dozen people were milling around in the mint-green room waiting for one to begin. Mari was happy to see Kalia at the front welcoming people and taking payment for the classes. It had been several days since she'd had a real conversation with her sister, and she was sick of catching attitude from Kalia. She walked up to the counter, hoping she'd get a nice reception.

"Can I help you?" Kalia smirked, tapping her pencil on the counter.

"Ha-ha, very funny," said Mari, walking behind the counter as Kalia and Colby exchanged hellos. "So what's going on in here? Is Ma giving away money?"

"No. She put this ad in the paper with a coupon, and those flyers we posted and passed out in those apartment buildings are working."

"There's a lot of people here," said Colby. "That's really good for your mom."

"Thank you very much," said Elaine, walking up, wiping her brow with a towel. "Hi, girls. How's it going?"

"It's going good for you, I see, Ma," said Mari.

"It is, it is. And it's all because of you guys' genius. Thanks so much for suggesting that coupon idea. As you ladies would say, it's off the chain up in here."

"Oh no, Mrs. Jefferson's gettin' crunk up in here," said Colby, pumping her hands in the air. Her sweater slid up exposing a small round belly.

"So how are you feeling, Colby?" Elaine asked. "You know yoga is good for pregnant women. I could show you some things sometime if you'd like."

"That would be great, Mrs. Jefferson. I'd really love to, but I'm really on kind of a budget these days."

Elaine grabbed Colby's hand. "Sweetie, you don't have to worry about that. Just let me know when you're ready and you come on in. Don't sweat the money."

"Thanks, Mrs. Jefferson," said Colby.

"Yeah, that's so sweet, Ma. Thank you," said Mari, kissing her mother on the cheek.

"Of course, darlings...listen, I want you guys to meet the new yoga instructor I hired to help out," said Elaine, looking around the corner toward the mint-green room. "His name is Peter, and he's about to teach his first class. Let me grab him before it starts." Elaine did a little pirouette as she flitted away.

"Your mom seems really happy," said Colby.

"She is," said Kalia. "And it's good, but weird good. We haven't seen her this happy in so long. It's kinda strange."

"Yeah, it is a little strange, isn't it?" said Mari, nodding with Kalia.

Elaine came trotting back, pulling Peter by the hand. Mari, Colby and Kalia looked at the rippling muscles of the attractive, tall, dark-skinned man in front of them, then looked at one another and burst out giggling.

"What's so funny, ladies?"

The girls tried to smother their chuckles to no avail.

"Peter, two of these silly girls are my daughters. That's Kalia and Mari. And this is their friend Colby," said Elaine, frowning at them. "I wish somebody would let me in on the joke."

"Nice to meet you, ladies," said Peter, gripping each one of their hands firmly. "Is everything all right?"

The girls looked at one another and then at Peter and nodded. Not one of them said anything. Elaine shook her head.

"Okay, Peter, I just wanted you to meet them. I don't want you to be late for your class. Let's talk about schedules later."

"Okay. Nice meeting you, ladies," he said, waving as he rounded the corner.

"Byyyyyeeee," Mari, Colby and Kalia sang in unison, craning their necks to catch a last glimpse of Peter's well-defined legs.

"Oh," said Elaine. "No wonder you guys couldn't speak."

"Ma, he is *so* hot," said Mari. "How can you hire a hot guy like that to teach yoga?"

"What do you mean?" Elaine asked.

"Nobody's gonna try to become one with themselves when he's in the room," said Kalia.

"They're gonna be trying to become one with him." Colby snickered.

"All right, ladies, as long as I don't see one of you in here trying to become one with him. You feel me?" said Elaine sternly. "That's a grown man and even more importantly, he's my employee, and this is a place of business. Let's keep it professional."

"Yes, ma'am" filled the air just as Ronald stepped through the glass door.

Kalia and Mari greeted their father while their mother fiddled with the bulletin board above the counter.

"I see things are going well down here," said Ronald, walking up to Elaine.

"Yes, they are," said Elaine coolly. "Did you happen to bring those check registers with you? I really need them."

"Damn, woman, can I get in the door good before you ask me for something? I mean if you can't remember something as simple as a check register, you may not need to be running a business. I never had to ask anybody to remember to bring me my check registers."

Fumbling, Elaine dropped all the papers she had in her hand. When Kalia, Mari and Colby bent down to help her, Mari saw the look of hurt and embarrassment on her mother's face. An awkward silence followed.

"How'd you get all these people in here?" Ronald asked.

"It was the girls' idea. We've been distributing flyers, and I put an ad in the paper with a coupon, and it's really paying off," Elaine said in a strained voice.

"That was a good idea. I see I've taught my girls well," he said, walking behind the counter. Elaine pursed her lips, seemingly stifling some remark.

Just then Peter came jogging around the corner. "Laine, where are the extra mats?" he asked before he was even visible.

When Peter came into the room, it was like everything started moving in slow motion to Mari and Kalia. Peter had started his class and had his shirt off, exposing a six-pack of tight abs. They watched their father turn around to see Peter. They saw his face register surprise then slight disdain when Elaine introduced the two men. As Peter heartily shook his hand, Ronald looked Peter up and down and said to Elaine, "I see how you've been getting all these people in here now, especially the ladies."

"Excuse me?" said Peter, a look of bewilderment crossing his face.

"I'm just saying, man. You walking around here looking like LL Cool J or something," Ronald said, huffing.

"Oh, I usually have a shirt on, but I was showing this one student how the vertebrae in the back should be, and I was just using myself as an example. You know," explained Peter.

"Yeah, I know, buddy," said Ronald, turning to leave. "Looks like you've got everything you need here, so I'm going to work." He smirked at Elaine then at Peter and back to Elaine.

Peter furrowed his brows, grabbed some extra mats from the side closet and went back to his class. Kalia, Mari and Colby said their goodbyes, and Elaine followed her husband out the door. When she came back in, the girls saw the forced smile on her face and wished for the earlier genuine happiness that had Elaine dancing in her Studio of Peace, Love and Soul.

After Mari and Colby left, Kalia stayed around to help, and it became a little part-time job for her in a few days when Elaine realized she really needed another trusted employee. When she wasn't taking payment for classes, doing her homework or straightening up one of the rooms, Kalia observed the classes. The participants looked so at peace that she seriously considered taking yoga regularly. She felt like her mother had suggested it to her hundreds of times, telling her that it would help her relax into her performances if she was able to connect with her center.

One evening Kalia was waiting in the car for her mother, who was in the studio locking up, when she decided she was going to take her mother's advice and take a class. She went back in the studio to get the new schedule and was rummaging through the flyers on the counter when she heard voices in the back.

"I've got to go. My daughter's waiting for me in the car."

"Don't go yet, Laine. We need to talk about this."

"No, we don't. I don't have anything else to say."

The voices started coming toward her, so Kalia edged toward the door, but her curiosity wouldn't let her leave. It was like watching a train wreck. She knew she was witnessing something terrible, but she couldn't turn away. The voices got fainter, so she moved closer to the counter.

"Please, baby. I think we could have something here."

"I've got something, okay? A family. And I'm trying to keep it."

"But you can't deny what's going on with us. You can't deny this."

Kalia didn't hear anything for several seconds.

"Okay, you're right." She heard her mother breathing hard. "Let me think about it, Pete."

"I can make you happy, Laine. I'll do whatever I need to make sure you're happy."

"It's just not a good time. My daughters are about to go to college. I just…why didn't I meet you earlier?"

"Sometimes love doesn't show up when you want it to. Come here, baby."

Kalia inched around the corner and saw her mother and Peter kissing. She put her hand over her mouth, holding in some sort of sound she knew she would have made and tiptoed out the door and back to the car. The ride home was excruciating, even though feigning sleep kept her mother from talking to her. As soon as she got to her room she picked up the phone, but she put it down immediately. She didn't know who to call. She wanted to talk to Dewayne, but she wasn't sure where they stood. She couldn't tell Mari, so in a moment of weakness, she dialed the digits of someone she hoped would be sympathetic and want to listen.

"What's up, baby?" said Malcolm. "I just knew I was never going to talk to you again."

"Are you busy?" Kalia asked, sniffling.

"Kinda, but what's the deal? You sick or something?"

"No."

"So what's going on?"

"Malcolm..." Kalia hesitated, fingering the name chain he'd given her.

"Yes...hold up. Man, let me get a Rainbow Roll and some extra wasabi and uh, some sweet tea...okay, so talk. Go 'head tell me your problems."

Kalia couldn't believe this was the same Malcolm who left her sitting by herself at the table on Valentine's Day. Maybe not calling him had made him think twice about his behavior. Feeling he was in full-on listen mode, she told him all about Peter and her mother.

"Well, what did you think was gonna happen?" he said through a mouthful of sushi. "Your parents are separated."

"What?" said Kalia. She didn't expect him to say that.

"Your mother is a woman in the prime of her life. She's gotta get it where she can, especially if your father isn't laying it down like she needs it."

"Malcolm! These are my parents. Stop talking about them like that."

"Like what? Like people who have sex? Baby, how do you think you got here?"

"Shut up. Just shut your nasty mouth up. You make me sick," Kalia shouted. She heard Malcolm saying something but she was screaming so loud she drowned him out.

"Why do you have to be so mean? I hate you. I don't even know how you got a deal, you fake-ass deejay! You can't even be yourself. Don't you ever call me again," Kalia screamed, slamming the phone on the hook. The image of her mother with Peter melded in her mind with images of her father kissing her mother in happier times. Tears were blinding her steps as she got up from the bed. She tripped over the cord of her keyboards and pulled down half the clothes in her closet, falling on top of her neatly organized shoes. She was lying in her closet, partially obscured by her wardrobe, when her mother flung open her door.

"Kalia, are you okay? What was all that yelling about?"

"I'm just fine," she said curtly, trying to find her way out of a mound of shirts, pants and hangers.

"Well, you don't look fine," said Elaine, walking over to her. "Here, let me help you up."

Freeing herself, Kalia moved out of her mother's reach, glaring up at her. "I said I was fine."

"Okay," said Elaine, stepping back, eyeing her daughter. "What was all that shouting I heard up here?"

Kalia was torn. She wanted to tell her mother about breaking up with Malcolm, but she couldn't get the image of her mother and Peter out of her head. "I—I—I don't have a boyfriend anymore."

"Oh, sweetie," said Elaine, sitting down on the bed. "I'm so sorry. Do you want to talk about it?"

Kalia didn't answer. She really couldn't tell her mother that the straw that broke the camel's back was when Malcolm tried to tell her that her mother's affair was natural. She hated everybody right then—Mari for stealing her best friend, Dewayne for abandoning her when she needed him, her father for neglecting her mother and her mother for cheating on her father. She sat up and looked at her mother, wanting to hurt somebody.

"Why are you cheating on Daddy?'

A look of horror followed quickly by one of guilt flashed across Elaine's face. "What—what are you talking about?" she asked in a high-pitched voice, getting up from the bed.

"I saw you," said Kalia, getting up, too. Her voice was a low rumble. "I saw you and that Peter," she said a bit louder.

"What? Saw us what?" Elaine was at the door.

"I saw you kissing him," spit Kalia. "I saw y'all at the studio tonight."

"You don't know what you're talking about, Kalia," said Elaine, rubbing her hand against the door. "You misunderstood. You're confused."

Kalia started reciting the lines she'd heard her mother and Peter say earlier that evening. "Why didn't I meet you earlier?" she said, taunting her mother with her own words, then she went in for the kill. "Sometimes love doesn't show up when you want it to."

"Kalia, baby, let me explain," said Elaine, inching toward her daughter.

"Don't you come near me," Kalia screamed, tears streaming down her cheeks.

Mari came to the door and looked at her mother and her sister, both crying. "What is going on in here?"

"Tell her, Ma," Kalia demanded. "Tell her what positions Peter's taught you."

"What?" said Mari, looking from Kalia to her mother. "Ma, what is she talking about?"

"Mari...Kalia...I—I didn't mean for it to happen," whimpered Elaine, leaning against the door.

"You didn't mean for what to happen? Something happened between you and Peter?" Mari asked.

Elaine looked at Mari and started to say something, then she looked at Kalia, whose face had hardened.

"Will somebody please tell me what the hell is going on?" Mari shouted.

Elaine wiped her eyes and walked past her younger daughter out of the room. Kalia bent over and started hanging up her clothes methodically.

"Kalia...I know you hear me," said Mari, walking up behind her sister. "What's going on between Ma and Peter?"

Kalia turned to Mari, her face in a snarl. "Figure it out, genius. It shouldn't be too hard. You're the expert at stealing people's best friends. You probably got that shit straight from Ma. She can't be trusted either."

Mari watched Kalia turn around and continue hanging up her clothes just as she heard her mother's car screeching out of the driveway. She ran to her room to see her mother speeding off up the street. She wondered if she was going to see Peter.

Sitting on her bed, Mari didn't know what to do. Her mind raced. Her mother was seeing another man. Her sister hated her. All hell had broken loose in her house. She picked up the phone to dial Colby, who didn't answer. She needed someone to talk to, but Dewayne wasn't supposed to be home for another half hour, and she didn't want to try him on his cell and interrupt his meeting with the professional animator he'd spent weeks setting up. She sat on her bed in the dark counting the seconds of the next thirty minutes, trying not to think about her splintering family.

It was freezing as she walked across the lawn to Dewayne's house. She'd almost reached the front steps when she thought she heard his voice come from behind the house.

"I'm so sorry about your mom. I wish there was something I could do. How is Mari taking it? Is she okay?"

Before she even heard her sister's voice, Mari knew Kalia had beaten her over to Dewayne's.

"Mari, Mari, Mari," she heard her sister say. "Is that all you ever think about? I'm the one who saw them. I'm the one who needs some damn understanding and sympathy. Can't you forget her for just a minute?"

"No, he can't," Mari shouted, jogging up to the gazebo where Dewayne and Kalia were facing each other, "and he shouldn't."

Kalia turned to her sister, her breath streaming from her mouth like smoke in the cold. "He was my friend first," she said, "and I need him now."

"Well, so do I. He's my man now," said Mari, coming nose to nose with Kalia.

Dewayne stepped between them. "Look, we all need each other now, so let's just calm down."

"You stay out of this," Kalia told Dewayne, shoving him out of the way.

"Yeah, this is between me and my sister," said Mari, not even looking at Dewayne.

Dewayne couldn't help but crack a smile. "So I've got two women fighting over me, and I don't even have a say?"

Kalia and Mari glared at each other, neither willing to back down.

"I guess we're going to stand out here in the cold until one of you cracks," Dewayne said. "Correction, y'all are going to stand out here. I'm going inside."

He walked down the gazebo steps and started toward the house. Turning to look back over his shoulder, he looked at the sisters, who were beginning to shiver, but were still holding their ground.

"My parents always said they wanted a statue back here. I guess in the morning they'll have two frozen Jeffersons," he joked. Neither sister moved, but Mari's face softened. "They wanted a waterfall, too, so maybe you two could start crying every afternoon around four, then they could have tea parties and stuff back here."

Kalia smiled, and Mari chuckled. "He is so corny," she said to her sister, shivering.

"I don't know why you like him," said Kalia.

"Because she has good taste," said Dewayne, walking back toward them.

"No, because my sister has good taste," said Mari, putting her hand on Kalia's shoulder. "She knows how to pick a best friend."

When they hugged, Mari and Kalia's embrace was just the warmth they needed.

"Aw, ain't that sweet?" said Dewayne. "So, y'all not gon' throw some punches over me?"

"Shut up, Dewayne," said Kalia over her sister's shoulder.

"No hair pulling, no scratching? I wanted to see a catfight."

Mari and Kalia looked at each other then at Dewayne and slowly started descending the steps toward their friend.

"Wait, ladies, I meant I wanted you all to fight each other," he said, trotting backward.

As Mari and Kalia chased Dewayne around his backyard, an unspoken truce materialized.

chapter 14

I hate when I'm right, Mari thought, stomping her feet to keep warm. She looked around at the rest of the track team, all shivering at the beginning of East Moreland's horse trails, waiting for Coach Little to start them on their warm-up. Everybody's breath was making clouds in the air around them, and no one looked particularly pleased about having to run in thirty-degree weather. No one, that is, but Asha. To the annoyance of Mari and the rest of the team, she was the only chatterbox out there, rambling on about how she'd dressed appropriately for the climate and how she'd once run several miles in Switzerland when the temperature was in the teens. She was getting on everybody's very last nerve. They were all ecstatic when Coach Little started them off.

Mari was just getting into her stride when Asha came up beside her.

"I've got a little secret," she sang breathily, blowing ghostlike smoke in Mari's direction.

"I don't care," Mari sang back, quickening her pace. They only had about half a mile to go, and she was determined not to let Asha throw her off. Asha didn't try to keep up with her, but sang her little song again as they were getting dressed in the locker room.

"Okay, what is it?" Mari asked, putting on her sweatpants, "'cause you're not going to leave me alone until you tell me."

"I've got an admirer who's signed to Fire." Asha smirked.

Immediately Kalia popped into Mari's mind. She looked at Asha, trying to ascertain if she was telling the truth. Asha raised her eyebrows.

"For real," she said. "You don't have to believe me. Just listen to Rob RideOut's show today. He's going to give me a shout-out."

The suspense was killing Mari. "So who is it? And how do you know he likes you?"

"'Cause I just know. You know when a guy digs you. He was trying to kick it to me when I was in the Versace store the other day."

"Ooh-wee, the Versace store, I'm *so* impressed," said Mari.

"Don't hate 'cause you're a Greenbriar Mall girl. One day you'll be able to hit the big time."

Mari wanted so badly to say something smart to Asha, but she was more concerned with finding out who her admirer was, so she bit her tongue. "Well, who is it?" she asked again.

"You know what? I don't think I'm going to tell you," said Asha, putting her bag on her shoulder and walking toward the door. "You'll find out on Rob RideOut's show."

Asha dipped out of the locker room. Mari sat there steaming, angry that she'd fallen for Asha's little game. Waiting just inside the gym doors for Kalia to pick her up, she wondered if she should tell her sister about Asha's little secret. Kalia pulled up, and she jogged down the steps and hopped into the car. As soon as she saw her sister's face, she knew that it wasn't the time to tell her that her major competition in the Fire contest might have an edge on her. She had to listen to Rob RideOut's show, which came on at six o'clock.

"What's up?" she said, putting on her seat belt and looking at the clock on the dashboard. It read 5:56.

"I forgot about a paper I was supposed to turn in today in musical theory," Kalia said, peeling off.

"Whoa. Slow ya roll. I'm trying to make it home in one piece," said Mari, holding on to the door.

"Sorry."

"Well, it's only one paper."

"Yeah, but it counts for twenty percent of our grade. I'm trying to get an extension until next week, but I think my teacher is only going to give me a couple of extra days," said Kalia.

"That kinda sucks, huh?"

"Especially since I'm not doing so hot in the class."

"You'll be able to knock it out. I'll read it for you if you need me to," said Mari, eyeing the clock, which read 5:58.

"I'm sick of having my little sister help me out. I want to be able to do my own work," said Kalia, banging her hand against the steering wheel.

Mari didn't know what to say. Her mind was really on listening to Hot 103.5. She went back and forth several times before making her decision. Plus, it would give her a good excuse to change the subject.

"Kalia, I heard they were going to be talking about the contest on Rob RideOut's show," she said, leaning over and punching the button on the car radio to Hot 103.5.

They listened to the intro for Rob RideOut. Several songs later, he broke in with a special in-studio guest, JD.

"It's JD, baby. Just like the joint says, this cat is cold as ice. Boy, you are really representin' with that single."

"Thanks, man. I 'preciate the support."

"So how's it doing? What's it doing on the charts? Are people feeling it?"

"You tell me, man. Are people calling up here and asking about it?"

"Well, you know we always support our hometown heroes. It's like the only song people are requesting. We can't play it enough."

"That's all good. It's doing pretty well on the charts. I think it's like number three right now. Ciara and Jeezy got me."

"Pretty good? That's hot, man! Number three. You can't be mad at that your first time out of the gate, and you're in the top three with two other AT-aliens. Who else is in the top five? Ain't it Luda? Another brother from the ATL?"

"Yeah, and I think Lil Wayne is up there, too."

"You can't hate on him. He's putting his thing down."
"Yeah, he's doin' it."

Kalia sighed and rolled her eyes at Mari after a few minutes had passed. "I thought you said they were going to be talking about the contest?"

"Well, I don't know exactly what time they're going to talk about it. I just heard it was going to be on Rob RideOut's show."

Kalia rolled her eyes again as they listened to Rob RideOut and JD talk about when his debut album was dropping and how he'd probably go on tour with some other Fire artists in the summer. When they finally started talking about the show, Kalia was pulling into their driveway. They were a captive audience, unable to get out of the car.

"So what's going on with Who's Got That Fire? Are you involved with that in some kinda way?"

"Yeah, well you know the final show is next month, and they're really cranking up at Fire for it."

"For real?"

"Yeah, man. They've been there rehearsing already. Those contestants are really serious. As a matter of fact, I need to shout one out that I bumped into in the Versace store the other day. She and I were looking at the same jacket I wanted to hook my sister up with. I can't say her name, but baby, you know who you are. You've got good taste, sweetie. Maybe we'll catch up with each other again one day."

"Who is that? What contestant is he talking about?" Kalia whispered urgently.

"Shh," said Mari, turning up the radio. "I can't hear."

"Sounds like she might have you open, dog."

"She was hot, man, I can't front, but you know I gotta keep my distance. Wouldn't want to throw her off her game, you know."

"That was ridiculous," said Kalia, turning off the radio when a commercial came on. "They didn't even say who it was."

Mari followed her sister into the house. "Okay, I have something to tell you," she said as they walked up the steps.

"What?" Kalia asked, walking into her room.

"I know who he was talking about."

"So who was it? That blond chick. She's probably the only one shopping at Versace."

Mari pulled off her coat and sat on Kalia's bed as her sister placed her shoes in her closet. "Well no, it's actually Asha."

"Ugh," said Kalia. "It would have to be her. Wait, how do you know?"

"'Cause she was the one who told me about him being on the Rob RideOut's today, and she said she had an admirer at Fire who she saw at the Versace store."

Kalia sucked her teeth, sitting down at her desk and looking out the window. "Do you think he really likes her? No, do you think he can help her in any way?"

"I don't know, K. I really don't know." Mari paused. "What I do know is that you can't worry about that, and you don't need to. I've been hearing you practice anyway. You're going to blow her away, and those old stinky judges aren't going to have any choice but to crown you Miss Fire Records."

Kalia smiled at her sister. Ever since she, Dewayne and Mari had come to an understanding, everything had been great between them.

"Thanks, Mari, for being such a great sister."

"Oh, please. The only reason you love me is because I'm getting the low on Asha and I'm going to figure out something to do about her, too. She's just too cocky," said Mari, standing to leave.

"Don't do anything, Mari. I want this to be a fair contest."

"Umm, hmm," said Mari devilishly. "I wish I could put a spell on her."

Kalia laughed at her sister. "Okay, you've been watching too many *Charmed* reruns. You'll mess around and turn yourself into a frog."

"Ribbet, ribbet," said Mari. She hopped across the hall to her room.

With only a few weeks left until the final show, Kalia was in full preparation mode. Driving down to Fire, she thought about how hard she'd been working. She practiced for several hours twice daily every day except Sundays when she figured she needed a rest, so she only practiced once. There were fittings for her outfit, sessions with hairstylists and visits to every makeup counter in a fifty-mile radius of their house, all of which had been done with her sister because she couldn't stand being in the company of her mother.

She turned onto the highway, and for some reason Peter flashed in her mind. The thought of his tight and toned body that once turned her on now sickened her. All she could think about was his voice, begging her mother to let him make her happy. Wondering if her father had ever said words like that to her mother, Kalia tried to remember if she'd ever witnessed the type of passion between her parents she'd glimpsed between Peter and her mother. She wished she'd never seen them together. It was affecting everything in her life—her schoolwork, her singing, her playing and how she felt about men. She thought about the days her mind would wander in class or while she was practicing.

What if I'm like Ma—a cheater? she pondered, swerving slightly to avoid a bump in the road. Even though she knew they weren't happy, she never imagined that one of her parents would do something like have an affair. Another thought entered her mind as she parallel parked in front of Fire. What if her father was cheating, too? Kalia shook her head and made a concerted effort to purge all parental disturbing behavior from her mind.

She walked into the label with that determination on her mind. Sitting in the lobby, she contemplated how there were only three more rehearsals with the live band that accompanied each of the contestants. Luckily, she hadn't had to think too hard about what she was going to sing. She was happy she'd decided to stay in the same vein and go with an Alicia Keys song. At least that was a load off her mind, her parents' drama not withstanding. Every time she met up with one of the contestants at Fire, they all talked about how concerned they were with the song they'd chosen, but she was completely comfortable with her choice.

She was also cool with the order in which she found out the contestants would perform. Instead of singing directly after Asha, there would be several contestants between them, and since she went on seventh, she was closer to the end, which she believed would leave her performance fresher in the minds of the judges.

In terms of the contest, things were going well, she thought as yet another video girl–looking receptionist called her back to the waiting room for her turn to practice with the band. There were some more forms to sign. She wished either of her parents were there so they could read whatever she was about to sign, but she wasn't sure if she could handle the sight of either of them. If her mother was there, they probably wouldn't be talking, and lately she'd been feeling guilty around her father because she knew what was going on with his wife, but he didn't.

Kalia tried to distract herself, flipping through several *Essence* and *Vibe* magazines that were on the table, but for some reason she'd gotten anxious about this rehearsal and wanted Mari to hurry up. She'd promised to show up and support her whenever she had a rehearsal, especially because their mother had been noticeably absent in their lives since they'd confronted her about Peter.

When she heard footsteps in the hallway, she knew it had to be Mari. To her surprise, Asha walked into the waiting room.

"What's up?" she asked Kalia, sliding into a chair and crossing her long legs. Kalia noticed her butterfly toe ring and wanted to ask Asha where she'd gotten it, but her competitive spirit kept her quiet.

"Ain't nuthin' up," said Mari, walking in right behind Asha. "Hey, K."

"Hey," Kalia said to her sister. She still hadn't spoken to Asha.

"Well, lookie here," said Asha, lowering her Gucci sunshades down her nose to peer at Kalia and Mari over them. "If it isn't the Sisters Jefferson."

Mari sat down and ignored Asha, who turned to Kalia.

"I hear that you and your sister think you can beat me. It's going to be such a shame when I wipe the floor with you both."

"You might be the one on the ground when we're done with you," said Mari.

Kalia looked from one to the other. "Did I miss something here?" she asked.

"Yeah," said Asha, running her fingers through her long, wavy hair. "Your sister here thinks that she's going to whip me on the track and that you're going to shut me down on the stage. I hate to say it, but you're both sadly mistaken."

"Whatever," said Mari. "You've got no talent and no speed, so we won't even have to try hard."

"Well, how did my slow butt beat you in cross-country last year? And, I think I got a standing ovation and your sister, if I'm remembering correctly, got clowned—isn't that right, Kalia?"

Kalia hesitated for a moment. "Well, maybe I could have loosened up a bit, but—"

"But nothing," said Mari, raising her voice. "You don't have to explain anything to her. Don't say a thing, just let your actions speak for themselves." She turned to Asha. "Stop trying to psyche her out. You aren't going to throw her off her game—me either."

"Me?" said Asha, feigning concern with her hand over her chest. "Oh, I would never try to do that intentionally. I don't have to cheat. I have all the support I need from my family and from my sweetie."

"What are you talking about, Asha?" asked Mari, immediately sorry she went there.

"You know, my man from Versace."

"JD don't care about you," said Mari, wondering why she was allowing herself to be antagonized by her classmate. "He probably just saw you drooling over him outside Versace and took pity on you."

"Yeah, well we'll see who's feeling sorry for who in a few weeks, won't we Kalia?" said Asha nastily.

Kalia opened her mouth to respond just as the receptionist stopped by to tell her it was her turn to rehearse.

"JD's not a judge, so even if for some unknown reason he is feeling you, it won't make a difference. You should have flung that hair in Big Spinner's face. He seems more like the type to fall for your fakeness," she said, standing. "Play nice, Mari. I'll be back in a few."

Although there was a lot of sighing and coughing and generally unnecessary noisemaking, not a word was spoken between Mari and Asha the entire time Kalia was in rehearsal. The same uncomfortable silence that hung between them had taken hold in the Jefferson household. When the sisters got home from Fire, their mother was in her room with the door closed and their father was in the guest room, door closed as well.

Sick of coming home to a house that might as well not have any parents at all, Mari banged on her mother's door first and then her father's. No answer led her to Kalia's room. Her sister didn't want to talk about it or even think about how to save their parents' marriage. She'd successfully practically avoiding her mother and her father since the Peter incident several weeks ago.

Mari was angry with her mother, too, but it wasn't as intense as Kalia's ire, probably because she didn't catch their mother in the act, she thought, sitting at the top of the steps to the kitchen. She wondered what was going to happen to her family. Was her mother going to run off with this yoga guy? What happened if her daddy found out? Were her parents going to get a divorce? That thought was so upsetting that she hopped up to call Colby. She needed distraction immediately, and Colby was always good for a complaint about how she was feeling or how Sean was clueless about pregnancy.

The next rehearsal to which Kalia went coincided with Asha's again. She wondered how it was that she and Asha had been scheduled for the last two rehearsals right after each other. *Maybe we're getting taped for some reality show,* she thought, her paranoia working overtime as she sat in the waiting room with another contestant, anticipating her main competition's arrival. She looked hard at the light fixtures in the ceiling, the phone on the coffee table and even the rivets in the floor, searching for hidden cameras. Shaking her head, she decided she was letting the pressure get to her. She leaned her head against the wall behind her and took some deep yoga-inspired breaths, trying to calm down. *Only two more rehearsals left, and that's it,* she told herself.

The receptionist came and got the other contestant, and as she left, Asha walked in, with, of all people, JD.

Asha hadn't even gotten into the room good before she was dragging JD in front of Kalia. "Kalia, this is JD. JD, this is Kalia, my competition," she said, trying to hold his hand. Kalia noticed he wasn't really cooperating.

"What's happenin', Kalia?" he said, extending his hand. Kalia looked into his hazel eyes and lost her capacity to speak for a second.

"Hi," she said, finally taking his hand. "Nice to meet you."

"So, you nervous?" he asked. "About the contest?"

"Um, yeah, kinda." She smiled, but she wasn't sure why. He was looking directly in her eyes as he was speaking to her. Malcolm was always looking everywhere else but at her when they were together.

"What's so funny, cutie?"

"Nothing," Kalia said, giggling a bit.

Asha coughed horribly all of the sudden, and they both looked at her, neither asking if she was all right. Kalia doubted she was really choking.

"Whew," she said, placing her hand on her chest theatrically. "I thought I was going to need the Heimlich for a few seconds there. Would you have saved me, JD?"

Her purring was making Kalia ill. JD whipped out his cell.

"I don't know how to do the Heimlich, but I know how to dial 911."

He and Kalia burst out laughing. Asha twisted up her face.

"All right, ladies, I gotta jet. Thanks for the ride, Asha. I don't know how you ended up at that studio," he said. "Nobody knows where it is. As a matter of fact, what were you doing back there anyway?"

"Oh, I just got turned around, you know," she said, smiling shyly. Kalia knew she was faking. Asha was a lot of things, but shy was not one of them.

"Okay," he said, frowning at Asha's response. "Anyway, I'm checking out the rehearsals today, so I'll see you inside."

"Bye," Kalia said.

"Yeah, see you later, baby," said Asha, wiggling her fingers at JD.

He looked at her strangely and walked out of the waiting room.

"That's my sweetie," Asha said, sitting down.

"Umm, hmm," said Kalia, sitting as well.

"On the ride down here, we had the best conversation, you know, exchanging industry info."

Kalia rolled her eyes. Asha wasn't even on stage, but she sure was hamming it up. "What industry info do you know?" she asked Asha.

"You'd be surprised," she said, flipping through a magazine.

"I sure would," Kalia said, leaning her head back against the wall.

"I think you're just jealous of me and JD. You can't take it that we're going out."

Kalia chuckled at Asha.

"What's funny?" Asha demanded.

"You are," said Kalia. "You're the star of your own sitcom, but you have no audience 'cause I'm certainly not paying attention anymore."

"Well, you will be when I win this contest and my song is on the radio and you're standing in line at Wal-Mart to buy my album."

"Dream on, silly goose," said Kalia without moving her head.

Asha huffed, and they sat there in silence until the video girl came to collect Kalia for her rehearsal. While singing on stage with the band, she tried to peer into the audience to see JD, but the overhead lighting blinded her, so she sang her heart out and hoped he was paying attention. She was back in the waiting room putting on her jacket to leave when JD appeared.

"That was really tight," he said, standing half inside the door.

Kalia knew she was blushing. "Thanks," she said. "That means a lot coming from you."

"No, for real, I mean it. You've really got some skills," he insisted.

"Thank you," she said again, not really knowing what else to say. She stuffed her hands in her pockets and tried to control the ridiculous grin on her face.

"I'll walk you out, if that's cool."

Kalia had a hard time answering verbally. She just nodded and walked out into the hallway with him at her side. On the way to the lobby he told her all about how he had been spending a lot of time in the studio recently with professional backup singers. In the few months he'd been signed, he'd recently learned how to distinguish between the singers who were theatrical and those who could actually throw down.

"You've got it, that thing that all singers want—incredible skill, maturing technique, a willingness to try different styles and deep soulfulness."

Kalia just nodded and kept saying, "Thank you" at his assessment of her talent. She wasn't used to hearing him so articulate. Every time she'd heard him on the radio, he was all "youknowwhatI'msayin'?" She couldn't help herself. She had to ask.

"Sooo, can I ask you a question?"

"Shoot," he said.

"Okay." She stopped and turned to him a little too dramatically. "What do you really want to do?"

JD furrowed his brows and tilted his head forward, pausing to think for a minute, stroking his chin. "I wanna be a producer, and, you know, have my own label, then maybe I can branch out into producing films and maybe own a network or something."

Kalia smiled and opened the door to the lobby. "Big dreams, Bob Johnson," she said.

"Well, you know hip-hop is for the young folks. Can't spit lyrics forever," he said, following her to the front door. "So what do you want to do?"

"Um, I think I want to do Broadway and musicals like *The Wiz* and *Dreamgirls*—you know, produce some theater one day after I've toured the world fifty times headlining my own shows."

They were at her car. "So who's got the big dreams now?" he asked.

Kalia laughed a little, feeling kind of special when two girls walked up to JD and asked for his autograph, which he gladly obliged them.

"All right, little lady," he said, backing away with his hands in his pockets. "I'll check you later, aight?"

"Yeah, cool. See ya," she said, getting into her car. She tried to resist the temptation to turn around and look at him walk into the building, but she couldn't. When she looked over her shoulder, she saw him still looking at her as he continued to walk backward toward the building. She winced when she saw him bump into a group of teenagers, who immediately recognized him. Embarrassed, he grinned at her through her back window, and she waved at him.

Kalia rode all the way home lost in emotion, replaying the entire conversation between her and JD. She remembered every word he said, how he smiled easily, patted his chest when he was trying to make a point and spoke so intelligently about his dreams. Stopping at a red light, she watched a young couple cross the street in front of her. The guy was tapping on his Blackberry, and the girl seemed to be talking to him, but he obviously wasn't listening. Seeing the girl throw up her hands in desperation, Kalia realized she'd hardly thought about Malcolm at all since she'd met JD. Looking at the couple in her rearview mirror as she crossed the intersection, she caught a glimpse of the name chain Malcolm had given her. At the next stoplight she took it off. *No need for this anymore,* she thought, dropping the necklace into a cup holder. She was in such a good mood when she got home that the somberness on her mother's and father's faces when she walked into the kitchen was jarring.

"What's wrong?" she asked immediately. Her father was leaning against the kitchen counter and her mother was sitting at the table across from Mari.

Kalia looked from her father to her sister.

"Don't look at me," said Mari, raising her eyebrows. "They just called me down here. I don't know what the deal is."

"Sit down, Kalia," said Ronald.

"Okay," said Kalia, taking a seat at the table.

"Elaine, you start," Ronald directed.

"Okay," she said, taking a deep breath and turning to her daughters. "We have something to tell…well, your father and I have…we've made a decision."

"What are you talking about, Ma?" asked Kalia, worry heavy in her voice.

Elaine looked at Ronald.

"We've decided to spend some time apart," he said, "but we want both of you to know that this decision has nothing to do with you."

"Well, we know it's going to affect you, but what he means is that you aren't the reason for it," Elaine said.

"I don't need you to clarify for me, Elaine. The girls know what I mean," Ronald said harshly.

Elaine rolled her eyes. Numbed by their parents' news, neither Kalia nor Mari had been able to say a word. They watched their father open the refrigerator, pop open a beer and guzzle half of it before he put the can on the counter.

"Girls, are you all right?" their mother asked, reaching across the table to touch Kalia's hand. Neither answered as Kalia looked at her mother's hand on hers and felt sick.

Mari stood up abruptly. "Are you getting divorced?"

"Well, we're not saying that exactly," said Ronald. "We just know we need to separate right now to figure some things out."

"But you'll still be able to see us both," Elaine added.

Mari sat down on the back steps. "So who's leaving?"

"I am," said Ronald, taking another long swig. "Tonight."

There was silence in the kitchen. No one said anything for a while.

"Do you have any questions?" their mother asked in a choked-up voice.

Kalia shook her head, got up and walked up the steps. Mari followed.

"I'm going to be staying downtown. Your mother will have the number," they heard their father yell up the stairs after them.

Kalia had only been sitting in her room for about a minute when Mari came in with her jacket on.

"Come on," she said, picking up Kalia's car keys. "I gotta get outta here. Let's go for a ride. Ooh, I'll be glad when I can drive without the parents."

Kalia didn't say anything. She picked up her jacket and followed Mari down the front stairs. Not even bothering to tell their parents they were leaving, they walked out the front door and got in the car.

Listening to the oldies but goodies station, neither said anything for nearly half an hour. They drove through all kinds of neighborhoods letting Luther Vandross, Evelyn "Champagne" King, Phyllis Hyman and the SOS Band lead the way. They ended up at Grant Park, just as Stevie Wonder's "All Is Fair in Love" began playing. Kalia drove slowly in the parking area and backed into a space underneath a tree behind them. To their right they could see parents watching their children playing on the playground.

"Remember when we were kids, we used to play over there," Mari said, watching a little boy swing himself from one monkey bar to the next.

Kalia didn't say anything. When Mari turned to look at her, tears were running down her sister's cheeks.

Kalia wiped her eyes and turned down the radio when Kool and the Gang's "Celebration" came on.

"You think they're gonna get a divorce?" Mari asked.

"I don't know. I mean, maybe."

"It's going to be so strange going to visit Daddy somewhere else."

"Yeah," said Kalia. "God, what's going to happen to us?"

Mari returned her attention to the playground. "I remember when you fell off that seesaw and you busted your lip." She smirked. "You were so mad at me, and your lip was so big. Remember we called you bubble lip for like a month?"

Kalia couldn't help but chuckle. "Yeah, I remember, brace face." She smiled. "I also remember when you slid down the slide backward and landed on your head in the dirt."

"That hurt, too," said Mari, touching the back of her head.

"Remember Daddy came over and picked you up and promised he'd get you some ice cream if you'd stop screaming."

"Yeah, yeah. We drove around all night trying to find chocolate chip ice cream."

"We must have gone to six or seven stores."

"But I bet I got it. Ma made sure of that," said Mari.

"That was a fun night, back in the day," Kalia said solemnly. "I guess we won't be having any more of those."

"Them breaking up isn't why we won't be going out for ice cream anymore. We're just too old."

"You know what I'm saying, Mari. Life is going to be different."

"Yeah, I know, but we're just going to have to deal with it like everybody else does. Like who do we know whose parents are together? Hardly anybody except for Dewayne, and his parents are like zombies. It doesn't even matter."

"I mean, we don't even get to see Daddy much when he's here. Now we're never going to see him unless we go to the Frys," said Kalia, sighing. "I really need to go home and study for my midterms."

"Ooh, yeah, me, too, and I've got a five-page paper due in European history, but I don't really feel like going home right now."

"I need to practice, but I don't even feel like singing anymore. I really don't want to see Daddy leave. Do you?"

"Naw, not really," Mari replied, "but you gotta practice, Kalia. I know Ma and Daddy are going through their thing, but you can't just not practice. The show is in like two weeks."

"Maybe I won't even be in the show," said Kalia.

"Oh, you're really trippin' now," said Mari. "You need something to pour all of that emotion into, and I need for you to do it 'cause you gotta beat Asha. You know it's all about me, don't you?"

Kalia smiled at her sister. "I've got an idea," she said, starting up the car. They drove to the nearest grocery store, went inside and bought a half-pint of chocolate chip ice cream and plastic spoons. They went back to the park, sat in the swings, reminisced more about their childhood and finished the entire carton.

chapter 15

Mari was determined not to let Asha beat her in the one hundred. Even though she did pretty well in cross-country, short distances were her thing, and the one hundred was her race. She'd used all her frustration about her parents separating in a couple of extra hours of practice in the last week because she wasn't going to have a repeat of her losing streak in cross-country meets last fall. She was certainly not going to let Asha beat her in a track meet.

She adjusted her shorts and shook her legs out, preparing to get down in the blocks. There was something about the first meet of the spring season, she thought, looking around the stadium at the sea of faces in the stands and on the field. She loved that the temperature was always just perfect, not too hot and not too cool. Humidity and rain would kick in in April, but in March, Atlanta felt good.

Asha was in the next lane, stretching out her long frame. Mari thought it was so strange that although they were different in size they were competitive in the same race. She decided to run her own race and forget Asha was even there. She got into the blocks, and when the starter gun went off, she flew down the track. In her mind's eye, there was no one out there but her. When she crossed the finish line, no one had to tell her she'd won, because she knew it in her spirit.

She slowed down, and her world slowly came back into focus. The audience was clapping as she turned around to see her opponent bent over, breathing heavily. Asha straightened up when the winner was announced and her name wasn't called. Walking past Mari to the bench she said, "You're lucky I'm concentrating more on the Fire contest than I am on track."

"Whatever, loser," said Mari, grinning. She grabbed a towel and dabbed at her brow. "I got skills, and so does my sister."

"We'll see," Asha said, walking away.

"We sure will," Mari threw after her. The rest of the meet went great for her. Her four-by-four relay team won, and she came in second in the 400, but she didn't care because Asha wasn't in that race. After the meet, she got congratulations from Kalia, Dewayne, Colby and Sean, who offered to take her out for a celebratory dinner. She was so excited about beating Asha that she'd left her gym bag on the field. On the way back to the car to meet up with Colby and her sister, she stopped to talk to some other team members and saw Asha's mother, Roxanne, standing with a guy on the track.

"Hey, Mrs. Wright," she said as they walked by.

"Oh, hello, Mari," said Asha's mother. "Didn't I tell you to call me Roxie? I'm too young to be called Mrs. anything."

"Oh, I'm sorry." Mari giggled. "I totally forgot, Mrs....I mean Roxie."

"You had a great meet today, huh? Just ran on past my little Asha," she said, winking.

"I guess," said Mari, embarrassment creeping into her voice.

"Yeah, you're real fast," said the guy with Roxie. "You must practice a lot."

"Uh, yeah," said Mari, looking at the Sean John suit he had on, thinking he was a little overdressed for a track meet.

"I hope your sister is practicing," said Roxie, "because you may have beat my baby out here on the track, but on a stage? *Pfft*, that's another thing."

"With all due respect, Mrs....Roxie, Kalia is going to win next week. Trust me."

"Well, like Jesse Jackson says, you keep hope alive, baby." She laughed, grabbing her friend's arm. "Come on, Jackson. See ya, Mari."

★ ★ ★

Kalia was starting to get stressed. She'd had her last rehearsal with the band the day before, and it had gone well—actually even better than well since JD showed up and they'd gotten a chance to talk, she still couldn't get rid of the feeling that she wasn't going to win. There were only two days left until the final show and she was a wreck, she thought, closing her economics book. Trying to study seemed to be a waste of time. She'd read half a chapter on inflation, and she didn't even remember what it was about. Looking out her window into the backyard, she thought about Asha and wondered what she'd be singing. She looked frantically around her room for something to clean or straighten, but her room was immaculate. She was just about to get in the bed and pull the covers over her head like she did when she was a child, when Dewayne walked in.

"How's it going, champ?" he asked.

"I'm going out of my mind," Kalia whined, holding up her hands.

"Okay, okay," he said, sitting down at her desk. "Tell big daddy what the problem is."

Kalia sat on her bed with her legs crossed. "Dewayne, I don't think I can do this."

"Do what?" he asked, chuckling.

Kalia gave him the evil eye. "I'm not talking to you. You're laughing at me."

"No, I'm laughing with you," he said, leaning over and tickling her on her stomach.

"Stop making me laugh," Kalia protested weakly, swatting him away.

Seeing her smile, Dewayne took pride in his abilities. "The Chosen One is victorious again. See, that's what you needed, some good old-fashioned tickling. Now don't you feel better?"

"No," she lied, smiling widely.

"Umm, hmm. So how about you take the night off and we do something fun? You've got like forty-eight hours before the show starts. Kicking it for a few hours isn't going to hurt."

Kalia thought about it for a split second before she grabbed her jacket and they ran out the door. The next thing she knew, she was at the gaming restaurant, Dave and Busters, where after some chicken fingers, she and Dewayne got into a to-the-death battle of who could make the most free throws. At the end of the evening Kalia redeemed her tickets for a nice-sized teddy bear. Dewayne went home with a key chain.

The next afternoon Mari and Colby swept in to rescue her from her worries by accompanying her to the hair salon and the nail shop, then they helped her work on her performance techniques and answer crazy judge questions they threw at her. They even encouraged her to practice blowing her winner's kiss to the audience. Thinking that would jinx her performance, Kalia refused. Mari and Colby kept Kalia so distracted she really didn't miss her mother's involvement in the preperformance night shenanigans until she was snug in her bed. She thought about how much of a busybody her mother had always been the night before her performances when she was younger. She could never get her to leave her alone, checking and rechecking to see if Kalia had all of her costume or makeup or whatever she needed to be the star of the show.

One thing she didn't need was insomnia, she thought, fluffing her pillows. She couldn't help thinking about how weird it had been in their house the past couple of weeks. They'd only seen their father one time since he'd left, and that was when he called them and told them to meet him at one of the Frys for dinner one night. Their conversation had been strained, and their father was kind of sad and pitiful. He kept apologizing, which made them uncomfortable.

Turning over, Kalia thought her mother must be pretty uncomfortable, too, because she seemed to be making a point of never being there when she or her sister were. When she was home, she was closed up in her bedroom. Earlier in the week she'd walked up to her mother's closed door. When she got close enough, she heard her mother crying quietly and decided against knocking. As much time as she and Mari had spent together in the last week, they really hadn't talked much about their family situation. Ignorance *is* bliss, Kalia thought, drifting off. Her last thoughts were of her mother and how much she wished things would go back to the way they were when she was young and she knew in her heart that her parents were in love.

She got up the next day, refreshed and determined. She and

Mari grabbed a full breakfast of grits, cheese eggs, pancakes and sausage at the Waffle House and hit the road. Most of the next day was a blur. After a dizzying schedule of running around, including going back to the hairdresser for a touch-up of her style; to the tailor for her outfit, which had to be altered; and to the drugstore for some of her favorite Maybelline mascara, she made it to the Fox theater in time to relax for a few minutes before she had to get dressed.

Mari, Colby, Sean and Dewayne had just left the dressing room when her mother walked in. They hadn't really had a real conversation in a week, so Kalia was uneasy, although she was happy to see her.

"Hey, Ma," she said, swiveling from the mirror in her chair.

"Hi, sweetie," said Elaine, ducking under a dress that was being handed over her head from one person to another. "It's wild outside. There's some type of live radio broadcast going on outside the theater with a Cool Ice or something."

"Oh, it must be Cool Mike. He's been pumping the show up with JD on Hot 103.5."

"JD, okay, whatever you say," she said. "You know I don't know these hip-hop guys. You should see the theater. I don't want to make you nervous, but it's really packed out there. I don't think there's a seat available. Why didn't you tell me this was going to be on television?"

"Oh, so much has been going on that I totally forgot," said Kalia. "Do you know what channel?"

"I don't know. I heard somebody say it was going to be filmed like a local reality show or something."

"Really?" said Kalia, slightly distracted. Something was on her mind, and she didn't know what would happen if she asked her mother about it, but she did know that she wouldn't be able to perform if she didn't get an answer.

"Ma, is your friend here?"

Elaine got a quizzical look on her face.

"Your friend from the studio. Peter?"

Elaine's face dropped, and Kalia was sorry she'd brought up his name.

"No, he isn't here," her mother said curtly. "Why would you ask about him?"

Kalia copped an attitude—fast. "What do you mean 'Why would I ask about him?' I want to know if he's going to be out there watching, if you brought him to a family thing?"

"No, he isn't here, I said," whispered Elaine, guilt softening her voice.

Kalia kept at her mother. "Well, is Daddy here? Do you guys even speak anymore?"

Elaine really looked hurt, and Kalia was starting to feel guilty for pushing so hard. "Yes, your father and I have talked—several times in fact. He said he was going to be here. I'm sure he's somewhere out there."

"Oh," said Kalia, deciding to lay off her mother's personal life.

"Look, I wanted to give you something for good luck, and this is really all I could think of," said Elaine. "It was your great-grandmother's." She pulled a maroon jewelry box out of her purse and handed it to Kalia. When Kalia opened it, a diamond-and-pearl bracelet lay delicately on crushed velvet.

"This is beautiful, Ma. Thanks," she said, scooting out of her chair and giving her mother a hug, the first since her parents had told her they were separating. When she tried to let go, her mother held her a little longer. She felt her mother's heart beat against her own, and the warmth of her reminded Kalia of when she was young and used to snuggle in her mother's lap as she read her bedtime stories. She missed being close with her mother as much as Elaine missed their tight relationship.

Her mother fastened the bracelet on her arm, wished her good luck with a kiss on the forehead and rushed out of the dressing room, which was in a frenzy. The same madness from the preliminary show in December was going on again—contestants, parents, friends and stagehands were all zipping back and forth, questioning, shouting, laughing and generally turning the dressing room into a zoo, but Kalia didn't care. She didn't let anyone shake her inner resolve. Sitting in her chair, she looked carefully at herself in the mirror. She liked what she saw. She was ready.

And it was a good thing because the stagehands were rushing everybody into place for the beginning of the show. Funny that she hadn't seen Asha all evening until right before they were about to line up, then her fiercest competition ran in at the last moment in a fire engine-red minidress with sequins and spaghetti straps.

Her lips were so red, her stilettos so high and her hair so wind-blown wavy, Kalia thought she looked like a runway model.

All of the contestants held hands and mouthed "good luck" and "break a leg" to one another as the band started the Who's Got That Fire? theme song. Then LaToya, Fire's hottest female singer, came out on stage, sang the lyrics to the theme song and introduced the judges. Kalia rolled her eyes as Carter got the most applause then stepped out on stage with the rest of the contestants for their opening wave. Looking at all of the outfits worn by the contestants as they paraded around the stage, Kalia was pleased with her choice. Her shimmery rhinestone butterfly blouse and fitted tuxedo pants didn't scream look-at-me-I-really-want-to-be-a-celebrity like Asha's, but it also didn't fade into the background. With deep berry lipstick, strappy stilettos and a real gardenia tucked in her hair behind her ear, her ensemble had just the right amount of funk and flash, Kalia thought as she gave her last wave at the audience before stepping off the stage into the wings.

She started to go back to the dressing room, but changed her mind when she remembered that Asha went on second. Watching the first contestant completely let his nerves get the best of him had Kalia talking to herself about remaining calm and remembering to think about her performance as one that she'd done a million times in Williams High practice rooms or at home. She knew she needed to be that comfortable if she was going to perform well. Big Spinner clowned the first contestant, Lola felt sorry for him, and Carter rated him so poorly that Kalia thought the guy would cry. He walked straight through the rest of the contestants when he came off stage and Kalia bet right out the stage door.

If she was nervous, Asha sure didn't look it when they called her name, Kalia thought, watching her strut onto the stage swinging her hair like Naomi Campbell. When she heard the band play the first three notes of the song Asha had picked to sing, Kalia thought she would die.

"That's Alicia Keys," she said to herself. "She's doing Alicia Keys."

"Umm, hmm," said the contestant next to her as Asha launched into "Girlfriend." "I thought you always did Alicia Keys. Why is she doing it?"

"I don't know," said Kalia, her voice rising in pitch. She couldn't believe that Asha was stooping to such a level to steal her thunder.

"Well, are you singing this one?" asked the girl.

"No, but still," said Kalia, crossing her arms. She watched Asha work it out. The only person she'd heard sing "Girlfriend" better was Alicia Keys herself. Holding a long, drawn-out note at the end, Asha had the crowd on their feet, but if she wasn't mistaken, Kalia thought she heard a few boos as well.

"I guess we've got more than one person who wants to be Alicia Keys," said Big Spinner first off. Some members of the audience snickered with him.

Asha responded to his jibe with only a plastic smile and a nod.

"Well, I thought her performance was magnificent," said Lola, "and that dress is, well, what can I say, fire." Her comments elicited a roar from the audience, to which Asha graciously waved and mouthed, "Thank you" several times over.

When Carter opened his mouth, a hush fell over the theater. Everyone was listening. "Yes, Asha, you did a great job. Your performance was energetic and very entertaining, and of course no one can be mad at you for having the Fire spirit in that dress." The audience hooped and hollered. "I don't know if it's in the best taste to take someone else's thing," he added. "I mean Alicia Keys? What's up with some originality? Thank you very much, and good luck."

Kalia was waiting in the wings as Asha strutted off stage toward her. Thoughts of tripping or just straight out clocking Asha filled Kalia's mind. She resisted the urge and, instead, followed her to the dressing room. As she walked in Asha was with her mother and a guy.

"Oh, hi, Kalia. Wasn't Asha great?" Roxie gleamed, hugging her daughter's shoulders. The huge bouquet of red long-stemmed roses in Asha's arms perfectly complemented her outfit.

Kalia couldn't bring herself to answer Roxie, so she just smiled and nodded at all three of them and walked over to her dressing table, looking around like she had forgotten something. Picking up a tube of lipstick, she prayed she'd be able to scoot back by them and get out of the dressing room without further conversation. Luck was not on her side.

"So what did you think of my performance?" Asha called to Kalia, just as she was about to make a clean getaway.

Kalia thought she felt beams of electricity shoot out of her eyes as she turned toward her enemy. To her dismay, Asha didn't disintegrate, but stood smirking in her direction. "It was Alicia Keys," was all she could manage to get out.

"Well, yes." Asha chuckled, looking back and forth between her mother and Kalia, like it was obvious to everyone there who wrote the song she sang.

Kalia could barely contain herself. She turned on her heels and walked toward the door. "Good luck," she heard Asha shout after her, but she didn't stop walking. She wound her way around the backstage maze of the Fox, trying to get away before anyone saw her cry. Brushing past Sean, he caught her eye and tried to grab her hand, asking if she was okay, but she eluded his grasp, nearly running down the hall. Damn, she cursed herself as tears ran her eyeliner and mascara down her cheek. She tried several doors before she found one that was open. Looking around she realized she was in the same room she'd escaped to during the preliminary show.

Contestant number five was wailing on a monitor. Kalia searched around the room for the remote. This time she was able to mute the monitor. She sat on an oversized green couch and took several deep breaths and a tissue from a dressing table to dab her face. She thought about the industry chick from New Year's Eve. What would she do in a situation like this? she wondered. She'd probably take a few minutes to get herself together and then what? Kalia knew she was too angry to perform.

She got up from the sofa. *First things first,* she thought, pacing. *I need to calm down.* After doing several modified yoga positions, down she sat again, closing her eyes and leaning back against the plush fabric. She didn't realize she'd drifted off until she awoke, startled. Looking at the screen she saw the contestant before her walking onto the stage. Without a thought she jumped up and retraced her steps through the backstage hallways toward the dressing room.

Because she'd been crying she wanted to check her face before she went on stage, but as she came around the corner, a stagehand grabbed her. "We've been looking for you," he said, pulling her by the hand toward the stage. "You're on in like fifteen seconds."

"But…but…my face," she protested as he dragged her into the wings.

"No time. They're playing your intro," he said, shoving a mic into her hand.

She turned around to walk on stage, and there was JD. "You look so beautiful that you don't even need luck," he said, kissing her on the cheek. "Make it happen, baby. Show 'em what you got."

Kalia opened her mouth and started singing into the mic as she floated onstage.

The audience was on their feet instantly, but Kalia didn't notice. She was getting in her own zone.

She flowed into the second verse of "You Don't Know My Name," aching soul smoldering in her voice. She'd planned to just move on to the bridge of the long song and the chorus, but something made her walk over to the band. The electric bass player vacated his seat, and she sat perched on the stool.

She started her favorite part of the song. As many times as she'd performed in rehearsals, she'd only done the spoken word breakdown twice because the producer had told her it was too long. But that night was different. Swaying back and forth, the audience mouthed the words along with her.

Daring them to stop her midway, she laid her rap on thick and snuck a peek in the wings to see if JD was looking. He winked at her.

She wailed the ending, releasing all the emotion she had into her finish.

It took forever before the audience quieted down enough for Big Spinner to say something. Kalia stood tall and waited for his berating.

"Wow," he said. "All I can say is wow, wow, wow."

Kalia looked at him expectantly.

"That's all I got. Really," he insisted. "Wow."

"I second that emotion," said Lola, clapping, which started the audience's frenzied applause. "I guess I should say that I second all those emotions because Kalia you went through every one in the book. That had to be one of your best performances ever."

"Thank you so much," Kalia said. She was pleased and encouraged by Big Spinner's and Lola's comments, but she knew who really mattered. She turned her attention to Carter and braced herself.

"Kalia" he said, putting his finger to his lips, "I must admit that was one of the finest showings I have ever seen in an amateur competition. Congratulations. That breakdown put you over the top. Thank you and good luck."

Then she was in the wings with JD's arm around her waist, ushering her past the other contestants who were all giving her big ups. She'd only been in the dressing room a few minutes when everyone she knew and loved rushed in, congratulating her and taking pictures. She looked at her family and friends and started crying. She hugged them all, thinking that whether or not she won, she was proud of her performance and happy she was so loved. As everyone else went back to their seats, except Mari, who stayed backstage, Asha walked into the dressing room.

"That was pretty good," she said to Kalia. "You know you went over the time, though."

"She was good enough to," said JD, stepping from behind a rack of clothes.

Asha looked at JD, then to Kalia and back to JD. "Hey," she said to him. "What—what are you doing back here? Did you see me sing?"

"Yeah, you were cool," he said, grabbing Kalia's hand. Asha shifted her weight from one flaming red stiletto to another. "Look, they're about to announce the winners, and I've got to be on stage, so I'ma jet." He kissed Kalia on her cheek and jogged past Asha out the door.

Asha put her hand on her hip. "So, you're stealing my man?"

"You stole my artist," Kalia said defiantly.

"It doesn't matter," Asha said, "because I'm still gonna win."

"Really?" challenged Kalia.

"Really," said Asha, coming nose to nose with Kalia.

Mari walked up to Asha and pushed her back. "Move out of the way," she said, brushing past Asha. "Come on, K. You need to be front and center when they call your name."

"I'm out," said Asha, walking out of the dressing room. "I know whose night it is, and it's certainly not yours."

All of the contestants were crammed into the wings, waiting to see who was going to be called on stage by the announcer. The crowd was amped after JD finished his performance, and Kalia and Mari were clutching hands as the announcer described the winner's prizes.

"The third place winner will receive copies of all of the albums Fire has released this year. The second place winner will receive a roundtrip ticket to anywhere in the continental United States and three nights' accommodations at any four-star hotel, and the winner of Who's Got That Fire? will receive a one year, one album contract with Fire Records and will go into the studio immediately to record a song and film a video for his first single by summer. We'd like to thank our sponsors, our esteemed panel of judges and of course our audience. And now, for the winners…"

Kalia thought her knees would buckle. Mari was flexing the hand her sister was holding trying to loosen Kalia's vicelike grip. JD was in the wings on the other side of the stage, giving her the thumbs-up sign.

"The third place winner is Brian Price."

Kalia breathed deeply as she watched the young man walk out on stage to accept his winnings. She was happy that she wasn't in third place and hoping she placed at all.

"The second place winner is…"

Kalia closed her eyes and prayed in the pregnant pause.

"Kalia Jefferson."

The crowd went into an uproar as Kalia stood in the wings, frozen. Mari leaned over in her ear.

"Kalia, you got second place," she said urgently. "You have to go out on stage. Go ahead." Nudged forward by her sister, Kalia walked out on stage in a daze. She didn't even remember shaking the announcer's hand as he congratulated her and ushered her to the second place winner's place. It hadn't even hit her yet whose name was about to be called.

"Are we ready to see Who's Got That Fire?"

The crowd was on its feet, thunderously applauding and whistling. Kalia looked at the excited people in the balcony and on the floor, wishing she were right down there with them.

"And the winner of Who's Got that Fire? iiiissss...Asha Wright."

The audience erupted into screams and yells and some boos. Kalia watched Asha glide out on stage like this was a moment for which she'd been preparing all her life. As she got to the announcer, an escort handed her a huge bouquet of white roses, and a small trophy was placed in her hand. Smiling widely, she waved, blew kisses at the audience, then suddenly she snatched the microphone from the announcer. The band was already playing the Who's Got That Fire? theme music, but she still tried to get out a speech.

"I'd like to thank my mom, Roxie. You're right. You're always Wright. I'd also like to thank all of my competitors tonight. The competition was really rough, and I'd like to especially thank these two on stage with me right now. Winning is nothing if you don't have great talent to compete against. Thank you all very much."

Kalia kept a smile plastered on her face while Asha shouted into the mic over the band, but as soon as the curtains closed, she relaxed her face muscles and clenched her fist. Congratulators engulfed the whole stage, and Kalia certainly had her share. Everyone from stagehands and other contestants to JD and Mari expressed to her how much they thought she should be the one with the Fire recording contract. Accepting the hugs and pats on the back, all she could say to her admirers was "I wish you were right. I wish you were right."

chapter 16

Mari sat on the gym steps letting the April afternoon sun warm her face. Initially, she'd been happy to find out that track practice was canceled and Coach Little just wanted to have a meeting with the team, but when he announced who was going to be in what races for the East Moreland relays, she was outdone. *Why would he put Asha and me on the four-by-one relay,* she wondered, leaning back on her hands and tilting her face farther toward the sky. True, they were the fastest on the team, but they'd never been on the same relay team before. Why now?

A couple of her teammates trotted down the steps beside her, but she didn't move. She thought about Asha's face when Coach Little announced the four-by-one lineup. It had twisted up like someone had dropped a carton of rotten eggs. "I don't want to pass off to you either," she said aloud, sitting up and dusting off her palms. Ever since Asha had won the Fire contest, she'd been unbearable—or maybe it had just been unbearable going to school with her.

Mari had seen her on every local television news show, heard her on the radio, and her picture had been in several Atlanta newspapers. At school, she'd show up to the one class they shared together late, and the teacher would let her slide because of her "I had an interview" excuse. Even the students who really didn't pay black students much attention flocked to Asha the first few school days after she won. Her classmates ate up every bit of it, barely acknowledging Mari's existence in the process.

Normally the snub wouldn't bother her. She really didn't care about Asha, but she did care about her sister. Every time Asha would strut by smirking, or every time she saw her picture in the paper or heard her voice on the radio, she thought of Kalia. Even though she'd sworn to her a dozen times she was fine about winning second place, Mari knew her sister was devastated.

As she drove up to pick up Mari, Kalia had the same blank look on her face she'd had since the contest. Mari put on her well-worn cheery act.

"What's crackin', big sis?" she said, getting into the car.

"Nuthin'," said Kalia dryly.

"How was your day?"

"All right."

"Okaaaay, so did anything exciting happen today?"

"Nope."

Wanting to fill the dead space, Mari got chatty, telling Kalia all about how helping Colby had inspired her to pitch an idea to the *East Moreland Review* about doing a story on teen pregnancy. Getting no commentary from her sister, she went on about her classes and her track meeting, being careful not to mention Asha.

Exhausting all of her small talk, she resorted to the radio. "Let's see what they're talking about on Hot 103.5," she said, hitting the button on the radio.

"That Asha Wright…she's a stunner, ain't she?"

"Yeah, man, and she can blow, too. Don't let me catch her out one night. It's gonna be me and her."

"Man, please, she don't want your old butt. You'll catch a case messin' with a young hottie like that."

"You right. You right."

"Well, we caught up with her at Fire the other day, and she told us the type of guy she likes. We got the interview right here."

"So what you waitin' on, pahtnah? Cue it up."

Kalia frowned. Mari reached to punch another station, but Kalia pushed her hand away.

"So you laid 'em out down at the Fox last week, huh?"

"I tried to. I was kinda nervous."

"You didn't look nervous, especially in that dress. I mean that was hot. Does you mama know her baby is out there like that."

"My mama picked that dress out. You know I had to get fire on 'em."

"Yeah, well all of Atlanta knows now that you got that fire."

"Thanks, Rob. Thanks a lot. I really appreciate all the support you've been giving me since the contest. It means so much that I've got some fans now. Who would have guessed that I'd have fans? It's wild."

Mari looked at Kalia, but couldn't tell what was going on in her sister's mind because of the hardened look on her face. She did know that they were flying down the expressway. They listened to Asha's humble act nearly all the way home, with Rob RideOut's gushing over her, making their stomachs turn.

"So now that we know what you're working on, you gotta let us in on what you got going on on the personal tip."

Asha giggled. "What do you mean?"

"Aww, you know what we're talking about. Are you seeing anybody? You know you're like new on the scene, and I bet it's a lot of cats out there trying to get at you."

"Well, they've been keeping me so busy at Fire, and you know I'm still in school, so I really don't have a lot of time for like dating and stuff right now."

"You mean to tell me there's no one out there you like?"

"Now I didn't say that. There was this one guy, but I think he's not feeling me anymore. You know he kinda got with this other chick I knew."

"You know she's talking about JD," Mari said. Kalia didn't say a word.

"Ooh, a love triangle."
    "Well, kinda. I just want to let her know if she's out there listening, and she knows who she is, that you may have gotten the guy, but I got the fire."

Mari flipped off the radio. They'd been sitting in the driveway for the last five minutes listening to the end of Asha's interview. Kalia had her head leaned back against the seat, her hand over her eyes.

"Are you okay?" Mari asked softly.

"Umm, hmm."

They were quiet for a minute, then Kalia spoke.

"I just don't understand how she could win. I've been going over it and over it in my mind—every bit of her performance, every bit of mine—and I just don't know how she won. I know that I did my best," she said, turning to Mari.

"You did. You did, and that breakdown was tight. I mean I don't know how she won either."

"I'm so sick of thinking about this," she said, abruptly opening the door and getting out of the car.

Mari followed suit, trotting around the front of the car and up the front stairs after her sister.

"Well, maybe it's time to think about something else," she gingerly suggested.

"Like what? College? Yeah, I got accepted into Penn like Daddy wanted, but I haven't heard one thing from Howard or Juilliard. They had the performing arts programs I really wanted to get in," she said, walking through the kitchen and up the back steps. "Maybe I'm just not good enough. I mean maybe I need to take a hint. I lost the contest, didn't I? What made me think that Howard or Juilliard would want me anyway? I'm trippin'."

"I don't think so," said Mari, following Kalia into her room. "I just think that you haven't heard from those schools yet. You'll hear. Of course you're good enough. You got second place. That's great out of more than two hundred people who tried out."

"Oh yeah. No one ever remembers the name of the person who got second place," Kalia said, kicking off her shoes. "They only remember the winner, and that isn't Kalia Jefferson. It's Asha Wright."

Mari leaned against the doorway, not knowing what to say to her sister, so she changed the subject.

"Hey, I need a favor," she said.

Kalia looked at her, annoyance registering on her face. "What? What do you want?"

"I need someone to help me throw a baby shower for Colby."

"And you're asking me?"

"Yep. You're my big sister, and I need your help."

Kalia threw her hands in the air. "Why not? I sure don't have anything else to do."

"Cool. We can come up with some ideas a little later, okay? I'm gonna hit the books. I've got a quiz in poli-sci tomorrow, and I haven't even done the reading."

"Okay, whatever," said Kalia, walking over to her window.

Mari stood there in the doorway looking at her sister, wishing she had some words of wisdom or a great idea that would make her feel better. Luckily her father swooped in to the rescue. Later that evening, he showed up at the house with three tickets to see Sade. Sitting in the audience, Mari looked to her right. There sat her sister entranced by the depth of Sade's performance. If the building were on fire, she doubted Kalia would move one inch. She looked to her left and there was her father, just as caught up in the show. The only thing missing was her mother. As Sade padded shoeless around the stage, Mari sat back in her seat thoughtfully, realizing this was how their lives were going to be from now on. Even though they hadn't been on a family outing in a while, the fact that all four members of the Jefferson family might never go out again made Mari wistful for her childhood. Willing back tears, she closed her eyes and let Sade take her away.

When the alarm went off the next morning, Mari hit Snooze three times. She didn't feel like getting up. She knew Kalia was probably already downstairs finishing up some homework or rummaging around in the fridge for something to eat. Her cell phone rang, and she dragged her body over to the side of the bed to answer it.

"Turn on the radio," shouted Dewayne.

"What? Why are you calling me on my cell?" she grumbled "You know I'm at h—"

Dewayne cut her off, literally screaming. "Mari, turn on Hot 103.5 right now, and get Kalia."

Mari rolled back over to the other side of her bed and slapped the snooze button again on her clock radio.

"Man, I can't believe it!"

"I know, right? The Fire contest was rigged."

"And by the winner's mother!"

"Woo-wee...that's wild... Look, we gotta get some weather and traffic now, but we'll get right back atcha with the dirt on the Fire contest."

"Seems like somebody's throwin' water on that fire..."

"Kaaaaaahhhliiiiiiaaaaaa!" Mari screamed, dropping her cell phone and scrambling out of bed. "Turn on the radio."

She ran to the bathroom, throwing open the door, passed her sister's room, and seeing she wasn't in there either, stood at the top of the stairs and yelled again. "Kaaaahliaaa! Girl, turn on the radio."

"What?" Kalia shouted from downstairs. "Why are you yelling? You're gonna wake up Ma!"

Mari ran back to her room and turned her clock radio up full blast. Kalia appeared in her doorway, followed by her mother.

"What is it, Mari?"

"Yeah," said Elaine, tying her robe sleepily. "Where's the fire?"

Mari grinned and pointed to the radio, then put that same finger to her lips.

"The dude at Fire. He was vice president or something, right?"

"Yeah, yeah, and he was dating the mother of the winner."

Elaine's eyes widened as she put her hand over her mouth. Kalia walked over to the radio, an incredulous look growing on her face. Mari sat on the bed, leaning toward the radio.

"So Asha Wright's mama was getting with a Fire Records VP?"

"That's what I heard."

"Man, I don't know 'bout you. You be gettin' your info from your baby's mama's hairdresser's cousin's play sister. Who knows if what you say is true."

"Aw, how you gon' try to play me like that? You know I stay in the know."

"What happened? Who is this VP? What happens now? Does Asha lose? Is Kalia the new Fire girl?" Mari shouted at the radio. "I wish they would shut up all that silly mess and tell us what happens now."

The three Jefferson women sat in Mari's bedroom, captive to the morning antics of the Gerry and Trina show. After suffering through seconds that seemed like hours of ridiculousness, they got down to the nitty gritty.

"Okay, so our producer just got off the phone with someone at Fire, and it's official. Asha Wright is not the winner of the contest."

"Wow…dang, that must hurt to know your mama jacked you out of a record deal with a major label. Woo…I'd hate to be sitting at the Wright breakfast table this morning 'cause it's probably wrong up in there."

"So who won? Is it the second place winner?"

"I asked that, but they're not saying any more about it right now. The girl who won second place is Kalia Jefferson. I bet she's going crazy right now."

Without saying a word, Mari started jumping up and down on the bed. "Oh my God," said Kalia, sliding along the wall down to the floor, her hands on either side of her face in disbelief. Elaine stood in the door beaming as the phone rang.

When Kalia hung up the phone, she sat on the bed, smiling.

"Well?" Mari said, hitting Kalia so hard on the shoulder that she fell backward.

"Oh, oh, oh, that was JD," she said, holding her shoulder and giggling. "He said he got wind of it last night and that he's been trying to find out information since then. He said he didn't want to call me until he could find out whether it was true. He did say that the VP's name they were talking about was some guy named Jackson Trane."

"Jackson. I met a guy with Asha's mama named Jackson," Mari shouted. "And you know what? He is VP at Fire. I heard them talking about it."

"When was this?" Elaine asked.

"At the meet where I whooped Asha in the one hundred. He was there, and it was so strange. Roxie never introduced him to me."

"Maybe 'cause she knew she was doin' some dirt." Kalia snickered.

"Well, whatever. That's enough to confirm it for me. So did JD say anything about who was gonna be the winner now? Are they gonna have another winner?" asked Mari.

"Nope. He said that's what he was trying to find out, too. So we just gotta wait," said Kalia. "I don't even want to go to school."

"Ooh, yeah, me neither," said Mari. "Ma, can we stay home from school today? It's just like a holiday, and what if we miss hearing whether Kalia is the winner? We need to be close to a radio or a TV or something."

Elaine turned around, shaking her head. "Don't you both have text messaging on your phones? You better use it 'cause if you're not deathly ill, you're going to school."

Kalia walked to her room, listening to Mari coughing theatrically down the hall. She stood in front of her closet and picked out the brightest thing in her closet, a fire engine-red sundress. Yeah, it was a little early to break out the summer gear, she thought, but she was feeling fire, and everybody was going to know it.

When Kalia and Mari stepped in the house that evening, her mother was sitting in front of the television, watching the news.

"Come in here," she called. "Fire's on the news."

They rushed into the family room just in time to see Jackson Trane's picture on the screen. A well-coifed black anchorwoman detailed how Fire Records was accusing Jackson and Asha's mother of conspiring to rig Who's Got That Fire? As they talked about how long Roxie and Jackson had been dating, they ran clips of her in infomercials for the Wright Touch.

"Wow, I haven't even seen these," said Mari.

"Shh!" Kalia and her mother hushed.

The anchorwoman reported that Asha's recording contract had been nullified, Jackson was on administrative leave from Fire, and he and Roxie were being called people of interest in investigations both Fire and the police were conducting.

"Woo-wee," said Mari as the segment ended.

"It's on the news," said Kalia. "I guess it's real then. Oh, and I forgot to tell you, Mari, guess who left me a voice mail today?"

"Who?"

"Malcolm."

"For real? What did his tired butt want?" Mari asked.

"He wanted to congratulate me, talking about how we should get together and do a track now that we were on the same team."

"K, you betta not even think about it," warned Mari.

"Please," said Kalia. "I am so done with that boy."

"Umm, hmm," said Elaine. "He's trying to be down now that he thinks you're the winner."

"You've got that fire, that fire, that fire," Mari sang, dancing around the room.

"Oh, yeah, you got a call from Fire today, too," said Elaine suddenly. "They want you to call them immediately."

"Ma! Why didn't you tell me this when I walked in the door? It's after six," said Kalia, picking up the cordless phone in the kitchen.

"Well, Fire was on the news and I don't know, I thought you might be home earlier," said Elaine, following Kalia into the kitchen.

"Oh, crap. All I'm getting is voice mail," Kalia said, pacing.

"Oh, you need to dial extension 243," Elaine remembered.

"Ma," Kalia said.

"I'm sorry, I'm sorry," said Elaine, flexing her hands. "I guess I'm getting old."

"No, this is just comedy," said Mari, walking into the kitchen and sitting down at the table.

"Hello, this is Kalia Jefferson. Someone left a message for me?" they heard Kalia say into the phone.

"Travis Howard," said Elaine, grimacing.

"Travis Howard," Kalia said into the phone, rolling her eyes. Mari doubled over in silent laughter.

"Okay…yes. Hi, this is Kalia…yes, I've heard about it, of course… Oh, they aren't sure…well, okay…yes, I understand… and thank you…okay…that's okay… Thanks for letting me know…okay. Bye."

Mari and Elaine's hearts sank as they watched Kalia lean back against the refrigerator.

"They said they didn't know how far the investigation would take them and they couldn't be sure who all was a part of the conspiracy, so right now they're not going to name another winner," she said quietly. "They may revisit the contest in the next few months, but that's going to depend on how many people were in on it."

"So how many more people were involved in it? Were Jackson and Asha's mother running Fire or something?" asked Mari, beating her fist on the table. "I mean, how come you just can't be the winner? This really sucks."

Elaine got up and walked over to her elder daughter. "I'm so sorry, Kalia," she said, embracing her. "I wish it was in my power to never have you feel this type of disappointment. I want you to know that watching you practice hard these last couple of months has really been an amazing experience. I'm very proud of you. You did your best, and you won. Even if nobody else wants to admit it. You won before you even went out on that stage."

"Yeah, K, I'm proud of you, too," said Mari, walking over and hugging both her mother and her sister. The phone rang, and Mari reached over to pick it up off the counter.

"Hey, Daddy. All right… Yeah, she's right here," she said, handing Kalia the phone, just as her sister's cell phone started ringing. Seeing that it was Colby, Kalia handed her cell to Mari, who walked off into the living room. The Jefferson women didn't get a break for much of the rest of the evening. Everybody was calling to find out what was happening with Kalia and whether she was the new winner of Who's Got That Fire?

By the time she'd spent an hour and a half telling three people the deal, Kalia got tired of talking about it. She let her mother and Mari inform the rest of the callers. A few minutes later, she found herself in her parents' bathroom, standing over their Jacuzzi. She closed the door, turned the water on full blast and poured in entirely too much rosemary bubble bath. Sinking into the hot water, she tried to let the heat melt her cares away, but it wasn't working.

Kalia closed her eyes and let the tears fall. "Why? Why? Why?" she whimpered. "Why couldn't I win? Why can't I catch a break?" She let it all out, splashing the water, hitting the tile on the wall, even letting out a frustrated howl she just knew would bring her mother rushing to the door.

She calmed down when no one came. Her mother was right. She'd done her best, and she knew it. If she had to, she was going to force herself to be proud of herself. She just had to trust in her talent.

Mari couldn't believe she was going to have to accept the baton from Asha in the four-by-one in the livest meet in the metro area. Teams came from all over the city and the suburbs to compete in the East Moreland relays. Mari never got to see so many black people at her school as she did during this event. With more than a dozen teams in the competition, those from mostly black schools did well, and all of their fans came to watch them slay the few mostly white teams.

Cursing Coach Little, she jogged down to the stadium, trying to mentally prepare herself for her races. She ran past Asha, who was stretching with the rest of the team, then stopped and looked up, searching the stands for her people. She spotted Kalia and her mother then saw Dewayne and JD, arms filled with drinks and snacks, scooting past people to get to Kalia and her mother. She smiled and waved. Kalia waved back as her mother was busy trying to help unload the guys.

Stretching out, Mari heard the announcer read the times for the last race. He then announced that the four-by-one would start in ten minutes. She stood, pulled off her lightweight athletic pants and walked over to Asha.

"You ready?" she asked.

"Are *you* ready?" Asha shot back, her three braided ponytails flapping in the wind.

"I wasn't even sure if you were going to show up. You haven't been in school all week."

"Gee, I wonder why," said Asha, jumping up and down and wiggling her arms.

Mari looked intently at Asha as she pulled one arm across her chest with the other, then reversed the stretch.

"Look, I just need to know if your mind is on this race," she said. "I'm sorry about your drama, but I just care about this race right now."

"And that's all I care about," Asha said.

"Good."

Asha turned to walk away, but changed her mind and walked up to Mari.

"Listen, I don't know if this is going to mean anything, but I didn't know what my mother and Jackson were doing."

"Umm, hmm," said Mari, looking at her skeptically.

"For real," said Asha. "I found out about it probably the same way that you did. Someone called me and told me they were talking about me on the radio, asking me if my mother was dating a guy from Fire. I didn't even know what he did at Fire until after the fact."

Mari just looked at Asha.

"You don't have to believe me. Just please tell your sister that I'm sorry and that I didn't want to win like that."

As Asha walked away, Mari noticed she didn't have her chin in the air as usual. She started to call her back, but the announcer began reading the lineup for her race. When he said Asha's name, several boos came from the stands. For some reason Mari felt bad for Asha as she walked to her starting position for the last leg of the four-by-one.

The gun went off, and Mari watched her teammate run the first leg of the race. They were in second place by the time the baton was passed to their second leg runner. As she approached Asha, they were tied for third. Everybody in the stands was on their feet as Asha came out of her start like she was shot out of a sling. "Go, Asha. Come on, come on," Mari chanted, turning her body forward while reaching behind her. The minute Asha touched the baton to her hand, she lunged forward and didn't think about anything else but the finish line. The race was so close she didn't know who won. Everyone was pointing and screaming.

"Ladies and gentleman, it appears we have a… Oh, I was about to say we have a tie, but I've been informed we do have a winner," boomed the announcer. During his pause Asha and Mari exchanged hopeful glances, walking toward each other.

"And the winner of the girls four-by-one is East Moreland with a time of 50.04 seconds."

Mari and Asha were so overcome with excitement they hugged each other before they even knew what they were doing. Pulling back, they smiled at each other, then hugged again. Mari looked up in the stands and saw her sister pointing to her and talking to her mother. Her arm still around Asha, Mari knew it looked like she was snuggling up to the enemy, so she threw the okay sign up to her sister and pointed at Asha. She saw Kalia tilt her head to the side, raise her hands and shrug.

"I'll be right back," she said to Asha, motioning for Kalia to meet her behind the stands, then she changed her mind, grabbed Asha's hand and dragged her toward the stands.

"What are you doing?" Asha asked, trotting behind her.

"You gotta tell Kalia yourself. It'll be more believable coming from you," said Mari.

"Oh, my God," said Asha. "She's not going to believe me."

"Well, you gotta tell her anyway," said Mari, leaping up the steps two at a time.

"All right, all right," Asha said, huffing, a half step behind.

Dewayne, JD and Kalia were waiting for them when they got to the back of the stands. Asha and Kalia walked off, talking.

"Congratulations, speed demon," Dewayne said to Mari.

"Yeah, you guys were flying around that track. I thought you were going to sprout some wings for a minute there," said JD.

"Thank you, thank you," Mari said, bowing deeply.

JD nodded in the direction of Kalia and Asha. "So what's up over there?" he asked.

"Asha said she didn't know what her mom and Jackson were doing. She said she was completely out of the loop," said Mari.

"For real?" said Dewayne.

"I can believe that," said JD. "This is the music industry, and stranger things have happened. Money and celebrity bring out the worst side of people sometimes."

"Do you believe she's telling the truth?" Dewayne asked.

"Yep, and I think Kalia does, too. Look," Mari said. Asha and Kalia were walking back toward them with smiles on their faces.

"I guess I'm not going to have to duck any claws around here," said Dewayne as they walked up.

"Shut up, Dewayne. No. All is cool. We're cool," said Kalia, looking at Asha.

"Good," said Mari. "'Cause you know even though my sister gets on my nerves sometimes, I would've had to be on her side if y'all had issues."

"It's all good," Asha said. "Kalia and I are cool, so I'm outta here. I don't have any more races."

They all watched Asha trot down the steps.

"I still don't trust her," said Dewayne as soon as she was out of earshot.

"Aww, ain't nuthin' wrong with Asha. She just a little bourgeoisie," said Mari, laughing at her boyfriend. "She probably didn't know what her mother and Jackson were doing."

JD and Kalia chuckled, walking along beside them.

"I don't know," Dewayne persisted. "You know what they say about apples."

"Apples? What in the world do apples have to do with anything we're talking about?" asked Mari.

"They don't fall far from the tree."

Kalia and JD burst out laughing.

"You are so corny," said Mari, running up behind Dewayne and thumping him on the back of his head. "I think you fell from a tree and bumped your head."

She squealed as Dewayne picked up her petite frame and threatened to drop her on the ground. Instead he put her down gently and took her hand. She didn't pull away. Neither did Kalia when JD grabbed hers. They walked all the way back to the gym that way, two sisters with their boyfriends, laughing and joking, their hearts light as feathers.

Kalia got out of her car and walked to the mailbox. If she didn't hear from Howard or Juilliard that day, she was going to go right back in the house and call them. It was the middle of April. *School is going to be over soon,* she thought, placing her hand on the mailbox door. *I'm sick of waiting. I've got to know what I am doing with my life.* She said a silent prayer and opened the box, reaching in without looking. She pulled out three envelopes. The first was a telephone bill, the second was from the electric company. Her heart almost stopped when she saw the return address on the third envelope. It was from Howard. She ripped it open.

We are pleased to inform you that you have been accepted into the freshman class of Howard University was all she read before she clutched the letter to her chest, closed her eyes and mouthed, "Thank you, God."

She was reading the rest of her acceptance letter when she heard someone bumping a hot beat. Looking in the direction of the sound, she watched a midnight-blue Maybach coupe pull up in her driveway.

"Whatcha got there?" said JD, leaning out the window.

"Whatchu got there?" asked Kalia, walking up to the car, looking it up and down.

"You first," he said, turning off the engine and pulling off his cell-phone earpiece.

She waved the letter in his direction. "This is an acceptance letter from Howard." She grinned.

"That's what's up! Congratulations, baby," he said. "That's great."

"I'm so excited. I know I haven't heard from Juilliard yet, but at least I know I'm in somewhere I want to go. Now you tell me what's up with this car."

"Oh, I'm just test driving it. It's kinda fire, isn't it?"

"Yeah," she said, walking around the front of the car. "I must admit, it's hot."

"Speaking of Fire, I've got a surprise for you," he said with a devilish look on his face. "Get in."

"Tell me what the surprise is."

"Get in."

"Okay," she said, running around to the other side of the car and getting in. "Ooh, these seats feel good. Okay, so what's the surprise?"

JD leaned over and turned down the radio.

"They're looking for some singers to do some studio work down at Fire, and I mentioned your name, and they want me to bring you down to check out your skills," he said.

"Oh my God! Thank you," said Kalia, leaning over impulsively and kissing JD on the cheek.

"It's all good, baby doll," he said, leaning back and putting the car in Reverse. "You ready to ride out?"

"We're going to Fire right now?" Kalia asked, nervous excitement making her voice rise.

"No time like the present, huh?" said JD, handling the steering wheel with one hand and rubbing the fingers of her left hand in the other.

"Yeah," she said, watching her Southwest Atlanta neighborhood roll by. "It's my world, ain't it?"

"It's your world, baby," JD said, smiling at her.

Kalia didn't know if she was going to college, if she was going to be the next Alicia Keys, or both, but what she did know was that she was riding in a Maybach, her boyfriend was the hottest new artist on Fire Records, and she was on her way to becoming a professional background singer. Yeah, her senior year had brought her more drama than Whitney and Bobby, but the weather in Atlanta was doing its spring thing, and she was about to have the best summer of her life.

"So let's make it happen," she said, almost to herself.

JD turned down the music. "Did you say something, baby?"

She squeezed his hand and smiled at him. "Nope. I think it's gonna be a hot one this summer."

"I think you're right," he said. "I think it's gonna be fire."